WHERE DREAMS RESIDE

HEIDI CHIAVAROLI

Hope Creek Publishers, LLC

PRAISE FOR HEIDI CHIAVAROLI

"Chiavaroli delights with this homage to Louisa May Alcott's *Little Women*, featuring a time-slip narrative of two women connected across centuries."
PUBLISHERS WEEKLY on *The Orchard House*

"As a longtime fan of Louisa May Alcott's *Little Women*, I was eager to read *The Orchard House*.... [It] invited me in, served me tea, and held me enthralled with its compelling tale."
LORI BENTON, Christy Award-winning author of *The King's Mercy*

"This story... *Hope Beyond the Waves* tugged at my heart from page one, and I was totally immersed in the seemingly insurmountable challenges of both the past and present day characters. Kudos to Heidi Chiavaroli for pouring out this beautifully raw and moving story about finding love and hope in the most unexpected of places."
MELANIE DOBSON, Carol Award-winning author of *The Winter Rose*

"Captivating from the first page....Steeped in timeless truths and served with skill, *The Tea Chest* is sure to be savored by all who read it."
JOCELYN GREEN, Christy Award-winning author of *Between Two Shores*

"[*In Hope Beyond the Waves*,] Heidi Chiavaroli paints a beautiful portrait of loving the unlovable, of forgiving the unforgivable, and of finding hope in the least likely places. This is a story that lingers."

KAREN SARGENT, author of IAN Book of the Year, *Waiting for Butterflies*

"*The Hidden Side* is a beautiful tale that captures the timeless struggles of the human heart."

JULIE CANTRELL, *New York Times* Bestselling author of *Perennials*

"First novelist Chiavaroli's historical tapestry will provide a satisfying summer read for fans of Kristy Cambron and Lisa Wingate."

LIBRARY JOURNAL on *Freedom's Ring*

"*The Edge of Mercy* is most definitely one for the keeper shelf. "

LINDSAY HARREL, author of *The Secrets of Paper and Ink*

ALSO BY HEIDI CHIAVAROLI

The Orchard House

The Tea Chest

The Hidden Side

Freedom's Ring

The Edge of Mercy

Hope Beyond the Waves

The Orchard House Bed and Breakfast Series

Where Grace Appears

Where Hope Begins

Where Love Grows

Where Memories Await

Where Dreams Reside

Where Faith Belongs (January, 2023)

To Gramummy,
One of my favorite memories as a child was curling up with a Little
House on the Prairie book in your small library downstairs.
Thank you for helping to instill the love of books in me at an early age.
I love you!

‖   1   ‖

I passed the quaint sign that welcomed travelers to my hometown of Camden, Maine. I pressed the gas pedal harder. On the radio, Trisha Yearwood crooned about second chances and I flipped the station.

If I've learned one thing from my quarter-century of living, it's that second chances are the stuff of fairytales. Trish might be raising the hopes of other listeners, but not this girl. I knew better.

If only I could drive fast enough to turn back time, to undo all that was done here eight years ago.

I eased my foot from the gas and pushed the thought away. No good would come from carrying my past around like a child's well-loved, dirtied blanket. I was here to build a new future. One in which I didn't distance myself from my family and hide away in shame. One in which I would be an active participant in my new niece's life. One where I faced the past like an adult.

No matter how grueling that might be.

As I pulled into the familiar drive, doubt curled cold fingers around my spine. Maybe I didn't have to do *this* part of facing my past right away. I could at least see my family first, check in with the landlord at the apartment I'd found online, unpack my suitcase . . .

But my Mazda was already pulling up the drive, parking in the spot I'd parked a thousand times during high school. The one to the left of Isabel's spot, out of the way of the basketball hoop.

The hoop was gone now. The driveway sported new cracks along its surface. The landscaping was neat as always, despite the shrubs that had grown too close to the house.

With trembling hands, I pushed open my car door and shoved my phone and keys into the pockets of my winter coat. Though the last days of March had come and gone, winter didn't release its stubborn grip from the coast of Maine without a fight.

I strode to the front door, preparing myself for the worst. There would still be hard feelings, of course. Eight years wouldn't have erased that. But I refused to come back into town without facing Mr. and Mrs. Davis. Words needed to be said—my words. Better to see Isabel's parents now instead of allowing them to stumble across me in the library or in one of Camden's many downtown shops. I *must* do this.

I rang the bell before shoving my hands in my pockets. I glanced at the greenery along the porch so as not to stare into the house. When no one answered, I started back down the steps, relief stirring my insides.

I had tried. There was always tomorrow.

But as I made my way down the walkway, the door behind me creaked open. Slowly, I turned. At the sight of the familiar figure before me, I released a pent-up breath and smiled. While Isabel's parents scared the living daylights out of me, the sight of Isabel's grandmother, small and wrinkled and brown as a California raisin, eased a sore spot in my spirit.

"Miss Esther." I started back up the stairs.

Isabel's grandmother's eyes remained blank behind her glasses. My sister mentioned several months ago that Miss Esther suffered from some sort of dementia. Would she not remember me?

"It's me, Miss Esther. Morgan. Isabel's . . . friend."

Quicker than a Fourth of July firecracker, Miss Esther's eyes lit up. "Morgan! Honey, what are you doing out in the cold? You come in here quick and we'll get you a cup of tea, darling."

I stepped into the house, warmth encompassing me. *A lot* of warmth. Sahara Desert warmth. Isabel's grandmother had always liked the thermostat on high. I looked around. Were Mr. and Mrs. Davis home?

"Thank you, but I don't mean to impose . . ." My gaze flicked to the woman's chocolate eyes. Any minute now, she'd remember everything. Then, what would she do?

But her eyes remained light and sparkly. "Ha! An imposition? No friend of Isabel's is an imposition, as far as I'm concerned. Now, come sit down. Ruth has the box of tea here somewhere." She planted her hands on her hips and looked around the kitchen —nothing had changed about it from when I'd last stood here during my senior year of high school. Same gingham curtains. Same white sugar and flour containers. How many times had Isabel and I sat at this very table, finishing off a row of Oreos while talking about boys or stressing about colleges?

My heart squeezed and I reached out to touch Miss Esther's arm. "It's okay. Perhaps we could just sit. I—well, I was hoping to speak with Mrs. Davis. Do you know if she'll be home soon?"

With what appeared to be much effort, Miss Esther tore her gaze away from the kitchen counter where, from all accounts, she still battled her memory for the whereabouts of the tea.

"Mrs. Davis . . . my daughter . . . Ruth!" She said Isabel's mother's name as if it were a hard-sought victory, as if it were a precious jewel she'd found buried in the depths of the couch cushions.

"Yes, Ruth."

Miss Esther pressed her lips together and looked down at the table. "Ruth . . . where did she go?"

"It's okay, Miss Esther. We can sit and chat if you'd like."

"Oh! I know! She went to pick up Isabel from basketball practice." She grinned at me, revealing a space between her two front teeth. My insides deflated. If only Mrs. Davis *were* picking up Isabel from basketball practice.

"Okay, I'll wait until she gets home." I read once that it was best not to disrupt the delusions of dementia patients. So instead, I pulled out the chair closest to Miss Esther. "Would you like to sit?"

She worried her bottom lip between her teeth, suddenly looking uncertain. My heart went out to her as she lowered herself to her chair.

"How is the Camden Quilting Club? What have you ladies been working on lately?" Surely this line of conversation would put her at ease.

Again, her eyes lit up. "Priscilla opened a bed and breakfast!"

Priscilla Martin, Miss Esther's longtime friend. "I heard about that. The Orchard House Bed and Breakfast, isn't it?" I asked, although I knew very well, having researched as much as I could regarding my new landlords.

Miss Esther beamed. "Yes."

Out of the corner of my eye, a tall shadow peered around the door of the kitchen. It couldn't be . . .

"Marcus?"

Isabel's brother grinned before diving back across the threshold, hiding his dark, curly hair. I stood. The last time I'd seen Marcus, he'd been a small second-grader . . . now . . . was he in high school already? I wondered if he were on track to graduate. I wondered what his plans post high school would be. His autism had slowed his progress, but his winsome personality had always made up for his lack in formal education. "Marcus, you've grown so much! Do you remember me?"

He peered around the doorway again with wide brown eyes, gave me a lopsided grin, and nodded. "Ehmmmm . . ." He drew out the letter M long and proud. Tears pricked the insides of my eyelids. Isabel called me M. No one had called me that in years.

I swallowed. "Yes, it's M. It's so good to see you, Marcus."

The sound of the back door reached my ears and my blood froze.

"Mom? Sorry I took so long. The line was—" Mrs. Davis looked up, blinking behind the serious frames of her glasses and nearly dropping the bag of groceries she held.

My mouth turned dry and I backed away involuntarily. "Mrs. Davis. Hi."

Hi?

Mrs. Davis placed the groceries on the counter but didn't release them. Instead, she leaned against the counter, the bag still in her arms, a storm of emotion clouding her face.

"I—I hope it's okay I stopped in. I—I wanted to see you."

Isabel's mother released the bag of groceries, her jaw firm, her eyes shooting daggers. "You have no right to be here. Get out."

Heat rushed to my face. A thin sheen of sweat broke out over my entire body. I gasped for breath, but the warmth of the house combined with Mrs. Davis's words choked me.

"I—I'm sorry. I shouldn't have . . . I should have called. I—I'm sorry." I backed away toward the front door I'd come in.

"Morgan!" Miss Esther said. "We were going to have tea!"

Marcus began shouting Isabel's nickname for me. "Ehmmm!"

"Maybe another time, Miss Esther? It was good to see you, Marcus." I stumbled into the living room and bumped against an end table, knocking over a couple of chess pieces. I scrambled to pick them up, placed them flat on the board without minding their proper place.

"That was rude, Ruth," Miss Esther scolded her daughter. Behind her, Marcus cried, still calling out my nickname.

I took the last two steps out of the house, gulping in cold air. I practically ran to my car. I tried not to see Isabel's ghost shooting a layup or challenging me to a game of HORSE. But it was no use.

How stupid could I have been? A passing of eight years did not mean Isabel's parents would welcome me into their home any more than they'd had when I left. Miss Esther and Marcus were different, of course—they wouldn't hold a grudge against a fly. But then again, Marcus may not have fully understood what happened to his sister. And Miss Esther still thought Isabel was alive.

Miss Esther hadn't remembered that I, Isabel's very best friend in the whole wide world, had killed her.

$\maltese$ 2 $\maltese$

Bronson Martin considered himself a patient man. A decent man. A man who went above and beyond for his family.

But even patient men had limits. And right now, his younger sister was coming dangerously close to toeing the line.

"I don't see why you won't give her a chance, Bronson." Amie stood beneath the tree he was pruning, a yoga mat bag slung over one shoulder.

"I can find my own dates, Amie. Why don't you worry about your own love life? Speaking of, how's August anyway?"

She shrugged. "We're good."

He eyed her. Their brother-in-law Tripp's youngest brother had been hounding after Amie for years. A few months ago, they'd finally started dating. From the lack of enthusiasm in his sister's voice, he'd be surprised if it lasted.

He cleared his throat. Whatever. Amie's love life was not his business.

He attempted to focus on the task before him, studying the one-year-old branch, considering where to prune. Every choice mattered. Every cut had the possibility to stimulate growth—or stunt his harvest.

And he had big plans for the orchard this year. Real big.

"Besides," he continued. "I'm not sure you're as interested in me finding my soulmate as you're interested in finding a future sister-in-law you approve of."

"But Lacy's smart and pretty and really sweet. She's running an amazing, profitable business *and* she teaches classes at the Y for seniors on Saturday mornings—*voluntarily*."

"Wow, you sound pretty smitten. Maybe *you* should go out with her."

Amie swung her bag and hit him in the shoulder, narrowly missing a branch.

"Hey, watch the trees."

"You and your stupid trees. All you care about is this orchard."

He pointed his hand shears at her. "That's not true. I care about food. Which is why I need to finish up this tree before I miss dinner. You mind?"

Amie released a growl of frustration before stomping off down the hill toward their home—a Victorian their great-aunt had allowed them to turn into a thriving family business. The Orchard House Bed and Breakfast. Sometimes he still couldn't believe all they'd accomplished. And, Lord willing, it was only beginning.

Amie's blonde head disappeared among the branches of the apple trees and he exhaled a long breath, turning back to his work.

Between his mother, his aunt, his four sisters, and the bed and breakfast guests, it was hard for a guy to find a moment's peace. Thankfully, the weather was beginning to warm, freeing him from the confines of the house when he wasn't teaching at the middle school.

Not that he didn't care about his family with every bone in his body. He cared. Sometimes too much.

He moved on to another branch, assessing which cut to make,

keeping in mind the goal of an open center, which would allow the sun to reach as many branches as possible.

He imagined explaining the process to the kids who'd attend his summer camp in a few short months. Of course, he'd teach more than pruning. Some might be interested in pollination or irrigation or harvesting. Soil cultivation. Not to mention the business aspect of running a profitable orchard.

At least, he hoped it'd prove profitable.

An aggressive cut caused the shears in his hand to snap, and he stifled a curse. A spring from the tool leapt into the next aisle of the orchard. He stomped over to look for it, but after five minutes he resigned himself to a quick trip to the hardware store before dinner. With any luck, there'd be enough daylight after supper to finish up this section of pruning.

A half-hour later, he drove north on Route 1, satisfied with the new pair of pruners he purchased at Rankin's Hardware for a bargain price. A sign on the side of the road caught his attention. An apartment for rent. Man, what he wouldn't give for his own place. And this was a great neighborhood, too. But getting his own housing wasn't in the plans. Yet.

If his orchard camp took off, maybe then he'd be able to afford a monthly rent. For now, what could be better than growing young minds, creating a venture that brought memories and learning and, of course, good food. With any luck, it'd be a boon to the bed and breakfast business as well. Maybe he'd be able to tuck some extra money in his own pockets.

Out of the corner of his eye, he saw a woman struggling with a tire beside a black Mazda on the side of the road. He pulled into the breakdown lane in front of her. Amie'd ring his neck if he passed this girl by to get back to his "stupid" trees.

After a small row of passing cars whizzed by, he exited the driver's seat. "Need help?"

If the woman were like Josie, she'd shun him. It wasn't that he thought a woman couldn't change a tire—of course they could. But why do so alone on a busy road?

The auburn-haired beauty looked up from her trunk where she struggled with the spare tire. Relief washed over her face, and raw attraction tugged hard from the pit of Bronson's stomach. Maybe Amie was right. Maybe he *did* need to get out more if helping one damsel in distress was enough to stir his nerve endings.

She bit her lip, and nodded, her beautiful green eyes puffy and pink. Growing up in a house of five women had taught him what that meant—this damsel had been crying.

Oh, man. Nothing made him more uncomfortable than female tears. How many times had Amie won an argument between them with nothing but a few wet lashes? The mere sight of them made him feel utterly helpless.

Something about her looked familiar, but he couldn't place where he might have seen her. He pretended not to notice her emotional state as he took the donut from her. "I'll have you fixed up and back on the road in no time. No worries."

She blinked fast. "Thank you. I'm having a rough day, so I appreciate you stopping."

He searched the side of the road for a heavy rock to chock the wheel on the opposite side of the flat. "You're lucky—flats are my specialty."

A trace of a smile lit her face, illuminating perfect white teeth against lips the color of his mom's pink roses. She lifted her phone. "So, you think it's safe to put the You Tube video away, then?"

"I'd say so." He got to work loosening the lug nuts, jacked the Mazda up, and switched out the tires.

Once he finished, he fit the faulty tire and jack back into her trunk and closed it. "You'll want to get a new tire on there soon. This one's only temporary—I wouldn't do any highway traveling either, if you can help it. Definitely don't go over fifty."

"I'm not going far. Thank you so much." Her face brightened. "One second." She held up a hand and ducked into the passenger's seat, highlighting the well-fitted curve of her jeans.

He looked away. If Amie hadn't gotten his thoughts on finding a woman, he'd not be noticing more than he ought to be. But then, what if that meant something . . .

A moment later, she extricated herself from the car and handed him a Subway gift card. "There's ten dollars on it. At least I can say I bought you lunch for the trouble of playing my guardian angel today."

Guardian angel? Him? Bronson shook his head, pushed the card back in her direction. "That's not necessary. I'm happy to help."

Those sharp green eyes studied him, and she shrugged, slipped the card in the back pocket of her jeans. "Suit yourself. Thanks again. I'm not sure You Tube would have cut it."

"No problem." He kept his mouth open—for what, he wasn't certain. Amie would prod him to ask her out. He *wanted* to ask her out. But he didn't want her to think he was some kind of creep who preyed on helpless women struggling with flat tires on the side of the road.

He smiled. "Maybe I'll catch you around town sometime?"

She returned the smile, a crease denting the corner of her cheek, her eyes not quite so puffy. "Maybe."

He had made those tears disappear. A chivalrous—or was it chauvinistic?—pride filled his chest.

"Well, bye." She gave a small wave, and he forced his legs to move back toward his car. An irrational urge to turn around and say, "How about I take *you* out to lunch sometime?" surged through him, but he ignored it. No need to scare the girl off. Besides, he had too much on his plate as it was—no sense adding a new relationship to the mix.

Relationships could wait until after he got his summer camp off the ground. Until he was out from under his mother's roof.

He gave one last wave to the auburn-haired woman, checked his mirrors, and started for home, ignoring the odd feeling of loss that snaked through him.

A few minutes later, he pulled into the driveway of the bed and breakfast, the stained-glass sign welcoming him home, the naked branches of the orchards filling him with excitement and possibilities.

What would his father think of the work he'd accomplished? Hard to believe he'd been gone for three years now. Though the pain wasn't as severe as it used to be, on days like this, when so many possibilities lay before him, the ache came with renewed vigor. What he wouldn't give for just one day to show his dad the orchard, to pick his brain on how best to run the new summer camp.

Not that taking advice from Amos Martin would likely be in the camp's best interest. Most of his father's well-meaning projects ended up in financial ruin, with his family footing the bill.

Bronson sighed. He could only hope he didn't take after his dad in that regard.

He parked, glancing up at the empty apartment above the bookstore. After his sister Josie had married, Bronson had considered calling dibs on the apartment, but decided it'd be better to stay with his mother and help her out at the B&B so he could pay off his student loans faster. Besides, while being close to the orchards was convenient, when he moved out, he wanted more than a driveway separating him from his family—or it'd feel like he hadn't moved out at all.

He headed toward the Victorian when a familiar black Mazda pulled up the drive. He blinked, watching the woman from earlier park beside his truck. A moment later, she exited, shouldering a bag and smiling brightly at him with that alluring mouth.

"I guess I caught you around town sooner than either of us expected," she said.

Caught him . . .

He shook his head. "I really don't need the Subway card, honest. I—"

She pointed to the bed and breakfast. "I'm not following you. This is my destination. I guess it was yours, too?"

Was this a second chance to ask her out? An orchestrating of events from the Almighty?

His tongue explored the inside of his mouth, but no words came out. He tried again. "I—I live here."

Her eyebrows raised. "You're Bronson Martin? You've . . . changed a bit since high school."

He'd been a shrimp in high school. A late-bloomer. Even his younger sister had towered over him. How many times had he gone to bed, begging God to make him tall? God hadn't answered the prayer until senior year, but when He answered, He *answered*.

No one would ever call Bronson a shrimp again.

He stared at the girl. That was why she looked familiar. They'd gone to school together. But surely, he would have remembered those green eyes, the way her hair curled over one shoulder . . .

He shook his head. "I'm sorry, I can't remember your name."

"It's Morgan."

Morgan.

In a flash, he remembered. Something in his gut turned to lead. "Morgan . . ."

She pressed her lips together before answering. "Dalton," she whispered.

He recovered quickly, pushing aside what little he knew about the biggest scandal that had caused a hubbub the summer after his senior year. "Didn't we have a class together freshman year?"

"Sophomore year. Honors Chemistry."

He groaned. "I suppose you weren't absent the day the sprinklers went off?"

She crossed her arms over her chest, one corner of her mouth pulling up in a smile. "Oh, I was very present. Could never figure out how you caused that much smoke."

He couldn't, either.

He rubbed the back of his neck, gave her a sheepish grin. "Sorry I didn't remember you right away." Clearly, he'd made an impression on her, but that's what happened when you messed with ammonia and hydrochloric acid without reviewing the lab manual.

"Probably better off." She spoke the words so quietly he almost missed them, and for a moment he pitied her.

It could have happened to anyone, really. Well, maybe not *anyone*. But what did Dad used to say? *We are all one choice away from altering our futures. Be it for the good or the bad.*

Still, the woman in front of him had been irresponsible and reckless. Now, she had to live the rest of her life with the consequences of her decisions. Couldn't be easy, no matter how careless her choices had been.

"Are you checking in? It's right around the side. I'll show you."

She brushed a long curl out of her face. "Not checking in, exactly. I'm renting the apartment."

So, this was their new tenant. Interesting. *Very* interesting. "You probably spoke to my mom, Hannah."

She scrunched her face, and he tried not to notice how the gesture made her ten times more attractive. He really needed to tamp down whatever feelings—or hormones, rather—were acting up. Hadn't he already decided his focus needed to be on his new venture alone? And Morgan's history ought to be giving him far more pause.

"I spoke to Maggie . . . I think."

"That makes sense. She runs the front desk. I'll introduce you." He started around the side. "I can help you with your bags after we grab the key."

He pushed open the door to see his oldest sister at the reception desk. She hung up the phone and pushed her dark hair behind one ear. "Oh, hey, Bron." She ducked behind the desk. "What have the trees been telling you today?"

The tips of his ears heated. Their new tenant did not need to know that he spoke to the trees.

He cleared his throat. "Maggie, this is the new tenant, Morgan."

His sister stood from her crouching position and came around the desk, hand extended. "Morgan. We spoke on the phone. It's nice to meet you."

"I know I'm early, but I thought I might get settled in before visiting my family."

Maggie waved a hand through the air. "You're fine." A piercing shriek sounded from behind the heavy door of the butler's pantry that separated the Martin family living quarters from the bed and breakfast guest area. "Oh my, that would be Grace—my eight-month-old." She fished around in the top drawer of the desk and pulled out a key. "Bronson, would you mind taking Morgan over?"

"Sure thing." Normally, he scoffed at any business surrounding the bed and breakfast—not that he thought himself above it, but if he didn't set some boundaries his sisters would have him chained inside the house, serving fruit in fancy glass dishes and folding toilet paper rolls to end on a point. From the beginning, he'd made it clear he wanted to invest his time in the outdoor work.

But it wouldn't be any trouble to show Morgan around. No trouble at all.

He took the key from Maggie and led Morgan back outside. They stopped at her car, where he grabbed her one suitcase.

"This it?"

She shrugged. "I'm a bit of a minimalist."

A minimalist, huh? He didn't think that was possible for a female—at least it wasn't for the females in his family. Even Josie, who could be content with little more than a notebook and pen, had been talked into building an extravagantly large house by her well-meaning husband.

Bronson carried Morgan's small suitcase up the stairs.

"I never thought I'd be living above a bookshop."

"My sister, Josie, runs the gift shop. Feel free to stop in and say hi."

"That's right. You guys are the *Little Women* family. I should have put it together with the name of the bed and breakfast."

They'd reached the landing, and Bronson jiggled the key in the lock while he tried to keep from growling out his answer. "That's us."

He opened the door, stepping into a three-by-three tiled space that served as a foyer before giving way to the small, two-bedroom apartment. "Here it is. Nothing fancy, but it's got a great view." He gestured out the two windows along the wall of the sitting area to acres of orchards that would soon be in full bloom. And across the street, beyond the library, lay the sparkling bay. Past that, the wide blue of the Atlantic Ocean swelled with endless possibilities—one of the reasons he loved this place. One of the reasons thoughts of setting off on his own sometimes made him sad.

"This is amazing. Perfect. More than perfect." Her voice cracked, and he tamped down a sense of panic. Was she going to cry?

He cleared his throat, gesturing to the small, half-kitchen. "Just the toaster oven and the mini-fridge, but if you ever need to cook something bigger, let one of us know. Mom's generous to a fault—I'm sure she won't mind you using our kitchen now and then."

She raised an eyebrow. "To a fault, huh?"

His neck heated. "Yeah." No sense straying into the occasional disagreements he and his mom had over her generosity—the latest involving a man from Dad's mission they'd hired to do yard work. After telling the guy to help himself to whatever food they'd had in the kitchen, the man had done exactly that. Bronson would never get over the stolen pot roast, but his Mom had brushed it off, insisting the man would enjoy it more than they would have.

Bronson couldn't bring himself to agree. There was something about being taken advantage of when offering help that rubbed him the wrong way. Maybe because it had happened to his father one-too-many times. Maybe because his mother's charity cases never made it up to her.

Morgan placed her bag on the floor of the sitting area. With the movement, a faint hint of something flowery and sweet wafted toward him. "So, why do you hate the *Little Women* thing so much?"

Had he been so obvious? "I'm a guy who grew up in a house of *Little Women*—all named for the characters . . . need I say more?"

She giggled. "I think it's endearing. That was one of my favorite books growing up. I need to read it again."

"There're copies galore for sale downstairs." He rolled his eyes.

"Isn't there a *Little Men*, too? Maybe I should read that one."

Yeah, like he'd not heard that joke when he'd been stuck at five foot two for a hundred years. He started for the door. "All the best, Morgan."

"The *Little Women* stuff really bothers you?"

His jaw tightened. "When my dad was around, it wasn't . . ." It wasn't so lonely. Sometimes, he even liked being the only son. Him and his dad, taking on the world—or at least sympathizing with one another in their small house full of women.

Now, he alone struggled to find his space in a house awash with women. Though once he moved out, he wasn't sure it'd be any better. He'd likely feel like a scumbag for abandoning his mom.

Get a grip, Bronson.

It was the twenty-first century, after all. The Martin females were capable. More than capable. He'd never known such strong-minded women.

"It wasn't . . ." Morgan prompted.

Bronson shook his head. No use unloading on their new tenant. "Nothing. Hey, it was nice meeting you. I mean, re-meeting you." He could have smacked himself for the slip-up. "If you need anything, let us know."

She raised her arms, palms up. "I think I have everything I need. Unless, of course, you know of any job openings for special education teachers?"

He perked up. "You're a teacher?"

"I am."

"No kidding. So am I. My sister Lizzie, too. She teaches music."

Morgan straightened, her eyes widening. "Maybe I'll fit in around here, huh?"

Did he mistake the longing in those green eyes? It'd make sense she'd be worried about being accepted, considering her past.

She stuffed her hands in her pockets. "What do you teach?"

"Eighth-grade English."

"Phew, glad you didn't say chemistry."

He laughed. "I learned my weaknesses early on."

"So, what's your favorite thing to teach in English?"

"*Wonder*. It's a novel."

Her eyes lit up. "One of my favorites. You have good taste."

"How about you? What grade do you teach?"

"I was at the high school up in Presque Isle, near the Canadian border. I'm hoping and praying I can find something down here."

"I'll pray with you. Good luck on your job search." He opened the door. "Guess I'll be seeing you around."

"Thanks, Bronson. For everything."

The way she said his name made him want to help her again. Maybe *he* could be a sort of answer to her prayer. "Hey, Morgan?"

"Yes?" She straightened from where she'd been unzipping her suitcase, flinging her wavy, auburn hair over one shoulder.

Without warning, the gossip from high school crowded his mind. Probably wasn't wise to ask if she was interested in helping with his summer camp before he got to know her. And if she'd moved in the middle of spring semester, that meant she left her school high and dry. Something didn't add up. He shook his head. His hormones were clouding his judgment. "Nothing. I hope you enjoy your time here."

She flashed him a grin that had his stomach flipping again. "Thanks."

He turned and shut the door behind him. Best to keep as far away from her as possible now. He couldn't afford to get involved with a woman with such immense baggage, no matter how drop-dead gorgeous.

He had big plans, big goals. And he would not allow a beautiful woman to distract him.

$\approx$ 3 $\approx$

I peered out the window of my new apartment and watched as Bronson walked through the back door of the bed and breakfast. The guy wasn't gifted at keeping his feelings off his face—he'd remembered what happened senior year. But I gave him credit. He'd been gracious. Then again, what had I expected —for him to kick me out?

I sighed, and left the window, tackling my suitcase again. I'd nearly chickened out on following through with my stay. If it hadn't been for the flat tire and the help Bronson had offered on the road, I'd be halfway to Pesque Isle by now. But the turn of events had changed my mind—not to mention the fact that I still hadn't met my little niece yet. I'd thought long and hard about returning to Camden, and now that I was here, I needed to follow through with my decision.

I needed to make things right.

But my first hour in Camden had proven the difficulty of that feat. Mrs. Davis couldn't get me out of her house fast enough. And what had I expected? Open arms? Forgiveness?

I needed to get real. Building a relationship with the Davises would require nothing short of a miracle. A miracle, and time.

Like it or not, I was here to stay.

I finished unpacking my things. I hadn't exaggerated when I'd told Bronson I was a minimalist. After high school, after hours of therapy, I'd decided to concentrate on simplicity and utility. A handful of outfits, a couple of shoes. I'd had the same quilted coverlet since high school, the same worn slippers and winter coat. Simplicity served me well. Besides, beautiful things only reminded me of what Isabel would never experience.

My therapist said that sort of thinking was harmful. But the one time I'd tried to splurge on a new outfit for my cousin's wedding, I'd left the store practically hyperventilating, the thought of spending my money on something decadent threatening to eat me alive.

And so, I saved and I gave. Mostly to Mothers Against Drunk Driving and Isabel's scholarship fund.

And my saving had done some good, for now it afforded me a few months without employment. A few months to come back to Camden and figure things out. Hopefully.

After I'd stored my empty suitcase neatly beneath the full-size bed, I grabbed my phone and my wallet and left the apartment, locking the door behind me with the key Bronson had given me.

I ducked into the bookshop on a whim, a bell above the door greeting me. A pretty woman with straight brown hair looked up from where she stood at a desk. "Hello!"

My gaze swept over the generous windows, the rustic bookcases, and a ladder to reach higher shelves. A spiral staircase led to a second-story loft, and a couple sat playing a game of chess beside a rustic fireplace.

I returned my focus to the woman behind the desk. "Hi. My name's Morgan. I'm the new tenant living upstairs."

Her face lit up. She came around the counter, holding out her hand. "It's so nice to meet you."

Clearly, this woman didn't remember me from high school. "You're Josie?"

She shook her head. "I'm Lizzie. Josie ran out for a bit."

"You're the teacher Bronson was just telling me about."

"I was a music teacher, but I've been out of a teaching job for several months now. I'm staying busy."

She practically bounced on her toes, as if she wanted to say more, as if she had secrets to tell that she could barely contain. I wondered what it would feel like to be that excited about life again.

"I'm looking for a teaching job, myself."

"What do you teach?" she asked.

"Special education."

Her eyes grew wide. "That's a special calling, indeed. I bet you're great with the kids."

I shrugged off her compliment. What about me, in the few minutes she'd known me, made her think I was good at my job?

"Bronson must have told you about the camp for students he's starting, then."

"No. No, he didn't." We'd only spent all of fifteen minutes together. Maybe thirty if I counted watching him change my flat tire, the way his hands slid the new tire into place, those strong fingers confident and sure. Everything about him spoke of dependability, stability, safety. Was that what I was drawn to? Whatever the reason, I wouldn't dwell on it. That road was not one I planned to walk down.

Lizzie's face fell. "Oh. I'm sure he can tell you about it better than I can, but I'm so excited for it. The kids will work in the orchard and help plan the apple business, go kayaking on the harbor, get good and dirty. Just experience life out in the open."

I licked my lips. "That sounds fabulous."

And it really did. It shouldn't bother me that Bronson hadn't said anything about it. After he realized who I was, there'd been a shift between us. Could I blame him?

After a couple more minutes of chatting with Lizzie, I took

my leave. This day wouldn't get much easier, because the next item on my list was visiting my parents.

I could only hope their reception would be warmer than the one I'd received from Isabel's mom.

WHEN I PULLED INTO THE DRIVE OF MY PARENTS' SPRAWLING waterfront home, I breathed a sigh at the sight of my sister's new minivan in front of the house. Jenna had a way of softening life all around. Jenna was the reason I'd made the difficult decision to come home in the first place.

The door to my Mazda felt ten times heavier than when I'd opened it twenty minutes earlier. Shoving my phone and my keys into my pocket, I started up the cobbled walkway. The path lights flickered on, signaling the end of daylight. Was my family sitting down to dinner? Had Jenna told them I was in town?

I stared at the front door, vacillating between ringing the bell and inching the door open. If I chose the latter, what would I say? Somehow neither *Guess who?* or *Anyone home?* seemed appropriate.

I decided on a light knock. More personable than a bell, more formal than simply entering the house as if I'd never left.

A moment later, the door opened and I was enveloped in my older sister's arms, her joyful shrieks piercing my eardrum.

I clutched her tight, inhaling the familiar scent of her Victoria's Secret perfume, relishing the slight squishiness of her. How often had we stayed up late at night, trading secrets from one bunk to the other? And although I was the younger sister by two years, Jenna never scoffed at hanging out with me and Isabel. She wasn't the perfect sister, of course—we fought better than most, but we loved better than most, too.

When Jenna finally released me, I was shaking, my cheeks wet. She'd visited me up in Presque Isle often, but it had been a good nine months since I'd seen her.

"Oh my."

I swiped at my tears to see my mother standing at the threshold of the foyer, her hand hovering at her throat.

"Morgan . . . it's . . . it's really you."

"Hey, Mom."

"What's all the—" My father stopped beside my mom, his mouth falling open at the sight of me.

"Hi, Dad. I—I hope it's okay that I came."

He looked older since I'd last seen him. His hairline had crept farther back on his head and wrinkles creased his eyes, but the deep brown orbs themselves were exactly as I remembered, and now they washed over me, drinking me in.

A sob escaped my throat. Really, I'd never cried so much. Had thought juvenile detention had squelched any emotions I had left. Turns out I was wrong.

"I—I'm sorry it's been so long. I hope it's okay," I repeated.

They'd come to visit me now and then, but it couldn't be lost on them what a big step this was for me—coming back to Camden. Coming *home*.

And then I was in their arms, my forehead pressed against my father's lips, my mother's hair tickling my nose. "Of course, it's okay, sweetie," my father said. "It's more than okay."

❦

"I can't get over her. She's absolutely perfect." I gazed down at Jenna's newborn daughter, cradled snug in my arms after a dinner of chicken pancetta. Wisps of light hair feathered the top of her head. Round, rosy cheeks above a puckered mouth. Everything about her endeared her to me, causing a foreign and fierce sense of protectiveness to swell over me.

Though I never considered myself maternal, this feeling swirling within proved the instinct wasn't dead. I ran my finger down my niece's arm until it reached her tiny fingers. She curled her fingers around mine, and I thought of Isabel. With newfound clarity, I glimpsed the sorrow Mrs. Davis knew. I understood why she couldn't stand to look at me, let alone forgive me. If anyone ever caused harm to this little bundle—even unintentionally, I'd be tempted to string them up by their heels.

"We're kind of attached." Greg, Jenna's husband shared a smile with my sister and my belly lurched. I was happy for my sister, truly I was. What then, was this ugly jealousy fighting to the surface?

I shoved it aside, sank deeper into the newborn warmth of my little niece. Amelia.

Mom swirled the last of her red wine around in the bottom of her glass. Her gaze turned dreamy as she stared at me. I shifted in my seat.

"Oh." She sat up straighter, her petite fingers tapping the table. I could imagine her sitting at a conference table at her interior design firm, mimicking the gesture. *Oh, let's try some chintz fabric on that corner chair.* Or *Oh, the kitchen should absolutely have a two-tone color scheme to accent the island.* "I need to put fresh sheets on your bed," she said.

That she still thought of it as *my* bed warmed me at the same time it freaked me out. Surely, she'd turned my room into an exercise studio or office by now? Surely, she hadn't kept it as a memorial to me all these years?

"I—I'm not staying, Mom. I rented a place not far from here."

"Oh?"

This time, the one small word sounded quite different than it had a moment earlier. More like *Oh, you don't think the chintz fabric is the best choice?* Or *Oh, you didn't tell me we needed to plan for a* double *oven.*

"Yes. I'm renting a small place at The Orchard House Bed and Breakfast. It's not a room, exactly. It's a rental above their gift shop."

"Well, honey, there's no need for that. If you're staying long term, you should stay with us. Do you even have a job?"

I swallowed, trapped. Suddenly the weight of little Amelia threatened to crush me. I stood, carefully handing my niece to my sister. I refused to tarnish her in any way—even if it was something as little as sensing my anxiety. "Not yet, but I have some savings. I really think—"

"Teaching jobs are hard to come by in a close-knit town like this. Besides, don't you think with everything . . ."

Dad placed his hand on my mother's arm. A warning, an attempt to reign her in.

Must she point out the obvious? Didn't she realize how difficult it was for me to show my face in this town? I wasn't stupid. I knew my past would be an obstacle in the school board hiring me on. I would be in charge of molding young minds, after all. Every day.

Perhaps they'd consider inviting me in for an assembly about drinking and driving—the kind where the speaker tearfully recounts the horrible decisions she'd made on a single night that killed her best friend. I could picture myself standing before a group of high-schoolers, telling them how I badly misjudged the way a few drinks could affect my judgment. How I would give anything to go back and change my actions that night.

And I would. I'd give anything. But God hadn't agreed to that deal yet. And while the decent people of Camden would likely consider me for a good old school assembly, I wondered if the thought of me with their impressionable children day after day might be a major hang-up.

I leaned down and planted a kiss on Amelia's forehead. "I better get going." I had no reason to leave. I didn't have a job to wake early for the next day, no boyfriend waiting to spend time with me. For goodness sake, I didn't even notice a television in my new apartment. No, what I had was a date with a pint of Ben &

Jerry's Chunky Monkey ice cream and the latest Kristin Harmel novel.

"Honey, don't leave. I didn't mean—" Mom started.

I leaned over the table and placed a hand on hers. "I know, Mom. It's okay. Maybe we could take a walk sometime this weekend?" I didn't want to leave anything heavy between us.

Mom's eyes lit up. "I'd love that."

I smiled and bent to kiss my father goodbye.

When I reached the foyer, Jenna chased after me. "I'll walk you to your car."

We strolled down the lighted path, silent at first.

"Morgan," Jenna started when we reached my Mazda.

We faced one another. My sister's hazel, almond-shaped eyes landed on me. She was beautiful. Though we shared the same auburn hair, it had always looked more stylish and elegant on her.

"You are the bravest woman I know."

I rolled my eyes. "There's nothing brave about slinking out of the family dinner early."

She slapped my arm gently with the back of her hand. "You know what I mean. For coming back here. For facing your fears. For facing the past."

Maybe more stupid than brave. If my own mother couldn't spend one night in my presence without bringing up Isabel, how was I to expect that anyone else in this town would look past my sins? How was I to expect that Mrs. Davis would forgive me?

"Amelia is the most precious little person on this planet," I said, changing the subject to what may well be my new favorite topic.

My sister beamed, the lights from the window reflecting off her straight white teeth. I wondered if she still wore her retainer at night. I'd left mine behind when I left for juvie, and my bottom teeth had shifted.

"She is, isn't she?" She bit her bottom lip, and blinked fast, her next words quieter. "I'm glad she'll have her Auntie Morgan nearby as she grows up."

Warmth stirred in my chest. Auntie Morgan. It was like an entirely new identity I could cling to—one in which I could be proud. Here was a new beginning. I could be the best aunt in all of Camden, in all the world, even.

Jenna wrapped me in a hug and I closed my eyes, soaking her up. My beautiful, perfect sister beside my beautiful, perfect childhood home. Inside were my supportive, loving parents. I'd had it all.

I'd had it all, and I'd thrown it all away.

4

Bronson leaned back in his chair at the kitchen bar, surveying the seeds of his dreams taking root before his eyes. The middle school and high school had agreed to email the parents of every student in the sixth through ninth grades with the PDF flyer he'd created. They'd also post it on bulletin boards and inform students of the opportunity over morning announcements.

It was happening.

"And what do you have there, young man?"

He jumped at the sound of his aunt's voice from behind him. The woman sure was stealthy for her age.

"Aunt Pris, I thought you were taking a nap." He'd set up his laptop downstairs off the kitchen rather than in his room, choosing the rare quiet and the view of the orchards over his small, third-floor bedroom.

"I did. Twenty minutes is all one needs, you know. More than that and I'll be tossing and turning tonight."

Amie breezed through the back door, her cheeks flushed from the cold.

"Besides, Ed's taking me out for an early dinner."

"Aunt Pris." Amie walked straight to her, then stooped to kiss their aunt's cheek. "You and Mr. Colton are the cutest thing since Ron Weasley and Hermione Granger."

Bronson rolled his eyes.

"Hermione who?" Aunt Pris asked.

"From Harry Potter, Aunt Pris! I'll lend you my copies."

"I much prefer a good Agatha Christie novel, thank you very much."

Amie shrugged off her jacket. "Either way, you two are adorable. Where's Mr. Colton taking you today?"

"*Natalie's*, I think."

"Good choice. Good food." Bronson imagined their lobster and his mouth watered. What was for dinner tonight, anyway?

"Good atmosphere," Amie said. "That's just as important as the food."

"Not in my opinion." Bronson closed his laptop.

"The way you two go on, you might think Ed and I were in high school. We simply enjoy the companionship."

"Aww, come on, Aunt Pris. It's obvious Mr. Colton has the hots for you. Don't fight it." Bronson ducked out of the way of Amie's playful slap.

"The hots?"

"He's into you, Aunt Pris," Amie's mouth twitched.

Aunt Pris swatted a hand through the air and bent to pet Cragen, her rather fat Bichon Frise, before turning to Bronson. "Never mind all that. Show me your new project."

Bronson hesitated before reopening his laptop. "It's a flyer I'm making for the summer camp. What do you think?"

The two women peered over his shoulder.

"Wouldn't a little apple tree be perfect in the upper corner?" Amie pointed to the top of the screen. "Why don't you let me do it for you, Bronson."

He'd looked at clip art, but it all looked too cartoonish, too childish. Maybe he should accept his sister's help, she was the artist after all. "Yeah, sure. Can you get it done tonight? I plan to send it out next week."

"You bet."

"Sometimes you're not half bad, little sister."

"Does this mean you'll reconsider a date with Lacy?"

"Nope."

She sighed, grabbed her coat, and headed up the stairs. "Worth a try, I guess."

Silence enveloped the room with her absence. Aunt Pris still looked over his shoulder.

"So, what do you think, Aunt Pris?"

"A bit pricey, isn't it?"

He stared at the numbers at the bottom of the page. He'd formed monthly and weekly sessions, had tried to formulate the lowest number possible to fund the materials for the projects. At least another teacher on board to help him, maybe a counselor if he could swing it. The kids would need to eat. They'd take trips now and again. They'd have to rent kayaks and fishing poles. And he'd need to get paid at least a small stipend for his time. His school loans wouldn't pay themselves.

He leaned back in his chair. "I've crunched the numbers over and over. It's not a steal, of course, but the fact is, a camp like this requires money."

The amount wasn't that bad, was it? Old people thought paying a few bucks for a coffee was highway robbery. They were still stuck in the fifties or sixties, when a gallon of milk was ninety-five cents and a decent home went for under twenty grand.

Still, Aunt Pris was right. When he began this endeavor, the goal had been to work with underprivileged kids. And while that could still be his long-term goal, he'd never get the camp off the ground if they didn't start with a little profit.

The last thing he needed was a well-intentioned camp that failed after the first year. The town would have a field day. He could hear the gossip now.

I guess the apple didn't fall too far from the tree with the young Martin's apple camp, did it?

What can you expect from Amos's son?

Good heart, bad business.

"I take it you are expecting a certain . . . clientele for your camp, then?"

Aunt Pris's question unsteadied him, and his defenses rose. "It's the first year. Maybe once things get rolling and we start making a profit off the orchard, we could offer a few scholarships. I'd like to help kids from all sorts of backgrounds, but you're right. This year, our camp will probably be filled with kids whose parents have deep pockets."

If it was filled at all. Maybe kids wouldn't want to join the camp. Maybe they'd rather stay inside with their video games and air conditioning. The age he targeted didn't exactly need a babysitter while their parents went to work. If kids attended, it would be because they found genuine interest in an outdoor camp that would expand their mind and benefit their physical health, or because their parents wanted to find a way to keep them out of trouble and allow them a little fresh air.

Another gust of cool air met his skin as his mom bustled in with a bag of groceries, Maggie's son Davey tearing in behind her.

"Hey," she said, placing the bag on the counter. "Aunt Pris, Ed just pulled in. I told him I'd let you know he was here, but he insists on coming to the door like a gentleman."

"That old coot." Bronson's aunt wriggled one arm into her jacket. He helped her into the other. "No need for such fuss at our age, I'll tell you." She gave Bronson a rare smile. "Thank you, dear."

"Uncle Bronson!" Davey launched himself at Bronson, raising his hand for a high five.

"Hey, little dude. How was school today?"

"Great! We made an animal allegation."

Bronson looked at his mom for help, but she was already

sorting through the groceries. Two dozen eggs, a sack of flour, bacon, blueberries, kiwi, and sugar. With the five-course breakfast she served guests, she may be the market's best customer.

"An animal *allegation*? That sounds pretty intense. I'm afraid you'll have to teach me what that is."

Davey dropped his backpack to the floor and unzipped it, pulling out a lunchbox, a water bottle, and a handful of papers. "Here. An animal . . . allegation!"

He handed Bronson a drawing of a lion with a yellow oval in his pawed hand. At the top in his nephew's large, neat handwriting read, *Lions like lemons*.

"Oh, alliteration!" Bronson smiled. "This is some good alliteration, buddy."

"Thanks. I'll show Mommy." He grabbed the paper out of Bronson's hand and started off toward the front desk, where Maggie was likely finishing out the day.

"Hey, Bronson?" His mom stared distractedly into the refrigerator. "I'm having some mulch delivered tomorrow. You think you could help Lizzie spread it around the front garden beds?"

He bit back a groan. Saturdays were precious. He'd planned on pruning more trees, on working the soil and his compost piles. With the neglect of the orchard the last several decades, the best way to ensure a bounty of apples was constant soil improvement and adding new trees as he was able.

But of course, he wouldn't turn his mom down. He was the man of the house, after all. "Sure, Mom. We'll make a quick job of it."

Her face relaxed. "Thank you."

Once again, the door opened, a fresh burst of air sweeping into the breakfast nook and the kitchen. His older sister, Josie, bounced in, an eighteen-month-old Amos on her hip. "Hello!" she called out with her usual burst of energy. She dumped Amos on Bronson's lap. The toddler gave him a wide grin and Bronson tilted him back and tickled his stomach.

"Mom, what do you think?" Josie held a piece of square cardstock out to their mother.

"Oh, it's lovely. Beautiful, Josie. I love the flowers. It's exactly what Lizzie would want."

"Thanks. Although keeping it a surprise will be hard."

Mom leaned down to retrieve a cutting board from the cabinet. "Does anyone do surprise bridal showers anymore? It seems like brides these days always want to plan everything."

"Oh, we have to surprise her, Mom. She'll be too nervous about it, otherwise. Or stressing that we're going through too much trouble." She tapped her chin with a pointer finger. "Speaking of which . . . Bronson, mark your calendar for June 25th. We'll need help setting up the barn, and then of course, moving all the gifts out after—"

"Whoa, whoa, whoa. I thought we were putting events on hold this summer? I'm using the barn to run a camp."

"Events, sure. But this isn't just any event. This is for *Lizzie*. We're lucky Asher's footing the bill for French's Point for the wedding. The least we can do is give her the best down-home Orchard House bridal shower possible. Besides, your camp doesn't start until after Independence Day, right?"

"Wow, you actually listened," he muttered. "Sort of."

"It's one day, Bron. She's your sister. You're a smart guy—you'll figure out the logistics."

And he would. Of course, he would. Josie was right. Lizzie deserved the best. His sweet sister had not only fought cancer as a teenager, she had fought social anxiety and had lost her job as a music teacher last year. Meeting Asher Hill had been one of the best things that ever happened to her. Sure, it had taken Bronson a while to acknowledge that, but he was man enough to admit he'd been wrong about Lizzie's fiancé. His sister deserved a great shower—seriously, why did they call it that? But it would just be nice if someone in his family would choose to take his venture seriously. He wasn't asking for help with any of it—just a little space and freedom and *time* to get it all done.

"Yes, fine. Whatever you need." Bronson pulled one of Amos's chubby, wet hands away from the keyboard of his laptop.

Josie ruffled Bronson's hair and he craned his neck away. He *hated* when she did that. He wasn't five anymore.

She scooped Amos off his lap. "Shop's all locked up for the day. Hey, how's the new tenant? I haven't met her yet."

"Seems like she's pleased with the place." Mom peeled a carrot with long, expert strokes. "Her name's Morgan. She said she grew up here, but I don't remember her."

"Morgan . . . not Morgan *Dalton?*"

"That's it." Mom opened the container on the counter Bronson had set up for kitchen scraps and threw the peels in. Score one for the good bacteria that would inhabit his compost and feed his trees.

"Wow, I haven't seen her since high school . . . since . . ."

Bronson shot Josie a glare.

"Since what?" Mom asked.

Bronson stood, closing his laptop once again. "Come on, Josie. If anyone should know about needing second chances, it should be you. Maybe we shouldn't remind people who've already forgotten."

"What's that supposed to mean?"

His face heated. Josie had come home pregnant two years ago after having an affair with her college professor. It was probably the most scandalous thing that had ever happened to their family, and yet it had set into motion a new future for the Martin clan. Josie had been the brains behind the idea for the Orchard House Bed and Breakfast. If she'd stayed at college, if she'd never gotten pregnant, Aunt Pris's Victorian would be lifeless and empty, the orchard sold off to the highest bidder. Bronson would never be running an orchard and planning a summer camp, that was for sure.

Still, it had been low of him to bring up Josie's past. But the mention of Morgan's past sins made him want to defend her. Shield her from further pain.

Crazy, of course. Morgan hadn't asked for his help. Well, except for when he changed her flat tire.

"Sorry," he said. "I just don't think it's fair to talk about Morgan when she's not here to defend herself."

Mom's eyes traveled warily from Bronson, then back to Josie. "I don't need to know anyone else's business. As long as Morgan isn't some criminal or axe murderer, I don't need to know."

"Well, not an *axe* murderer, anyway . . ." Josie mumbled.

Bronson shook his head. Might as well just tell her, quick and plain. "Remember Esther's granddaughter, Isabel?" he asked his mother.

Mom's mouth pulled downward. "Yes, of course."

"Morgan was the one who was driving the night she died."

Mom bit her lip. "Oh, dear. Poor things."

"She's a special education teacher now. I talked to her yesterday. She got her act together." He narrowed a gaze at his sister.

Josie shrugged. "I have nothing against Morgan. I didn't mean anything by it, Bronson. Honest."

Mom brushed her bangs out of her face with the back of her forearm before slicing into a carrot. "If there's one thing I want Orchard House known for, it's for welcoming everyone, no matter their past—or their present."

It sounded so very *Martinish*. And while Bronson could get on board with the idea of it in words, all he could think about was the guy Mom had hired who'd stolen their food.

But Morgan wasn't a criminal. It had been one devastatingly, horrible mistake.

"Agreed," Josie said.

Bronson nodded. "I have to go check on Amie. She's working on something for me."

"Oh, hey, if you're not busy tomorrow afternoon, Tripp's shingling the roof. He could use all the hands he can get."

Sure. He'd lay some mulch, finish his flyer, turn his compost, plan his orchard and his summer camp, and help his brother-in-law build his dream home. He was Superman, after all.

"I think I called dibs on Bronson already." Mom winced. He hoped to high heaven it wasn't from guilt. She didn't need to feel guilty asking for his help. She was the one running a full-blown business. The least he could do was lay down some mulch.

"If Liz and I finish the mulch, I'll stop by and see if Tripp needs a hand, okay?" He really liked his brother-in-law, after all. They always had fun working together. If only there were more hours in the day.

Josie grinned. "You really are a good brother, Bronson."

"Yeah, yeah, yeah." He waved her off and ruffled Amos's head much like Josie had done a few minutes earlier to him. "And you're an okay sister."

He ducked out of the room, barely missing the swipe of her hand.

If he'd learned one thing growing up in the Martin household, it was that family came first. When it came down to it, nothing was more important than supporting his mother and sisters and aunt, making their burdens lighter any way he knew how.

If that meant his dreams came second, he'd simply have to work all the harder to see them to fruition.

❧   5   ☙

Sometimes, I'd forget about Isabel for hours at a time. In rare, glorious stretches, I'd forget about her for days. Sure, she was hidden in the back of my mind—the way she gave me all the whipped cream off her shakes and wouldn't eat the cherry until it hit the bottom. How she could dribble down a basketball court like nobody's business, a smooth seamless silhouette of coordination as she landed a perfect layup.

No one but me knew she abhorred basketball. I remember wondering how it was possible to be *so* good at something and still hate it. But Isabel proved it could be done. She'd received a free ride to Bowdoin College on a basketball scholarship.

She never even attended freshman orientation.

On days like this, with the sun about to dip behind the acres of the beautiful orchards, and the promise of spring in the air, Isabel wiggled to the front of my thoughts. She hung out there, as persistent as hot fudge on ice cream. And in a way, it was a relief. Because with her shining presence in the forefront of my mind, I could at least feel guilty. I could pay my penance—a penance I would never complete, but penance that, in some twisted way, soothed my spirit as it simultaneously tormented me.

It was when Isabel faded from my consciousness that I became scared. For what kind of a best friend was I to go on with life as if I hadn't killed her, as if all was well with the world—as if I had every right to live when she didn't?

Look at me, world! I'm Morgan Dalton, and I killed my best friend. Only you wouldn't know it today, would you? Because here I am enjoying a stroll through this beautiful orchard, watching the sunset, living my life as if I deserved to.

Thanks to a prominent defense lawyer my parents had hired, I'd only done two piddly years in juvie. He'd claimed my affluent, privileged lifestyle had done me a major disservice in knowing right from wrong. I'd pleaded guilty, acknowledged my sins in front of the world.

I deserved no less than life behind bars. But I remember how frightening the thought of giving my life over to the criminal justice system had been. If I really believed life behind bars was the just payment for ending Isabel's life, why hadn't I spoken up during the trial, asked to approach the judge's bench, no matter what my well-intentioned lawyer insisted upon?

Instead, I was found guilty but given a pathetic sentence on account of my being a minor *and* a poor little rich girl—two years in a juvenile detention center, rehab, community service, and a decade of probation in which I was not allowed to travel out of state.

In those early days behind bars, I'd been angry with my parents for hiring that lawyer, for going along with the defense story he'd created. Only in the last few years had I come to terms with the fact that I had no one but myself to blame. Of course, my parents wanted to ease my sentence. They wanted me to go on and live life, to redeem what I'd done.

And so that's what I'd strived toward since I walked out of juvie. I finished college. I vowed to give my life over to helping needy students, to helping kids like Isabel's brother.

Marcus . . . Isabel had been amazing with him, always carving out time for her brother, playing chess with him, coloring, building his Lego sets. Once, Jack Richards had made fun of Marcus at the bus stop and Isabel had laid him down flat, pinning him with the weight of her entire body until he cried "uncle."

Isabel loved Marcus with an intensity that proved, at least in my mind, that Isabel was a superior human being. While Jenna had taken me shopping before I was old enough to drive and sneaked me bubble gum and had even once given up a party with boys to take me to see *Harry Potter and the Deathly Hollows* (Part 2!), Marcus didn't provide Isabel with anything more tangible than his sweet, lopsided smile. And yet, Isabel loved him as if he daily gave her the sun and the moon.

Isabel's love for her brother prompted me to pursue a career in special education. Though never a career I dreamed for myself, I couldn't think of a better way to give my life in Isabel's honor.

Now, I opened my eyes to take in the view before me. Acres of rolling orchards, the bed and breakfast nestled at the bottom of the hill from where I stood at the very top. I craned my neck and could just make out one of the windows of my apartment. Beyond it, the harbor sparkled in the waning sunlight.

"Quite a sight, isn't it?" A deep voice from behind made me jump. I whirled to see Bronson, a pair of pruning shears in hand, his light blue t-shirt dirty.

"You startled me." I turned back toward the view. "It is beautiful." I squinted up at him. "I hope it's okay that I'm here. I needed a walk to clear my head."

"Of course, it's okay. This is the best place around to get some thinking done."

"I've certainly been doing a lot of that."

Bronson raised the shears to a tree and made a cut to one of the upper branches. "I asked around about teacher openings. Sorry, but I came up with nothing. Although the schools always need a good substitute."

I bit back a groan. The thought of corralling a new set of unfamiliar children each and every day ratcheted up my heartbeat. I did best with well-known schedules, well-known faces. With time to form relationships and bonds with my students. That's why this move back home had been such a big thing for me—I'd had to leave all of that behind.

"I'll keep that in mind. Thanks for looking into it, though." I hadn't gotten that far myself. But now that I'd met my niece, surely there was no going back. I'd *make* Camden work. I'd find something to do.

"Of course, positions for next year will likely be posted soon. In the meantime, if you're not crazy about substituting, I could hook you up with a contact of mine who has a tutoring business. He's always looking for good tutors."

"Thanks. I actually like the sound of that." One-on-one was more my jam, anyway.

Bronson lowered his shears and cleared his throat, seemed to wrestle with himself over whether to speak. "You know, I'm starting a summer camp this year."

"Your sister, Lizzie, mentioned that to me the other day. It sounds spectacular."

"I hope so." He looked over the orchards and his gaze clouded, but his smile grew. "I'll need some help if you're interested. There will be a lot of outdoor activities, teaching the kids about the orchards and all that, but some classroom time as well. Science experiments, basic accounting. Local field trips. We're starting an apple-picking venture and I want the kids in on it as much as possible."

A foreign emotion swept like a whirlwind through my chest. Bronson's excitement was contagious. Tangible.

Part of me was flattered he'd invite me, a virtual stranger, to be in on the start of his venture. Another part of me wondered if he extended the invitation out of pity.

And it was okay. I didn't hold it against him. My being here wasn't about me.

"It sounds wonderful, but I'm certain you can find more quali-fied candidates to help you." I wiggled my toes inside my worn sneakers.

Bronson shrugged. "I don't know about that. I've been asking around and it seems most teachers want their summers off. Go figure."

"Okay, keep me in mind, then, if no one more suitable comes along." My gaze landed on the flat, hose-like lines running on either side of the trees. "That's how you water all these trees, huh?"

Bronson perked up, laying the shears down. A foreign tug of attraction started in my middle at the sight of his broad shoul-ders, his t-shirt pulled taunt across his muscled arms as he bent and then straightened. "I took them out of storage today. It's called drip-tape. Efficient and cost-effective, as long as I don't miss any leaks."

"And it waters the entire orchard?"

He nodded. "It was my main project last spring. It made a huge difference in the harvest."

"We had a couple apple trees in our yard growing up. But the apples were always small and rotten."

"So were these when we moved in. This place was booming when Aunt Pris was our age though. Years of neglect caused the trees to grow more leaves, and with that, less desirable fruit." He gestured to the tree he cut. "Pruning is almost like a dance. I'm telling the tree which way I want it to grow, and it responds. There's a rhythm to it." He flashed me a grin and his brown eyes twinkled, doing nothing to quell the swirling in my stomach. "Too weird?"

I reminded myself to breathe. Hearing him talk about pruning as if it were a waltz . . . well, it wasn't doing anything to tamp down the attraction I already experienced when around him.

"I think it's fascinating. If you ever need help . . . I mean, I don't want to intrude, of course, but I love the outdoors and manual labor." In fact, yard work and exercise had been my sanity these last eight years. And when my muscles burned and I pushed harder, almost punishing myself, I'd occasionally reach a state of blissful emptiness. Pure exhaustion, where I didn't know anything but fatigued limbs and the sound of my own throbbing heart.

It was the closest I came to peace.

I blinked, pointing to the branch Bronson cut. "Are these the old trees? Are they still bearing fruit?"

"They are, though not as much as the younger ones. They're tired."

I raised an eyebrow. "So, you dance with them and hold conversations, do you?"

The tips of his ears grew pink at the mention of the comment Maggie made when I first arrived at the bed and breakfast. He cleared his throat. "As a matter of fact, as orchard manager, I consider it an important duty to talk to my trees."

I smiled. "I'll wager they're all the better for it."

He cleared his throat, picked up his shears. "If you're serious about helping, tomorrow after school I plan to run the rest of these lines. I can't pay you . . ."

I shook my head. "That's not what I was fishing for."

"Mom always makes enough for an extra plate at dinner. Maybe you'd want to join us?"

"Um, yeah. If you're sure it's not an imposition."

"We're in the business of hospitality, if you haven't noticed. No imposition at all." He gave me a wink that caused a tingle to race up my spine. "Enjoy the rest of your walk."

"Thanks." I watched the back of him, tall and lean, as he strode off toward the bed and breakfast. Eventually, the orchard branches hid him from view, leaving me with an empty, hopeful feeling I didn't quite recognize.

❧ 6 ☙

I clutched the file folder in my hand and buzzed the bell of the school door. Though I'd searched the school district's website for job openings, I hadn't found a single listing for a special education teacher. What would I do the following year if I couldn't find a job? I simply must get my foot in the door some way, even if it was as a substitute.

"Can I help you?"

"Hello." I hoped the lady in the office couldn't detect the slight waver in my voice. Probably not, considering the loud noise of the idling busses behind me, waiting to take students home as soon as the school day ended. "My name is Morgan Dalton. I'm here to drop off my resume."

The woman buzzed me in, and when I checked in with her, she pointed me to a door several yards down the hall. Before passing the threshold, I swallowed down my fear.

"Hello, can I help you?" A woman in her fifties with tortoise-shaped glasses and heavily penciled eyebrows greeted me.

"Hello. My name is Morgan Dalton. I just moved to Camden . . . well, I grew up in Camden. I just moved back here from up north."

Great. A teacher who tripped over her words. *Very professional, Morgan.*

I tried again. "I'm a special education teacher. I've looked at your teacher openings for next year but didn't see anything on the website in the special ed department." I paused, hoping her eyes might light up with excitement. *Why, we just found out we need a special ed teacher. What a stroke of fate that you walked in!*

No such luck.

I swallowed and pulled the papers out of my folder. "I thought I'd drop off my resume so you'd have it available if a position opened up."

The woman glanced at the folder in my hands but didn't make a move to take it from me. "I'm afraid what's posted online is all that will be available."

My gaze dropped to the nameplate on her desk. *Dorothy Silva.*

"I'd be open to subbing. I realize the school year's wrapping up, but if you needed another substitute, I'd be happy to jump on board."

The woman pushed back from her desk and held her hand out for my resume. I gave it over.

"I doubt we'll need any new subs this late in the year, but I can get you an application."

"Thank you. I appreciate that, Ms. Silva." I smiled. "Would it be okay if I check back in with you in a couple of weeks?"

She nodded as she opened a file drawer and pulled out a well-xeroxed bunch of pages. "Certainly. Fill this out and give it to the secretary out front. Have a good day, Ms. Dalton."

I left the office, fighting the discouragement building in my spirit. Last April, when the Pesque Isle school district was forced to consolidate their special education positions, two teachers had been cut, one of them being me. I didn't harbor ill feelings toward my coworkers who held seniority, I simply tried to roll with it. But I loved that school. I loved the kids and the faculty.

I'd decided to stay on as a long-term sub for an English

teacher going out on maternity leave in September. One of my special education colleagues, Nina, planned to retire the following year, and I'd received a verbal affirmation from the superintendent that I could have my job back if that were the case. But unexpected financial hardships and a falling stock market had disrupted Nina's plans. She'd told me she planned to stay on at the school when the teacher I'd been subbing for returned from leave.

That's when the notion of returning home first came to me. Then, when Jenna begged me to return to Camden after the birth of Amelia, I hadn't thought twice.

But now that I was here, would I find myself in the same predicament I was in at Presque Isle?

The school bell rang out as I turned right toward the foyer. Within moments, a sea of middle-schoolers surrounded me, most heading in the same direction I was, probably to catch their busses. I followed the flow, enjoying the chaos and bustle of kids calling out to their friends, backpacks bumping, notebooks and books in hands.

A tall man stood in the doors of one of the classrooms, bumping the fist of one of the students, saluting the next, and performing an elaborate handshake that looked more like a "Rock, Paper, Scissors" battle than a farewell handshake with another.

I blinked, recognizing the man as I came closer. Bronson.

"'Scuse me!" a girl from behind called out.

"Sorry," I mumbled, stepping to the side to allow her by, but not taking my gaze off Bronson as he said goodbye to each of his students—fifth graders, from the looks of them—with what looked to be a personalized handshake for each.

I watched, mesmerized as he turned on his heel in sync with a young girl before giving her a high five. The next was a high-step move followed by an elbow bump. And on down the line until only Bronson stood, watching his students make their way down the hall.

I came up beside him, my throat tight with emotion. "That was pretty amazing."

He blinked, jaw dropping. "Morgan. What are you doing here?"

"Thought I'd drop off my resume. There aren't any job openings for special ed here, but I didn't think it'd hurt."

His mouth turned downward. "It's always possible someone might turn in their resignation before the year's up."

I smiled. "Thanks."

"And if the teaching thing doesn't work out, you can find a job as a professional drip tape installer."

I laughed. I'd spent the last two afternoons helping Bronson lay down the rest of the drip tape in the orchards. The trees would stay well-watered this summer thanks to our hard work.

"As tempting as that is . . ."

His smile remained before he seemed to realize he stared. "If you give me a minute to grab my stuff, I could give you a ride home."

"Um, I have my own car, but I'll walk out with you?"

He shook his head. "I'm not thinking. Long day."

He stuffed papers, folders, and his laptop into a backpack and slung it over his shoulders. We walked back toward the foyer.

"So, the handshakes . . . you have a different one for each student?"

He grinned, and in it I saw the deep affection and enthusiasm he held for his job. For his students. "It started last year. One of my kids greeted me with a handshake and then tacked on a salute. Soon, the others were lining up after, creating their own handshakes. It's my job to memorize them."

"That is so cool."

"I think it makes them feel special, you know? Like they're seen. That's what I want for them."

He pushed open the door of the school and waved to a student through the windows of one of the last busses pulling out. When we reached my car, he opened the driver's door for me.

"Will I see you at supper tonight? You still haven't accepted the only payment I can render for all the help you've given me in the orchards."

"You can't even afford that. Your mother's feeding me," I teased.

"I pay her by doing dishes." He winked. "How about it? Humor me?"

Was it wise to spend more time with the Martin family? With Bronson, a man I was thinking about far too often of late?

"I'll be there."

What was the harm in a single, family meal?

⁂

MAYBE IT'D BEEN A MISTAKE TO INVITE MORGAN TO DINNER. He'd made the ridiculous assumption that his family knew how to behave around a guest. *His* guest. But he'd been wrong.

Dead wrong.

It started downhill when Mom had passed a bowl of peas to Amie. He knew what was coming before she'd even scooped them on her plate and handed them to him.

"Try to behave with these now, Bronson."

"Amie . . ." He used the same tone he'd use with one of his students who had misbehaved.

It had no effect.

Amie turned to Morgan, who sat beside Bronson. "When Bronson was five, he shoved a pea up his nose. Mom and Dad could not get it out to save their lives. They took him to the ER. How'd they get it out, Bronson? Forceps, vacuum, the jaws of life?"

"I don't remember. I was *five*," he ground out.

"The doctor said he had the smallest nasal passages he'd ever seen." Mom cut into her steak while smiling at Morgan. "But then again, he was such a tiny child."

"Mom . . ."

"I remember. We went to high school together." Morgan shot a radiant smile in his direction, seemingly oblivious to how mortifying this topic of conversation was to him. "You had to have been the shortest kid in our class, right, Bronson? But it's amazing how you grew."

"Oh, remember the church nativity play when you played Joseph?" Amie started giggling, eliciting the same from Aunt Pris and even Lizzie.

"You were adorable, Bronson," Aunt Pris said. She hardly ever gave compliments. Why this moment?

Between fits and starts, Amie continued. "The girl who played Mary was nearly five feet. They looked so awkward standing up on the church altar, but it really was sweet, Bronson."

"I have pictures!" Mom seemed to forget her strict rule of not getting up from the dinner table. She started toward the hutch where they stored old photo albums.

Bronson groaned. "Mom, can we *please* not do this now?"

"I'm sure Morgan would love to see them."

He glanced at the woman beside him. Something in his gaze must have conveyed his desperation, for she grew serious. "I don't want to interrupt dinner, Mrs. Martin. Maybe I could see them later?"

He released a long breath. Mom's smile faltered as she looked from Morgan to Bronson. "Yes, of course. Let's finish dinner first."

He'd never brought a girl home to dinner before tonight. Not that he and Morgan were dating, or anything more than friends. Not even friends, really. Colleagues. A fellow teacher. A woman who helped him in his orchards.

A beautiful, intelligent, hardworking woman.

She'd been a tremendous help in laying down the drip tape the last couple of days. She may be petite, but their new tenant was a hard worker—and all for the simple payment of a meal. She'd even turned down his offer of a water break and laughed at his corny water jokes—Where can you find an ocean with no water? (On a map!) Why are some fish at the bottom of the ocean? (Because they dropped out of school!)

Bronson took a hefty bite of steak and mashed potatoes, chewing carefully before trying to change the subject to something that wouldn't bring to mind his small nasal passages and former mini-stature. "How's August, Amie? I haven't seen him around in a while."

Amie straightened her spine. "We actually broke up last week."

The table erupted.

"Amie, what happened?" from Lizzie.

"Do you want to talk about it, honey?" from Mom.

"Ed didn't say a thing to me!" from Aunt Pris.

"That guy was the one good—" Bronson cut his words off beneath Amie's glare.

Amie pushed her blonde curls off her shoulder, her gaze uncharacteristically demure. "I'm okay. We're okay. We want different things, is all."

Bronson studied his sister. Was she actually okay?

Amie had always been unpredictable. But below the surface of her immaculate veneer was a discontent he'd always sensed but often ignored.

"*What* different things?" Bronson asked.

"A lot of different things, actually."

"Like . . ."

She huffed. "August didn't support what was important to me —my art, this new inter-faith group I'm starting . . ."

His head jerked up. "What faith group?"

She waved a hand at him. "It's just an idea I had to dig deeper into spiritual truths. It might not go anywhere. But that's not the point. The point is I'd like my boyfriend's support on things that are important to me."

What kind of faith group did Amie have in mind? He shared a look with his mother before speaking again. "So, you broke things off, or did August?"

Amie placed her water glass down a bit too hard. "Bronson, that is none of your business." She turned to Morgan. "I'm not sure if you're aware of it, but my brother is quite the interrogator."

"I am not." He turned to Morgan, ready to defend himself, but not before Lizzie chimed in.

"I don't know, Bronson. Remember when Asher first came around? You were on him like . . . what was it you'd said?" She cast a coy look at Amie.

Amie smiled, and it broke the tension. "White on rice."

Lizzie giggled. "That's right. You gave him such a hard time."

"And rightly so with his sketchy background. Lucky for him he turned himself around. But back to August." Bronson looked at his mom. "Did you know about this?"

Morgan cleared her throat, pushing back from the table. "I think I should excuse myself."

Amie reached across the table. "No, Morgan, please don't go. I promise we'll behave ourselves better. Won't we, Bronson?"

"Yeah, sorry about that." At least she'd been entertained by the trip into his humiliating past earlier. "Didn't mean to make things awkward for you—not exactly what you bargained for, huh?"

She smiled, showcasing a small dimple on her right cheek. "It's okay, really. I'm actually quite tired and think I'll turn in early. Mrs. Martin, thank you for dinner. It was so good."

Bronson stood. "I'll walk you over."

She laughed, and it was one of the most beautiful sounds he'd ever heard.

Wow . . .

The most beautiful? Where had his hesitancy about getting attached to her gone in the space of forty-eight hours? Maybe it hadn't been wise to accept her help in the orchards after all.

"I think I can manage fifty feet on my own."

He shrugged. "Mom raised me to be a gentleman. You'll have to take it up with her."

Bronson's mother held out her hand to Morgan. "It was lovely to have you, dear. You're welcome anytime. I mean that, okay?"

"Thank you, Mrs. Martin."

"Please, call me Hannah."

Lizzie twisted from her spot at the sink. "Bye, Morgan! If you're ever up for a walk in the woods, I'm always looking for a hiking partner."

"I'd love that." Morgan waved to Aunt Pris and said one last goodbye before crossing the threshold, Bronson behind her.

They slipped into the cool night and he closed the door, the quiet a distinct contrast to the warm noise and bustle of the house. The scent of fresh mulch lingered in the air.

"Your family is really nice."

"Kind of crazy though, right?"

She giggled. "A little, but you obviously care about each other. I love how you talk about everything and anything."

"We didn't have a television growing up. You learn to get in everyone's business if there's no option to veg out in front of a screen all night."

"Wow, you *are* the March family."

He groaned and looked up at the star-studded sky.

She laughed, again. "Sorry, sorry. You really do hate that, don't you?"

"I'll let it slide. This time." He winked down at her, a lightness stirring in his chest. It was on the tip of his tongue to tell her what a great laugh she had. But he caught himself. They'd just met. How well did he really know her?

"Thanks again, Bronson. I had fun working in the orchards. Anytime you need more help, let me know."

"I'll definitely take you up on that." He grinned down at her, and he thought how goofy he probably looked. Smitten. Besotted. Those are the words classic novels like *Wuthering Heights* would have used.

Lovesick. Crazy.

His words.

Ugh, what was with him?

"Goodnight." She started up the stairs, and something desperate within him caused him to open his mouth.

"Morgan."

She turned.

"What happens when you get water on a table?"

She rolled her eyes, but the smile on her face was worth the groan he was about to earn. "What?"

"It becomes a pool table."

She shook her head in mock sadness over his pathetic jokes. "Goodnight, Bronson."

"Goodnight, Morgan."

He waited until she was safely inside her apartment, then turned toward the headlights pulling up the drive.

Mr. Colton's truck pulled alongside Morgan's car. The older man turned off the truck and slid out of the driver's seat, his motions careful and slow. When he reached Mr. Colton's age, Bronson would probably be happy to still be driving, never mind racing about to see his lady-love.

"You just can't stay away, can you, Mr. Colton?"

The distinguished older man raised an eyebrow at Bronson. "Actually, Bronson, it's you I've come to talk to tonight."

❧ 7 ❧

"What's this all about?"

Bronson leaned over, propping his elbows on the tops of outspread knees. Across from him in the sitting room, Mr. Colton and Aunt Pris perched on a loveseat, Cragen content in Aunt Pris's lap.

"We have a proposition for you, young man," Mr. Colton said.

"Okay. Sure." What did they have up their sleeves?

His blood ran cold. Oh no. They were trying to dissuade him from doing the summer camp. Aunt Pris hadn't been pleased about his target audience. They didn't want to see him tarnish the legacy of the orchards.

But Aunt Pris had been ready to sell the orchards to a developer before Josie had proposed the bed and breakfast idea. This venture—carrying on the legacy of his father, growing young minds and producing something that would bring joy, memories, and good old tangible food—was his dream.

"We'd like to talk to you about the possibility of funding a few scholarships for your summer camp." Mr. Colton's eyes twinkled beneath bushy brows.

"I appreciate your concern, sir, but—wait. What?"

One corner of Aunt Pris's wrinkled mouth lifted. "I talked over the possibility with Ed the other night and we agreed it would be a meaningful investment the two of us could work on together."

"Wow . . . Aunt Pris, Mr. Colton . . . I'm—I don't know what to say."

"We hope you'll allow us to do it, young man." Mr. Colton shared a smile with Bronson's aunt.

Aunt Pris ran her hands over Cragen's wiry fur. "When I saw your flyer, it struck me that this is not the sort of school your own parents could have afforded for you when you were young. We'd like to do something about that."

This had the potential to change the dynamics of the camp entirely. Not to mention the influx of applications it would create, as well as publicity.

"Let's talk numbers," Mr. Colton said. "Pris tells me you're offering weekly and summer-long sessions. How many kids are you aiming to accommodate?"

Bronson cleared his throat. "To be honest, sir, I planned to see how many applications we received and go from there."

Aunt Pris made a tsking sound.

"I know, I know. Not the best business plan." He held his hands out. "I'm open to suggestions."

"Well, since you're asking . . ." Aunt Pris began. "I think starting small is best. Grow it, see what sort of a profit you make with the orchard this year. If it were me, I'd aim to pour one-hundred percent of the profit back into the camp for next year."

Bronson nodded. "That seems sound." It wouldn't make a dent in his student loans or enable him to move out of Orchard House quite yet, but it made sense. "What do you think, Mr. Colton?"

"Pris always did have a good head on her shoulders for business. How much did you turn over when you ran the orchards?"

Aunt Pris waved a hand through the air. "Never mind all that. I wouldn't want to make the boy feel bad. We did well enough."

Mr. Colton chuckled, dragging his gaze away from Bronson's aunt. Saints alive, the old man really *was* smitten.

"Are you hiring any help? How many kids would you feel comfortable with in one week?"

Bronson's mouth tightened. "I would need at least one other person. Maybe an older teen or two to serve as counselors. I don't want to take on too many kids, it would ruin the entire vision. I want a personal, guided experience." He leaned back, sighed. "I'd feel comfortable with fifteen. Twelve, more ideally."

Aunt Pris puckered her lips. "And how many weeks do you plan to run the camp?"

"Eight, starting the week after the Fourth of July. That will bring us to the beginning of school. Although it will also be the start of apple-picking season. My plan was to invite the kids who were truly invested in the camp to help run the business, if they wanted. Give them a part-time job of sorts."

She tapped her chin. "So, potentially ninety-six students throughout the summer."

"Some will sign up for a four or eight-week session, so potentially much less."

Aunt Pris stared at the throw rug at her feet. Bronson could practically see the numbers turning in her head, and a newfound respect for his aged relative swept through him. He'd nearly forgotten she ran the orchard herself for a time after her parents died and her first husband fell deep into the bottle. He should have gone to her sooner. No matter if more up-and-coming methods plastered themselves all over the internet, he could have benefited from her firsthand experience.

"I'm willing to offer six weekly scholarships and one summer-long session scholarship."

He scrambled for numbers. She offered a lot of money. The opportunity for seven kids to attend his camp for free. Kids who might not otherwise be able to attend. "Aunt Pris, that's overly generous." She hadn't even been keen on the idea of a bunch of adolescents running around her property to begin with. But the woman's tough exterior was no match for her soft heart.

"And I will match that, young man. As well as an extra five-thousand-dollar seed money to help you with startup costs, including hiring those teachers and counselors—and paying yourself, of course."

Bronson blinked. He opened his mouth, then closed it, emotion climbing his throat. He couldn't remember the last time he'd cried—when Dad died, probably. But these two were goading the tears to come.

His dream. Materializing before his eyes. Aunt Pris and Mr. Colton—they believed in him.

But what if they were wrong for placing their confidence in this camp? What if it flopped? What if no one wanted to come, even with a scholarship?

He shook his head. "It's too much. Thank you. Both of you, thank you so much for your generosity, and it's not that I'm not honored and absolutely grateful." He dragged in a breath, his thoughts whirling. "I'd feel okay accepting the scholarships, but I'm afraid I can't accept any additional money. It's just too risky."

"Risky? What do you call renovating my childhood home and inviting all my nieces and nephews to come live with me? What do you call inviting strangers into my home to stay the night? As far as I'm concerned, dear, any aversion to risk I've held went out the window a couple years ago when your brash sister approached me with her crazy idea of turning this place into an inn."

"Son." Mr. Colton scooted forward on the loveseat and slipped his hand into Aunt Pris's. The sight of their ancient, wrinkled hands all wound up together like tangled tree roots caused something to hitch in his chest. He wasn't the sentimental sort, but Aunt Pris and Mr. Colton were a testament to second chances and true love. What would it be like to know someone was there through thick and thin, for better or worse?

Oh, man. He must be getting old. When had he become such a softie?

Bronson dragged his gaze from the joined, gnarled hands to see Mr. Colton staring at him with serious eyes.

"Pris and I realize our time on this earth is shorter than longer. Allow us the privilege of being part of this endeavor. This place . . . these orchards . . . they mean a lot to us." Another look to Bronson's aunt. That's right. Aunt Pris and Mr. Colton had rendezvous in the orchards when they were young. When Aunt Pris's parents demanded she not see the poor boy intent on starting up a construction company, she had snuck out at night to meet him in the very orchards Bronson poured himself into now.

But . . . Bronson licked his lips, searching for words. None came, so he straightened, prepared to speak his mind. "What if it fails? What if it all blows up in my face?"

"Bronson," Aunt Pris spoke his name with such tenderness, he wondered if he heard things. But no, this was the same Aunt Pris who complained when her pancakes were a little under golden brown. The same Aunt Pris who muttered curse words under her breath when she couldn't figure out a crossword puzzle. The same Aunt Pris who held strong opinions about anything and everything under the sun.

"I don't know of a more capable young man to spearhead this project. Now, don't think I'm delusional. I realize you share many of your father's fine attributes. I also realize Amos was always starting endeavors—good endeavors—that often sat half-finished while he moved on to another undertaking. I've watched you bring our orchards back to life these last couple of years. I see your determination and heart. If it fails, dear, it will not be from lack of effort."

Bronson cleared his throat, but when he spoke, his voice came out hoarse. It was as if his great-aunt had seen straight through to his heart. For when it came down to it, he did fear the camp would follow in the footsteps of some of his father's well-intentioned enterprises. "That means a lot to me, Aunt Pris. Thank you."

Mr. Colton slid his hand from Aunt Pris's and slapped his thighs. "So, what do you say, young man? Will you accept our help?"

Bronson nodded, hard, before he could change his mind. "Yes. And I promise you I'll give this camp and your orchards everything within me to make them both succeed." He bent to kiss his aunt's thin cheek, and then shoved his hand into Mr. Colton's.

Mr. Colton shook his hand with a grip that belied his age. "I'll deliver you a check tomorrow."

"Thank you, sir. Thank you both. I can't tell you what this means to me."

He dashed out of the room, his mind on fire with possibilities and a list of tasks to add to his already long to-do list.

First and foremost, he needed to rework the flyer and ad copy. He'd need a separate application for the scholarship and he'd have to decide what criteria to use.

And then, he'd have to search out a small crew. Teachers and counselors held the power to make or break the camp.

His thoughts turned to Morgan. He'd offered her the job, and yet she'd brushed him off. Maybe it was better that way.

He sighed, forcing the pretty redhead from his mind. One step at a time. Before he hired teachers, he needed campers. Something Aunt Pris and Mr. Colton had just made much easier to attain.

﷯   8   ﷯

When I was in juvie, they made me cut my hair short. Shorter than it had ever been. I hated it.

I cried over my hair that first night it was cut. My cellmate, a girl named Mahlia, had whispered up from the bottom bunk at me. "You still pretty, girlie. Don't make no sense cryin' over hair. My Aunt Deidre's a hairdresser, and you know what she says? Hair grows."

Mahlia had the beefiest hands I ever saw on a girl, but every day I was grateful that I'd been paired with her and not one of the harder, more intimidating inmates. Mahlia was in juvie for four counts of burglary from an arts and crafts store. A sewing machine, a boatload of fabric, sewing novelties, and a Cricut. She said everyone should have the right to create art, and everyone should have access to art supplies. (She intended the Cricut as a Christmas gift for her aunt.)

I envied Mahlia in some ways. She didn't carry guilt around. Sure, she was a burglar, but Mahlia made me realize not everything was always black-and-white. She said she worked hard but her uncle stole all her money to drink it away. She wanted to sew, and so she found a way how.

Hair grows.

I could laugh about Mahlia's comment now. She had a way of simplifying things down to the bare bones.

And that's exactly what I needed to do if I were to help this young student in front of me—my first tutoring job. I needed to simplify things.

Three weeks had come and gone since I reached out to the tutoring service Bronson had referred me to. After they ran my background check—in which they certainly were made aware of my criminal history—they had hired me anyway, likely based on the recommendations from my previous school in Presque Isle.

"I hate math." The boy named Daniel slumped in his seat at the library table, his long hair hanging in front of his eyes. His hair was what made me think of Mahlia in the first place. Last I heard from my cellmate, she was living with her sister's family and had opened a sewing shop. Her aunt had left her uncle and was still cutting hair.

Because hair never stops growing.

I breathed deep, sensing the thirteen-year-old boy's tangible frustration, his desire to give up. "I know you can learn this. It takes some practice is all. Have you ever had to practice for a sport?"

He shrugged and stared out the window of the library to Harbor Park and the courtyard amphitheater down the hill. "Basketball, I guess."

Daniel's grandmother told me she didn't know how to help her grandson. From what I could gather, Daniel's parents weren't in the picture. While his grades had never been more than average, he was failing Algebra . . . badly. She couldn't begin to understand the concepts and had confessed to me that though money was tight, she wanted her grandson to have the very best chance at succeeding. She insisted he was a smart boy.

"What's your favorite thing about playing basketball?" I asked.

The boy shrugged again. "Making three-pointers." Daniel

sounded bored, as if a previous tutor had tried this basketball approach with him and he'd deemed it a waste of time.

I dug in my heels. The kid possessed a demeanor like many of the women I'd found myself in prison with. Tough. Guarded. They didn't want to let down walls and let anyone in. Letting people in meant the possibility of hurt.

I understood that all too well.

"And how many three-pointers did you make when you first started playing basketball?"

He snorted. "You're trippin', Miss Morgan. I was four years old."

"So, not many three-pointers, then?"

He released an exasperated breath. "My grandmother expects *you* to teach me math?"

While I didn't tolerate disrespect in my classroom, I decided to allow this to play out . . . for now.

"And how many three-pointers can you make now?"

"I can make them most of the time."

"Because you practiced," I said.

"Or because I grew." One corner of his mouth pulled up into a smile.

"Okay, I'll give you that. But you can't deny that practicing had something to do with it."

"Yeah, probably. But I *wanted* to practice basketball."

"You might not want to practice math, but don't you want to pass math?"

He flung a hand in the air, let it fall to the table. "I guess. Whatever. Better than summer school."

"That's the spirit," I teased, turning my attention to the work-sheet of linear equations in front of him. "We'll take one problem at a time." I wrote the first problem on a blank notebook page. My special education kids always did better when focusing on a single task. Many became overwhelmed with the sheer enormity of a worksheet filled with math problems. "Do you know where you might start with this problem?"

"Nope." He'd barely looked at it.

I wrote a group of letters at the top of his page. PEMDAS. "This is like a secret code that tells you what to do. It's the Order of Operations. Parenthesis, exponents, multiplication, division, addition, subtraction. There's a silly saying I used to remember to help me. *Please Excuse My Dear Aunt Sally*."

A slight twinkle brightened the boy's green eyes. "Or you could say Please Excuse My Dumb A—"

"Okay," I interrupted before he could blurt out the inappropriate phrase. I'd heard that one before. Maybe this kid knew more about linear equations than he let on. "Whatever works, okay? Just remember the saying." I tapped my pencil at the problem. "So, what would you do first?"

Daniel studied the problem, glancing at the acronym I'd written at the top of the page. "Get rid of the parenthesis?"

"Good! Do you know how to do that?"

He *looked* as if he were concentrating. Finally, though, he slumped back, hair once again falling in front of his eyes. "I don't know."

I pointed my pencil at the number in front of the parenthesis. "You want to distribute this number—multiply it—by the numbers inside the parenthesis." I drew little arrows to indicate which two numbers to multiply. "What would four times two-x be?"

"Eight-x?"

"That's right! And four times five?"

We worked our way through the first problem before I prompted him to work through the next one himself. He stopped once, a subtraction sign tripping him up, but after we'd worked through five problems, Daniel's confidence had grown by leaps and bounds.

I slid my pencil in my backpack. "Good job today, Daniel. You made a lot of progress."

"It's not as bad as I thought, I guess."

"I'll see you on Thursday?"

"If that's the plan." He scooped up his backpack and slung it over one shoulder. "Bye, Miss Morgan."

Miss Morgan. My previous students had always called me Miss Dalton. I couldn't help but prefer Daniel's name for me.

I sighed, soaking in the pleasure of helping one child. Tutoring could suit me. Working one-on-one with students held a lot of advantages over managing an entire classroom. I slid my notebook in my bag.

"Hey."

I startled at the masculine voice beside me and looked up, my body simultaneously relaxing and tensing at the sight of Bronson, tall and handsome in khaki pants and a polo shirt, so very different from the jeans and dirtied t-shirts I'd grown accustomed to seeing him in when we worked the orchard. Both wardrobe choices held their appeal.

"Bronson, hi. I just finished my first tutoring session."

"I know. I mean—" He pointed to an out-of-the-way cubicle across from the table I'd been working at with Daniel. "I was over there. Couldn't help but notice. I was going to say hello sooner but I didn't want to interrupt. You're a natural."

"You observed my entire tutoring session?"

"I didn't realize it was you until you were already deep into things. You have a gift."

His words warmed my insides.

I jerked my head toward the cubicle he'd indicated. "Grading?"

"Camp applications." He rubbed the back of his neck. "They've been pouring in. Actually, I'm a little overwhelmed. I need to choose the kids who'll receive the scholarships. I didn't realize there'd be so much interest."

"That's a good thing, isn't it?"

He grinned, and I noticed slightly crooked bottom teeth, an endearing contrast to that top line of pearly white perfection.

"A great thing. But I may have bitten off more than I can chew."

"I could help you look over the applications . . . if you wanted."

He brightened. "Really? Actually, I was wondering if you've given my job offer any serious thought?"

My brow furrowed. "Job offer?" I'd been helping him in the orchards a few times a week, but I didn't consider it work. I loved the quiet of the trees, the way their merry blossoms brightened the hill behind the bed and breakfast with fresh, white promise. He'd mentioned helping with the camp, but I considered that more a pity proposition than an official job proposal.

"I need another teacher for the summer camp." He poured out the logistics of timing, job duties, and the weekly salary figure. A small flame of excitement built in my chest. Maybe this was more than pity. Over the last few weeks, Bronson had observed my work ethic, had seen me one-on-one with Daniel. Was it possible he thought I deserved the job?

"I'd love to help out."

"You would?" His brown eyes shone, and my breaths came fast, an invisible magnet drawing me to him.

The attraction vanished and my insides shook at my next thought. He'd run a background check. He'd have to. My throat clogged, and I swallowed down the phlegm. "I do want to make sure you're aware that I—"

From behind Bronson, a frantic waving caught my eye. Coming toward us in skinny jeans and a baseball hat, Jenna swung a newborn car seat in her arm.

I gave a weak wave. "My sister," I explained to Bronson, my breaths loosening at the interruption.

I hugged Jenna before introducing her to Bronson. I didn't

miss the mischievous sparkle in my sister's eyes. I shot her a warning look.

Don't you dare embarrass me or I'll never forgive you.

At least, that's what I hope my look conveyed.

"Are you the Bronson Morgan's been helping in the orchards?" Jenna asked innocently.

As if there were dozens of Bronsons running around in Camden, Maine.

Bronson flashed my sister a smile that could just about ruin any heart. "That'd be me. Now I'm trying to get your sister to accept my job offer for the summer camp I'm running."

Jenna placed a hand on my arm. "That sounds fantastic!"

I groaned and ran a finger over the top of Amelia's sock. Her little mouth was puckered in sleep, her dark eyelashes fanned across rosy, plump cheeks. I swear, I could look at her forever.

"We should get on with our walk before Little Pea here wakes up, don't you think?" I stood, eager to tear my sister away from Bronson for fear of any embarrassing comments. Besides, it wasn't as if he'd not find out soon enough that I wasn't fit for his job—so it didn't have to be right this minute.

"It was nice to meet you, Jenna." Bronson turned to me. "We'll talk later?"

I nodded and followed Jenna out of the library. After dropping off my book bag in my car and grabbing Amelia's stroller, we headed down toward the water. I pulled my hat lower over my ears and Jenna zipped up the blanket covering Amelia's car seat.

"He is *cute*."

I shook my head. "Not happening, Jenna."

"Why not? He seemed into you."

"And how would you know after an entire thirty seconds?"

She shrugged. "I have a gift."

I rolled my eyes.

"It's okay to be happy, Morgan."

I didn't answer, but her words hung in the air like fog on a coastal morning.

Jenna stopped pushing the stroller. "Morgan."

I faced her, the back of my eyelids burning.

"You don't think you deserve happiness?"

I couldn't meet her gaze. "Do I?"

"What? What on earth are you talking about?"

"I don't—I don't deserve . . . a lot of things."

The weight of my sister's stare settled heavy upon me. "Morgan . . ."

"Isabel died because of me, Jenna. She will never get to fall in love, never get to have a family. It would be unfair to allow myself . . ."

"To live?"

I shrugged. "Yeah."

Jenna inhaled deep, gazed out at the naked masts of the boat in the harbor. "Morgan, how is denying yourself the possibilities of life—of *living*—going to help Isabel? Do you think she's up in heaven taking pleasure from your misery?"

"Of course not." Isabel didn't have a cruel bone in her body. I shrugged. "I think the guilt just makes it really hard *to* live, you know?" I wrapped my arms around myself. "I got two years. Two years, Jenna! People get more than that for stealing jewelry at Wal-Mart. I deserved more."

"So you plan to punish yourself forever?"

I'd never thought of it as punishing myself, exactly. I simply couldn't get past the guilt enough to imagine a happy future for myself.

"I don't know," I whispered.

Jenna squinted at me. "You need help, honey."

The comment pulled a thread of hurt clean through me. "I've been to several counselors. It's weird, but allowing myself to feel guilty actually gives me a sense of peace."

"That's self-flagellation, Morgan, and so not healthy."

"That sounds harsher than what I'm actually doing."

"Really? Because it sure seems that way to me. Honey, you made a stupid, stupid decision. And it sucks. And you shouldn't have done it. But your entire life is ahead of you. Don't you think a better way to honor Isabel's life would be to live a beautiful one yourself?"

Wasn't living a "beautiful life," as Jenna put it, a way of disrespecting all the pain I'd put Mrs. Davis and her family through?

"It's hard," I whispered.

Amelia made a tiny, disgruntled noise, and Jenna resumed walking. I followed suit.

A moment later though, my sister slowed again. "*Isabel* wanted to become a special education teacher." Her voice held a hint of wonder, as if she had been the first one to figure out who killed Mr. Boddy in the library.

"I love my career. I don't regret choosing it."

"You wanted to be a marine biologist. Morgan, this is so unhealthy. I only wish I had realized what you were doing to yourself sooner. What did your therapist say?"

"She helped me work through a lot of things. But this is something I think I'll always struggle with. I've decided to take it day by day. It's all I can do."

"Sweetie, you didn't purposely . . . I mean, it's not like you—"

I rested a hand on my sister's arm. "I know, Jenna. I know. But the end result was the same."

It didn't much matter to Mr. and Mrs. Davis if I'd premeditated Isabel's death or it was an accident. In the end, they did not have their daughter. Marcus didn't have his sister. Miss Esther didn't have her granddaughter. I'd done so much more than murder. I'd stolen—stolen all the could-have-been's for Isabel and her family.

❧   9   ❧

"These are a *lot* of applications."

I stared at the number on the top of the Google Form document on Bronson's laptop. We'd put aside orchard work that day to make some headway on getting through the applications. And though I hadn't talked to him yet about what he'd find on my background check, I had decided that if he still wanted my help after I fully disclosed my past, I would take the job.

"I'm surprised at the response. Aunt Pris and Mr. Colton putting up the scholarships made a huge difference. Still, it won't be easy deciding. I've been praying about it for days now."

Praying, huh? I had gathered from being with the Martins that faith was an integral part of their lives. While my parents hadn't raised me in any sort of religion, I had more than enough time in juvie to ponder my beliefs about the spiritual and the eternal. I had even prayed once, begging an unseen God to spare me from my own actions, to make it all disappear.

He hadn't. And who was I, anyhow, to believe I deserved that?

"How can I help?" I asked.

"If you start on one end of the applications and I start on the other, we can meet in the middle."

His ears colored in that adorable, alarmingly familiar way I now looked forward to seeing.

I bit the inside of my cheek to keep from smiling and opened my laptop, typing in the password Bronson gave me. "What am I looking for? What's our criteria?"

"For the scholarships, we're looking for disadvantaged kids—kids who wouldn't otherwise be able to come to the camp. But I want the students who genuinely want to come—who at least made an effort on the essay portion of the application."

I nodded. "Okay. And the rest?"

"We'll have to go with our gut, I guess. My main concern is that I have a group of kids who genuinely want to learn and won't be complaining about being outside most of the day."

I wondered if that might be asking too much of a bunch of middle-schoolers, but I clicked into the response portion of the form. "You want me to start at the beginning or the end of the list?"

"Beginning. If you can write down their names with a *yes*, *no*, or *maybe* beside it, along with what week or weeks they are requesting, that should give us a good start."

I dragged in a deep breath. "Here it goes." I couldn't believe he was trusting me with such an important task. It was almost enough to start me praying, too.

The first application was from a girl named Daisy. She hadn't applied for a scholarship but her essay was a full five paragraphs. Likely a star student. Straight A's probably—at least in English. Exactly the kind of student Bronson sought. I wrote her name and a *yes* alongside it.

The second application was from a boy named Tommy. His essay ran much shorter than Daisy's, and not nearly as well-written, but what it lacked in grammar, it made up for in heart. He wrote that his grandfather told stories of working in an orchard and it sounded like something Tommy would like to do. His grandfather died last fall.

Tommy had applied for a scholarship, and it looked like his single-parent income met Bronson's guidelines.

I marked a *yes* next to Tommy's name.

"So far, I'm two for two. Hope you have enough room in this camp of yours," I said.

Bronson's mouth turned downward. "I'm two for two, also. Saying no will be harder than I thought." He worried his bottom lip between his teeth. "But I can't take every kid. And most of them are probably applying for one of the scholarships—I only have so many of those to go around." He leaned back in his chair and raked his hand through his dark hair. The scent of spice and leather and earth wafted toward me, unsettling my insides.

More unsettling was the worried look Bronson directed at his computer screen. He really cared about these kids.

I glanced at the flyer for the camp on the table. At the bottom, Bronson's words were written in italics.

I want to help the Orchard House camp students wherever they're at. I want to help them become who they're meant to be, to sow honesty and courage in them. Industry. Faith in God. Faith in humanity. Faith in themselves.

I placed my hand on his arm. "Hey, we'll figure it out, okay? Let's stay the course and see where we're at in the end."

The muscles beneath my hand rippled and I withdrew my fingers, remembering my conversation with Jenna the day before.

I'd meant what I said. No relationships. But I tread on thin ice when around Bronson. He made me forget my guilt. At the same time, he made me long all the more for what I didn't deserve.

"You're right." Bronson turned back to his screen. "Thank you."

I clicked into the next application, redirecting my focus. A boy named Will applying for a scholarship. No essay and only half the form filled in. I wrote his name down and a *no* beside it.

There. A well-deserved *no*. I did have it in me, after all.

The next application belonged to a boy named Ned who applied for a scholarship. But no financial documents accompanied the application. I saw why when I read his essay.

Hello, Mr. Martin,

You might be wondering why I'm applying for a scholarship without sending any documents. The truth is that my parents have buckets of money and would have no trouble affording your camp if they wanted to. Trouble is, they aren't too keen on me attending your apple camp. They'd rather me go to military school for the summer. I told them you were offering scholarships and they said if I could go ahead and manage to get myself one, I could go to your camp instead of the military one down in D.C. So, I figured I'd at least try even though I know my chances are low. Maybe there's some other kid out there who deserves the scholarship more than I do.

The essay question is asking why I want to come to your camp. Here's the plain honest answer: I don't want to go to military camp. The idea of learning to grow things might not get my blood pumping, but I figured it's better than military camp. My parents insist I'll be better off for it, but I'm not sure I'm made for all that structure and running and shooting and yelling.

I think I could get used to the idea of learning to grow things. When I was eight, I asked my parents if I could have a garden. But they like their lawn all green and fertilized and trimmed. They wouldn't let me put a garden in it. I don't mean to complain about them—they aren't so bad most of the time, but I figured if I could spend the summer learning how to grow things instead of how to kill things, that would be a score in my book.

Thanks for the opportunity, Mr. Martin.

Ned Abbendroth

I groaned. Oh, man.

I wrote Ned's name on the lined paper, my pencil hovering to mark a checkmark in the *no* column. But something about the kid's words niggled at me. I was fairly certain they didn't simply go around teaching students how to "kill things" at military camp, but something about Ned's privileged life spoke to me.

I had grown up with every advantage under the moon. Our lawn that stretched out to the ocean was much as Ned described —lush and green and soaked with chemicals that would make it beautiful. I could see how a boy might long for a wild patch of land like the one Orchard House sat upon.

And what, really, did a privileged life of not getting your hands dirty give you? Despite all my wonderful raising, I had still made a series of bad choices.

I'd go over Ned's application with Bronson later. For now, I put a checkmark beside *maybe* and clicked over to the next application, a partially-filled out one, followed by two more just like it. I marked *no's* next to all of the names.

I smiled at the sight of the next name. Daniel Simmons. The boy I'd been tutoring the day before. Did he show a real interest in attending the camp, or had his grandmother prompted him to do so?

He'd applied for a scholarship, which didn't surprise me, considering what his grandmother told me. The application was completely filled out, and the essay, while a lump of a paragraph, was more than a little intriguing.

My grandmother says apples are kind of like people. They come in all shapes and colors and sizes. Some will fall to the ground and rot. Some'll end up in my grandma's pie. Some will be eaten with peanut butter and some dipped in caramel. Grandma says there are bad apples in this world and I think she's right because my dad is one. I guess deep down I don't want to be a bad apple, too. Grandma says maybe going to the orchard camp would help teach me about being a good apple, since it's an apple camp and all. And I'm wondering if you can teach me if it's possible for good apples to come from bad ones?

I swallowed down the emotion thick in my throat, and without hesitation, wrote down Daniel's name along with a heavy checkmark under the *yes* column. I would fight for him to be one of the scholarship winners even if it meant me giving up some of my pay as a teacher.

Wait . . . I hadn't agreed to that yet, had I?

I pushed back from the laptop. "Bronson?"

His gaze lingered on the screen. "Yeah?"

"How about a break? Got something to drink?"

He blinked, tore himself from the screen. "Yeah, sounds good." He walked to the refrigerator and grabbed two seltzer waters. "Are you hungry? We have fruit, cheese and crackers, left-over coffee cake . . . you name it, it's probably in this fridge."

"A drink is fine, thanks. But I think we should talk about me being a teacher at the camp . . . you know, before I get more involved in this process than I already am."

He handed me a water, twisted off the cap of his, and took a long swig. "I thought you helping me with the applications was sort of your way of agreeing." He winked at me, and my chest lurched. Almost as if Bronson was going fishing and had caught my heart. What was with me around this guy?

Not that my feelings were new—I couldn't deny the small crush I'd had on him in high school, though I'd never approached him, fearful my friends would make fun of me for pursuing a boy as short as Bronson. That's why I remembered chemistry class so well. I'd been hung up on him—while he hadn't even known I existed.

"Before you officially hire me, I want to make sure you know about my . . . past."

His mouth grew firm.

"You know what happened back in high school, right?"

I couldn't deny how I'd added the words "back in." As if it were *such* a long time ago. As if none of it mattered any longer.

I continued. "When you run a background check it will show up. I thought it'd be best you hear it from me."

He cleared his throat. "Isabel Davis."

I nodded. "It was my fault." *I killed her.*

"You want to tell me what happened? I mean, I've heard . . . stuff. But if you want to give me your side of the story . . ."

My bottom lip trembled. My side of the story. As if I could make what happened more palatable somehow if he knew everything. I cursed under my breath, blinking away unshed tears and shaking my head. "I just want to make sure you know what you're dealing with. People who remember me might not appreciate me teaching their kids. I don't know if I should even accept the position."

"You served time, didn't you?"

I rolled my eyes. "Two years in juvie." Seven-hundred thirty days for someone's entire life.

Bronson raised a hand in the air then let it fall back on his thigh. "Morgan, I'm not here to judge you. Sure, at first, I was . . . surprised that you were here. Esther's close with our family, and I remember how hard it was for the Davis family. But I'm not hiring you because you have a squeaky-clean past. I'm hiring you because I believe you're what these kids need. You have a gift."

The beginning of hope stirred in my chest, and if I'd been drawn to Bronson before, the words had served to intensify my attraction now. He believed in me.

I cleared my throat but couldn't manage a "thank you," so I nodded, then turned back to the applications. He did the same, both of us lost in work for the next hour.

I marked a handful of *yeses* and *nos*, along with a host of *maybes.* It seemed we may be getting nowhere fast.

I clicked to the next application and my breath caught in my throat.

"What's the matter?" Bronson peered over my shoulder.

I stared at the name on my screen.

Marcus Davis.

Currents of emotion built within me, riding waves of differing intensity. If Mrs. Davis knew I was involved in the camp, she never would have helped Marcus apply. It was surprising she allowed him to apply at all. While most kids were accepting of Marcus's quirks, some were not.

"That's Esther's grandson, right?" Bronson asked.

I nodded. "Isabel's brother."

Bronson's Adam's apple bobbed. I could practically see his thoughts, racing to choose his words with care. "It's not that I wouldn't love to have Marcus at our camp, but I don't see how we'd accommodate him. In school, he probably has a one-on-one. It was hard enough for me to find you—and you haven't even agreed to be a teacher yet, by the way—never mind someone qualified to be with Marcus. Not to mention the expense and the fact that we'll have our hands full with the rest of the kids."

I hated the relief that flowed through me. "You're right." Of course, he was right. I would write Marcus's name down on that piece of paper and put a checkmark next to the *no* column. Easy-peasy. Mrs. Davis would never know I had anything to do with the decision.

Yet, as I returned to my laptop, I couldn't make my finger click to the next potential camp-goer.

I scrolled down, past Marcus's address and emergency contact information to the essay, where a simple paragraph hung like an unfinished bridge over a ravine.

Please accept this application on behalf of my son, Marcus. I realize the chances of you accepting a boy with autism are slim, but he has not stopped talking about "picking apples" since he heard the announcement at school. He is not literate, but he is gifted at painting. Please accept his painting (attached) as a sort of essay.

Sincerely,
Ruth Davis

I clicked into the uploaded file, my mouth falling open at the gorgeous painting Mrs. Davis had attached.

Bronson's orchard. And yet, it was so much more. The view from the top of the orchard, looking down on the bed and breakfast and the harbor, captured a beauty deeper even than reality. And yet, I wasn't sure how that was possible.

A bruised sky denoted a sunset. Apples bright red amidst vibrant green leaves. Crisp colors and subdued shades and shadows made me want to sink my teeth into one of those sweet and tart apples.

I tapped Bronson's arm. He did a double-take when he looked at my screen. "Wow. That's—that's amazing." He inched closer, his thigh alongside mine, the slight muscles in his forearm moving taut beneath his skin. "Who's this kid?"

"I'm still looking at Marcus."

"He's sure got talent." Bronson squinted. "I wonder how he painted from that view? As far as I know, only a handful of people have been up there."

"I don't know, but it sure is accurate. And yet, it's more. It captures something almost . . ."

"Holy," Bronson finished.

"Yes," I breathed. "Yes, that's it." The way the light shone down, the way the clouds billowed, it was like I glimpsed the history and the story of the orchard, all in a single painting.

"I'll show Amie. She knows talent. Maybe she can hook him up with a good art camp or something."

I nodded. Bronson returned to his own laptop, and while I tried to focus on my work, my mind raced, refusing to move past Marcus's application. What if all of this was more than coincidence?

I swallowed. "I'm a special ed teacher," I began. "Maybe there's a way to accommodate Marcus."

What was I saying? Having Marcus at the camp would make everything one hundred times more complicated. Not to mention the fact that once Mrs. Davis found out I was one of the camp teachers, she'd drag her son as fast as she could in the opposite direction of Orchard House. Still . . . what if . . .

Bronson studied me with those deep chocolate eyes. "Morgan, I'm sure you'd be great with Marcus, but it's a matter of logistics. I need you for all the kids, not just one."

I need you.

The words stroked chords of pleasure against the strings of my rusty heart. I tamped it down, bit my bottom lip. I couldn't explain it, but all of a sudden it felt incredibly important that Marcus get his wish of attending Bronson's camp. Yes, if I were honest with myself, I'd acknowledge that deep down, I hoped this was a way for me to make peace with Isabel's family. But was that such a bad goal?

I released a long exhalation and clicked out of Marcus's application. "I'm too involved. Clearly. I'm sorry. You need to make the decision on Marcus and I need to take myself out of the equation entirely."

As if Bronson hadn't already made his decision.

It was logical. Understandable, even.

His gaze settled upon me. "This means a lot to you, doesn't it?"

I shook my head. "Bronson, forget it. I'm not thinking straight. I—"

"What happened that night?"

Heaviness surged within me. Like a chicken inside of a pressure cooker, I felt I'd pop any moment. "W-what?"

"The night Isabel died. I've heard rumors, but you deserve to tell it firsthand."

I *deserved* the chance?

What kind of malarkey was that? I deserved nothing.

"I told you. I was drinking . . ."

"There's more to it, isn't there?"

I shook my head, ordered my legs not to run as fast as I could from this room, from Bronson, from this heavenly piece of land I didn't deserve to live on, from Isabel's family and my family and Camden and all that was my past. All the worst parts of myself.

"Is this a job interview question, or . . ."

He leaned closer, and I couldn't bring myself to meet his probing gaze. "You already have the job if you want it, Morgan. I'm asking as a friend."

As a friend.

But I couldn't face that night again. Walking up to Isabel's old house had been terrifying enough. Would replaying that night, here to Bronson, help anything?

I closed my laptop and stood. "I have to get going. I can work on these later if you'd like."

He grabbed my arm, his fingers gentle on the skin beneath my t-shirt. The gesture sent ripples of apprehension surging straight to my bones.

"Don't go. I'm sorry. I shouldn't have asked."

A magnetic force compelled me to give in, to stay and convey all my fears, guilt, and insecurities to this caring man.

If it wasn't so painful, I'd do just that.

I pulled away from him. "I'll see you tomorrow, Bronson," I whispered. I scooped up my laptop and slid through the door of the bed and breakfast, hating to admit my reasons for running away from the conversation.

For as much as I wanted to run away from that night eight

years ago, there was something else I wanted to run away from all the more.

Those eyes. That caring touch. The way it all made my stomach swirl and lurch in a pleasant waltz.

There was no denying it—Bronson was stirring to life long-dead emotions and sensations. And he and his camp didn't deserve the complications I would bring.

Bronson closed out of the website for the inclusion camp with a loud huff, tapping his fingers on the breakfast bar.

"What's the matter, honey?" His mother poured batter into a coffee cake pan.

Bronson inhaled the scent of cinnamon and shook his head. "Nothing."

At times, the ache for his father waned. It was in those moments that Bronson found himself believing the mantra, "Time heals all wounds."

But as the reality of the Orchard House camp revealed layers of problems to be solved, plans to be made, and apples to grow, he couldn't deny how the longing for his dad had intensified.

And now the issue of Marcus Davis—something he never could have anticipated or expected. Of course, Morgan's involvement with the family made everything ten times more complicated. He'd prayed about the decision, sought information about inclusive camps for children with special needs, and still, he didn't have an answer.

He needed someone to talk to. The obvious answer was Josie's husband Tripp—the guy had always been the closest thing

Bronson had to a big brother—but Bronson was man enough to admit he was avoiding Tripp like the plague right now. His older sister and her husband were knee-deep in building their dream home. Any contact with Tripp would no doubt lead to Bronson spending a weekend he couldn't afford building Josie's home. He loved them, and he wanted to help, but right now, he needed to manage his priorities—and with Aunt Pris and Mr. Colton's financial support—he could no longer afford to put the camp on the back burner.

Maggie's husband, Josh, would have been a great one to talk to considering his background as a teacher, but Josh's father had just suffered a heart attack and was recovering from a successful surgery. No sense burdening his other brother-in-law.

"I'm a good listener," his mother said as she slid the pan into the oven.

He couldn't deny that. But he also couldn't deny he was seeking a logical, objective opinion. He was seeking an opinion that affirmed what he already believed—allowing Marcus to attend camp would not be beneficial for anyone—the other campgoers, the teachers, even Marcus himself. If he couldn't supply enough support, the boy would be frustrated. Bronson could imagine the scene that might unfold. He couldn't risk the camp's reputation. It was all too new, with too much riding on this first season.

But a woman who handed out hundreds of dollars in Subway gift cards to anyone who held up a sign in the busy city intersections, a woman who didn't fire on the spot the hired help who stole an entire pot roast from their very refrigerator, might not see things his way.

But what other options did he have?

"It's about a camp applicant. Esther's grandson, actually. Marcus."

"He helped your father plant some azaleas at the church

cleanup one year. Very enthusiastic young man, from what I remember."

"Sounds about right." Bronson cleared his throat. "Anyway, he applied to the camp." He paused briefly to take in his mother's raised eyebrow. "I don't see how we can accommodate him. Morgan thinks it could work, but she also has ties to the Davises . . ." He rubbed his throbbing temples.

Mom turned from her mixing bowl, the corner of her mouth tugging downward. "That certainly is a pickle." She tapped her chin. "I'm actually surprised Ruth wants Marcus to come. From what Esther says, she's very guarded of his time outside of school."

"I guess he has his heart set on it. He made this incredible painting." He opened his laptop and pulled up the file he'd saved to his desktop, spinning the screen toward his mother.

The door behind Bronson creaked open, then slammed. "Thank the *gracious* Father in heaven you guys are home." Josie bustled into the kitchen, a canvas tote over her shoulder that read *It's Not Hoarding If It's Books*. She heaved it onto one of the bar stools and pulled out envelopes and sheets of labels. "I need to get these addressed and to the post office before it closes today *and* before Lizzie gets home from Paramount. Any way you can help me? I'll give you anything you ask for."

Bronson exchanged glances with his mom.

"Anything?" he asked.

Josie hedged. "Within reason, of course."

He scratched his chin. "How great are your powers?"

Her brow furrowed. "Now's not the time to get all Yoda on me, Bronson. What's it going to take?"

"Help me come up with a solution to a camp applicant conundrum."

"Done. Now, get stuffing." She handed him a stack of envelopes.

He rolled his eyes. If only the issue of Marcus's application could be solved so easily.

"What's the rush getting these out?" Mom leveled off a cup of flour with a knife. "The shower's not for two more months."

"It's in June, Mom. If people don't save the date now, their Saturday morning might get booked. And Lizzie's helping Asher with a new display at the store tonight so that should keep her there late."

Lizzie's fiancé Asher owned Paramount Sports, a large chain sporting goods store. Lizzie helped him create realistic natural displays, something Asher was incorporating into all of his stores across the country.

Mom wiped her hands on a dishcloth. "I don't think people's calendars will fill up this weekend. You have a few days."

Josie handed Mom a stack of invitations. "Please?"

Mom shook her head, wiped her floured hands on a dish towel, and took the invitations from Josie. "I should have been helping you more all along. But business has been crazy this spring. And I haven't replaced Mike yet."

The man from Dad's mission who'd helped with lawn care. "Leave it to me, Mom. I'll find someone."

The creases on Mom's face eased, and Bronson told himself that the amount of time it took him to find a yard guy was worth easing his mother of even an ounce of stress.

"Thank you." She slid an invitation into an envelope. "Now, about Marcus—"

"Marcus who?" Josie sat at the bar and placed a pile of flowery invitations in front of her, Lizzie's name in flowing script at the top.

"The problem you agreed to solve for me," Bronson said.

Again, the door opened. This time, Amie bustled in. "It's getting to be spring out there!"

"Oh, good! Help, please?" Josie gave Amie a sheepish grin.

Amie placed her protein shake on the table, collapsing into a chair. "I'm exhausted from my yoga class. What is all this?" She wrinkled her nose at the small pile Josie placed in front of her.

"Shower invitations."

Amie perked up. "These are pretty! I can't wait to decorate the barn. I'm working on this large macrame backdrop to set up behind Lizzie's chair. It'll be gorgeous."

Bronson studied his free-spirited sister. Maybe *Amie* should help out around the bed and breakfast more. She was too busy creating macrame and jewelry and eco-friendly lampshades to worry about helping their mother, or anyone else in the family, for that matter. Save for trying to fix him up on dates.

"So, what's the problem, Bronson? You have the benefit of three brilliant Martin women all in one room to help you out." Josie placed an address label in the middle of an envelope.

Quickly, he outlined the crux of his problem to his family. When he finished, he leaned back in his chair, peeling off address labels and sticking them to the front of cream-colored envelopes.

"Honey, as much as I'd love to see Marcus enjoying your camp, I'm worried about you overextending yourself." Mom wet a paper towel, running it along the adhesive at the back of one envelope.

The niggling blister that had festered inside him since his conversation with Morgan about Marcus popped, the pressure of relief surging through him. If his own mother—one of the most compassionate people he knew—thought Marcus attending the camp was a bad idea, he'd take it as a sign. He needed to be practical, not Superman.

"But why shouldn't Marcus have the right to come to camp like everyone else? Besides, wouldn't it be good marketing to show your camp is forward-thinking and inclusive?" Amie's hackles had risen—it didn't take much these days.

"In theory, yes. Logistically, I'm not sure I can swing it." Bronson turned his laptop toward his sisters. "But the kid's a genius at painting. Maybe Mrs. Davis should send him to an art camp."

Amie peered at the screen. Her mouth fell open. "Marcus did that?"

Bronson nodded. "Good, right?"

Amie tore her eyes away from the computer. "*Good? Good* is a lacking and mediocre word that shouldn't come within a foot of this masterpiece."

Josie's mouth twitched. "What Amie said."

"Maybe I should research some art camps around here, give Mrs. Davis some resources and options. You know of any that would suit him, Amie?"

His younger sister licked her lips. He could practically see her mind reeling. "Yours could."

He wrinkled his brow. "What?"

"You should take him, Bronson. Why not include art as part of your camp? I could help."

Bronson let his hand fall to the counter. "Because I don't need *more* projects. I need to simplify so I can get things done."

"You said Aunt Pris and Mr. Colton gave you seed money to hire teachers. Why not hire me?"

Great. *Now*, his little sister wanted to get ambitious.

"You're not a teacher, Amie. You barely graduated high school!"

She crossed her arms over her chest and stuck out her bottom lip. "Who's to say I need to sit through a bunch of boring, stuffy classes on Shakespeare and curriculum design to guide some kids in a few art projects? Hire me on as a counselor, then. Come on, Bronson. I need the money and it could be good for everyone."

Bronson rubbed his face, closing his eyes against the pressure of his fingers. Was opening up an art program for the purpose of serving one student anywhere near practical?

He let his hands fall. "All I'm seeing is a whole lot of work and expenses for very little payout. Art wasn't in the brochures."

"Kids love art! It could be a great addition to the camp. You're always saying you want the campers to be exposed to the outdoors and hard work and science. Why not allow them to create beauty inspired by all that nature and work?"

Josie grinned. "Can't really argue with that line of thinking." She placed a hand on Bronson's arm. "Oh, I could do a creative writing class—free of charge. Maybe just a twice a week thing."

Amie gave a little jump of excitement. "That's a great idea! Why not have electives a couple afternoons a week? Josie could do writing, I could do art."

Bronson stood, pacing the area behind the bar. "You guys were supposed to help me find a solution, not make everything ten times more complicated. Doing an art project a couple times a week is not going to help me the other thirty-six hours of the week with Marcus. He likely needs constant attention, and as much as I want to include him, I don't want to take away from the other kids."

Amie looked longingly at Bronson's computer screen. "Let me be his one-on-one, Bronson. It's only a week, right? I'll volunteer my time. And you can just hire me for the art sessions for the rest of the summer."

Had he agreed to hire her? Seems he might have missed that part . . .

"I haven't worked any of this into the budget." Still, Amie helping Marcus was probably the least selfish thing he'd seen his sister do in a long time. He tried to picture her hair pulled back, dangly earrings swinging at her neck as she navigated a kayak with Isabel's brother.

"You do know it'll be hard work, right? It's not just sitting under an apple tree with a sketch pad. It's real honest-to-goodness manual labor that Marcus needs help with. Amie, you might have to *sweat*."

Josie stifled a giggle and Mom turned back to her mixer.

Amie swatted his arm. "I'm up for it. Really. I want to give Marcus this chance. I want to help."

"I'll have to talk to Mrs. Davis since you're not certified. If I can get her to sign off on it, I guess we'll give it a go."

"And the art classes? You'll hire me?"

"I can pay you a small stipend. I'm not sure it'll be worth your time . . ."

Amie held out her hand. "We'll negotiate."

Bronson shook his head, already regretting agreeing to his sister's whims. Nevertheless, he stuck his hand in hers.

Seemed he'd do just about anything to make the women in his family happy. But this would give Marcus Davis a chance to attend his camp.

Not to mention it'd make Morgan over-the-moon happy as well.

"We'll keep it clean and simple. Take some of the long tables we already have and set them up with chairs to serve as desks. I'll get a whiteboard and hang it near the windows." Bronson pointed to the corner of the Orchard House barn.

Beside him, I studied the area. "On nice days, we could keep the doors open for plenty of fresh air."

Bronson nodded, and I admired the firm square of his jaw. We'd worked closely together the last few weeks, finalizing the list of scholarship recipients and camp-goers. For the first time since high school, I woke each morning to a sense of anticipation and purpose. While I tried to pretend the camp was entirely responsible for this feeling, I could no longer deny that a ruggedly handsome orchard owner and teacher played a vital part in it as well.

Bronson clapped his hands together. "Oh, did I tell you Paramount's giving us a great deal on kayak rentals?"

I loved the excitement in his eyes, how he genuinely wanted to share every bit of the camp with me, how he valued my opinion.

"That's wonderful. Although, I've never been on a kayak. Aren't you a little nervous about taking twelve kids out on the water?"

"Paramount's providing a guide who's a lifeguard. And Asher said he'd like to come out a time or two. He's Lizzie's fiancé."

"I'm amazed at how you're turning this vision into reality." A deep and intangible sense within told me Bronson needed to hear the words. "It's going to be wonderful."

He shifted his feet, looking at me as if I were the only other person in the world. "That means a lot. Thank you, Morgan."

The sound of my name on his lips sent a shiver chasing up my spine. Other guys might have brushed off my compliment. But not Bronson.

He stepped closer and my senses heightened. His woodsy scent overpowered the faint smell of oil from the machinery used to clean the apples.

"I'm grateful for your help. With the orchards, the camp. Everything." He swallowed, shifting those long legs again. "I was wondering—if you don't find it too awkward . . . well, I was wondering if you might want to have dinner with me sometime."

My mouth grew dry. "Dinner? Like, a date?"

He moved closer, a hint of insecurity in his stance. "If I'm way off base here, just say so. I'll be nothing but professional from here on out. But we make a pretty good team so far, don't you think?"

Pretty good team . . .

I fought for shallow breaths around my compressed ribcage, couldn't push forth words. Instead, my body swayed forward of its own volition, almost as if an invisible force propelled me toward Bronson.

He responded by raising a hand to my face. His calloused thumb brushed ever so lightly over my cheek and I thought I might either keel over and die, or soar up to the rafters of this old barn.

The shadows of day's end played across his face. He'd consumed me with that single brush of a thumb. I could only imagine what the rest of his body might do.

"Would it be terribly inappropriate if I kissed you?" His voice came out gruff, stirring want in my chest where it spread outward, surging and tunneling through every blood vessel of my body.

Again, words—even one word of affirmation—refused to form. Instead, I sank into his hand as it slid along my jawline and then into my hair. I breathed in his presence and scent, my heart knocking out a crazy rhythm against my chest.

When he dipped his head closer, I closed my eyes.

A merry, tenacious ring broke through the air surrounding us.

Bronson's phone.

My eyes flew open. We shared a nervous laugh.

"Amie's always telling me not to carry it around in my pocket. Maybe this is why." He didn't remove his fingers from my face.

"Aren't you going to answer?" I asked.

"It can wait."

But the ringing persisted, enough to thrust me into reality. I shouldn't have let Bronson get so close—neither physically nor emotionally. He was not part of my plan. No matter how badly I wanted that kiss, it was dangerous. And I'd only hate myself for it afterward.

I stepped back from the sturdiness of Bronson's presence, and a chill swept through me. "You should answer."

The fingers in my hair fell to his side. Slowly, he reached in his pocket for the phone. His gaze flicked to me. "Mrs. Davis."

My breath hitched and I stepped back, as if Isabel's mother might know I was with the person she wanted to talk to, as if my presence might mar Bronson's simply by association. "Go on. You've been waiting."

We'd been waiting.

Bronson had told me about Amie's offer, and I couldn't deny my excitement in doing something beneficial for the Davis family, no matter how small. Nevertheless, we had agreed to be open about my part in the camp. We'd let Mrs. Davis make the final decision.

Bronson walked toward the back of the barn and I lowered myself into a student's chair and stared out the window, the echo of Bronson's voice bouncing off the high rafters. The adrenaline that had surged through me with Bronson's nearness changed course to flow for an altogether different reason.

"Mrs. Davis, thanks for returning my call . . . Yes, yes, the family's well . . . business is good. Oh, you know Aunt Pris, she's overseer of it all and not shy about her opinions in the least."

I could imagine Isabel's mother's voice on the other end of the phone. Polite, cheerful. Or maybe not as cheerful as I remembered. Were there snatches of time when she was happy, or had I stolen even that from her?

Through the barn window, I glimpsed the kitchen of the bed and breakfast. Mrs. Martin stood at the counter, a fixture in the room it seemed. Lizzie walked by with a basket of laundry.

Though the Martin family wasn't quite as perfect as I first assumed, I liked them all the better for it. It wasn't only Bronson I was becoming attached to. I loved it here, living at the Orchard House, mingling on the outskirts of the hustle and bustle of this family and their beloved business. How long would my presence be welcome? If I wanted, could I stay forever?

I blinked away the thought, tuning back toward Bronson's voice. The vague notion came to me that I should leave, or at least return to my apartment, but I pushed it away. I wasn't eavesdropping—Bronson knew I could hear him. If not for my insistence, Marcus would have been a solid checkmark in the *no* column of our applicants.

"Yes." Weeks of working with Bronson afforded me the ability to detect the slight tension in his voice. "Yes, that's one of the things I wanted to talk to you about. My sister, Amie, has agreed to stay with Marcus the week he's in camp. Not exactly as an aid, as she doesn't have any certifications, but a personal counselor of sorts, if that suits you."

Silence, then a laugh filled with relief. "Great. Yes, I'd have to draw up some papers for you to sign—for all the parents to sign, of course. Amie was impressed with his artwork. We're trying to put something together for all the kids regarding creativity in both writing and art."

If it wasn't Mrs. Davis on the other end of the line, if I didn't know what subject Bronson would broach next, I would almost enjoy hearing him converse with the parent of a prospective camp applicant. His passion for this project and these kids soaked through every word as he paced in the back of the barn.

"There's just one more thing, Mrs. Davis, for the sake of transparency."

He laughed again, and I could nearly picture Ruth Davis saying something like, "Well, sugar, you know you needn't hide anything from me."

My breaths trembled. Across the way in the Victorian, Aunt Pris bit a pencil as she looked down at what must have been a crossword puzzle.

Bronson cleared his throat. "I'll get straight to the point, Mrs. Davis. I called because I wanted to inform you that Morgan Dalton will be a teacher at the camp this summer. With the history there, I thought it best to let you know."

Silence. Though I couldn't see him, I sensed the smile on Bronson's handsome face falter. I tried to imagine Mrs. Davis's words but found it too painful.

Instead, I clutched the back of the folding chair until my knuckles turned white, waiting . . . waiting for Bronson to speak.

"Yes, I'm aware of that . . . she's been nothing but open with me, and I've observed her teaching. She's extremely suited to the job . . . Of course, Mrs. Davis. In the end, it's your decision. If you change your mind, let me know. We'll keep a spot open for Marcus for another week, just in case."

From within the depths of the barn came a tired sigh, then footsteps echoing closer to where I sat.

I didn't turn to face him. Instead, I kept my gaze on Aunt Pris, so concentrated on that crossword. I sniffed. "She's not interested, is that right?"

"Morgan, it's not—"

I brought my gaze to his. I'd been naïve to think Bronson's camp could make things right between me and the Davis family. Wishful, dreamy, foolish thinking.

"What if you hired another teacher to replace me for the week Marcus attends?"

Bronson gritted his teeth. "No. I was already jumping through hoops to help one kid—one family. I'd not replace you for any of the other applicants if they requested me to do so. I've done all I can. If they don't want Marcus to attend, that's their choice."

I shrugged. "Okay." My voice came out tinny and small, defeated.

Bronson strode over to where I sat and knelt before me, his hands on either side of my chair. "Morgan, look at me."

I dragged my gaze to his, its searing heat threatening to stir those embers again. Not just embers of attraction, embers lit by someone who cared—really cared. Embers lit by a man who didn't do anything halfway, who threw himself into life with a zeal I admired.

"I know you don't want to talk about what happened that night with Isabel, and I wish to God I could send you back in time so you could choose differently—but you can't beat yourself up over it day after day. You have a life to live, regardless of whether Mrs. Davis forgives you or not. Live it the best you can in honor of Isabel."

I released a small snort, tempered my voice to a whisper. "You sound like my sister."

"She must be a smart lady."

"Maybe I should try to talk to her again."

"Mrs. Davis?"

I nodded. "I visited when I first came back to Camden, but I wasn't welcomed."

Bronson's brow furrowed. "Wait . . . You hadn't been crying about the tire that day."

"The tire didn't help things." I closed my eyes. "It doesn't matter. I wrote Mr. and Mrs. Davis countless notes while I was in prison. I've apologized so many times. But I guess some things are unforgiveable."

Bronson bit the inside of his cheek. "You have a lot to offer these kids. Don't let this get in the way."

"What would you do, Bronson?"

He cocked his head. "What do you mean?"

"If you had killed your best friend, served a sentence that didn't justify your actions, and had to go on living your life with that knowledge and guilt hanging over you, what would you do?"

He swallowed, and his Adam's apple bobbed along the smooth skin at his neck. "You don't ask easy questions, do you?"

"With a life as messed up as mine? No."

One side of his mouth curved up into a comma before he grew solemn again. "I guess I can't say what I'd do for certain, and I understand why you want forgiveness from Isabel's family. I don't think that's wrong. But you are not in charge of whether they grant it or not." He shifted his weight. "Maybe all you can do is ask God for His forgiveness, trust His grace to carry you through each day. Live beneath that umbrella."

I stared at his handsome face, the slight stubble lining his jaw, those dark, hooded eyes. Something about his words drew me. The image of living under an umbrella of grace . . . I'd never thought that could be something for a woman like *me*.

"There was a time I thought God might take this burden from me in some way . . ." Her mouth tightened. "I've never met anyone who talks like you do. You're different, Bronson. In a good way."

He smiled and it was like the sun rising after weeks of rain. When he stood, he held his hand out to me. "Oh, and I'd do one more thing if I were you."

I slipped my hand into his, the calloused folds curving around mine, embracing my entire body in foreign heat. "What's that?"

"Accept my dinner invitation."

A blush worked over my face and I snatched my hand back from his. "What happened earlier . . . Don't get me wrong. I think you're a great guy but . . ." How did I finish this sentence? *I can't get too close to you. I end up hurting those I love.*

True, for a moment of time when Bronson and I shared that same space of breath, I'd fooled myself into believing happiness with a man like him was possible. But Mrs. Davis's call was like the loud gong of a warning bell, reminding me of reality.

The defeated look on Bronson's face made me wonder if I wasn't only punishing myself by means of my self-denial.

"Hey." He clapped his hands together. "What'd I tell you? Don't worry about it. Nothing but professional from now on. I'm sorry if I made things awkward."

He didn't understand my reason for turning him down. No doubt he thought I wasn't interested. Better to not correct him. "Not at all," I croaked, my chest aching.

He forced a strained smile. "I have to turn some compost. See you tomorrow morning to put together those packets?"

Packets for the camp-goers outlining schedules of activities and lunches as well as a few waivers and health insurance queries. Nothing but professional from now on.

I tried to mirror Bronson's smile. "Sure thing."

"Great. See you then."

I watched his languid strides as he walked out of the barn and toward the orchards, soon disappearing in the now-abundant foliage.

For a moment, I considered quitting the camp altogether. Quitting Camden altogether and returning to Presque Isle. But that would be the easy route. And if Isabel deserved one thing, it was for me not to take the easy way out ever again.

Bronson walked into Paramount Sports, envelope in hand. As always, when he entered the sporting goods store, a sense of awe filled him over what his future brother-in-law had built and created.

He waved to the cashier closest to him before turning down the corridor that led to Asher's office. He knocked upon the open door.

"Come in."

Bronson walked into the spacious workplace.

"Bronson." Asher's grin spread across his face and he wheeled his chair around his desk with little effort. Despite the fact that Bronson towered over Asher by at least three feet, Lizzie's fiancé possessed a powerful presence that commanded respect. It had taken Bronson no small amount of time to decide Asher actually deserved that respect, but now that he had, Bronson didn't hold back.

He shook Asher's hand. "Been missing you around the dinner table, man."

Asher's mouth thinned. "Springtime is always a killer around here, and I've got one more trip to LA before I can get my mind in wedding mode."

Asher often took trips out west to Paramount's headquarters. Though Lizzie wasn't one for travel, she accompanied him more often than not, choosing to bear the stresses of travel rather than be without him.

"I think all the Martin ladies are in wedding mode enough for you and Lizzie combined. And between you and me, if I get another RSVP text for her bridal shower, I'll lose it."

Asher chuckled. "Josie told me about the mix-up on the invitations. Sorry about that, buddy."

The Martin children had all received their phones at the same time, making them one number off from each other. Apparently, Josie had accidentally put a 9 instead of an 8 at the end of the RSVP number on the shower invitations, effectively making Bronson head of bridal shower attendance.

Lord help them all if she didn't get a good proofreader for that book of hers.

Bronson handed Asher the envelope. "The rest of the payment for the kayak rentals. Thanks again for the deal—I appreciate it."

Asher placed the envelope on his desk. "Happy to do it. How's camp planning going?"

"It's coming together. Morgan's been a big help. Nothing much left to do but to calm the nerves."

"Lizzie talks so highly of you and your work ethic—you might think you'd hung the moon and the stars the way she goes on and on."

Bronson's face heated. He loved all his sisters, but he couldn't deny the soft spot he held for Lizzie, the older sister he always treated as the younger. As shy and timid as Lizzie'd been as a child, and then fighting cancer in her teens, there had always been reason enough to step up and play the part of the big, protective brother—something headstrong little Amie would never allow.

Now, Asher would take that place. Bronson was happy for Lizzie, and he couldn't think of a better guy for her. But if Asher ever tried to up and move Lizzie to California, he might have a Bronson-sized obstacle to get through first.

Bronson glanced out the windows of Asher's office to the parking lot filled with cars, the elaborate landscaping and pond that adorned the front of the store hinting at the grandness within. "How do you do it all?" he asked.

"Do what?"

"Make running the largest sporting goods store in the country look easy when I'm bumbling my way through a summer camp, scared out of my wits to screw up."

Asher released a zesty laugh. "You're thinking too much, Bronson."

"It's what I do best." His sarcastic tone hung sour in the air. Thinking was Bronson's strong suit. So was *over* thinking.

"Listen," Asher said, not continuing until Bronson met his gaze. "All you have to have is guts."

"That's all it took for you to succeed?"

"Yeah. Stop doubting yourself and go after what you want—helping those kids."

Bronson rubbed the back of his neck. "You're right. But I keep thinking I'll mess up like my dad. All of his startups failed."

"That's a real possibility."

Bronson snorted. "Thanks a lot."

"Or it could be more successful than you even imagined. What if you helped one kid? What would you call that?"

A small smile tugged at Bronson's mouth. "Success."

"Make that your goal then, man. You got this."

Bronson stuck out his hand to the guy he'd be prouder than pie to call his brother-in-law in just two short months. "Thanks, Asher."

"Anytime, bro." He winked before wheeling back to his desk. "Now, who is this Morgan girl I've been hearing so much about?"

THIS TIME, WHEN I PULLED IN FRONT OF THE DAVIS HOME, I steeled myself for the confrontation. No illusions about welcoming hugs and forgiveness. I was doing this for Bronson as much as for myself.

I parked on the street and strode to the front door, hardening myself to my emotions.

It was a trick I'd learned at juvie—most of us did. I may have been born with a soft heart, but my experiences had painted a thick veneer around it. Yes, I'd cried myself to sleep those first nights of being locked away, but the jail had toughened me up, too. It was either that, or wither away.

While I'd released my hard exterior when I started teaching— a challenge in itself—I found that, most of the time, I could slip it on at will.

I knocked on the Davis's door, harsh and insistent, praying Miss Esther wouldn't answer. The kind-hearted woman would knock all the fight out of me with a single, wrinkly smile.

Mrs. Davis opened the door, her expression tight. "I thought I told you I don't want you coming here."

I firmed my jaw. "You did, but I need to talk to you."

She started to close the door.

"For Bronson's sake, Mrs. Davis."

She stopped the motion of closing the door, her face partly concealed by its edge. "What about him?"

I hitched in a deep breath. "Bronson has bent over backwards to find ways to accommodate Marcus. He went above and beyond to include him. You may not trust me—you may even hate me, but believe me, you can't hate me more than I hate myself for what I did. But I'm a good teacher, Mrs. Davis. I teach kids with Marcus's diagnosis all the time, and I'm good at it. Isabel's the one who inspired me to do it. All I'm asking is that you give Bronson, Amie, and Marcus a chance. Don't let how you feel about me ruin it for them."

She stared at me, and I couldn't read the expression on her face.

"That's all I came to say. Good night."

I turned and walked down the pathway to my car, my limbs trembling, but a victorious tune playing across my spirit.

Quite likely, my words wouldn't matter. But I'd spoken them. I'd stood up for Bronson, Marcus, and even myself.

And that was something.

I sipped my sparkling orange juice, attempting to hide behind my glass as I watched Lizzie open a lacy set of lingerie from Josie.

Squeals of laughter and a few raucous whistles came from the group of women seated in the Orchard House barn. Lizzie's face turned as red as one of the apples that would soon hang heavy on Bronson's trees. Thinking of Bronson, then of the lacy lingerie, my own face grew hot.

Beside me at the long table where we'd just eaten—a table that had been filled with a variety of quiche, petite sandwiches, fruit salad, artisan cheeses, tarts, muffins, and scones—Maggie shook her head playfully. "I knew that would embarrass her. Look at her, poor thing."

They watched as Josie turned to the pile of presents beside Lizzie. She handed her sister a pink and white bag with plentiful tissue paper exploding out of it.

Amie swatted her hand through the air. "It's her wedding shower! Of course, she should get some lingerie. She'd never buy it for herself, after all. It's nothing to be ashamed of, you know."

Beside me, Mrs. Martin rubbed a hand over her face and Maggie rolled her eyes.

"Is there anything else you'd like to lecture us on before we hand out the cake?" Maggie asked.

Amie's cheeks colored in uncharacteristic fashion. Whether the Martin sisters had invited me because they genuinely wanted my presence or because they feared I might feel left out living right above the merry party, I didn't know. Neither did I care. I'd thrown myself into helping them decorate the barn in a rustic style that suited the Orchard House barn.

Behind the food table, we'd woven lights through wood pallets and hung a sign pronouncing the word *Love*. We'd hung champagne pink, grey, and white balloons and decorated Amie's gorgeous macrame backdrop with a bounty of hydrangeas, peonies, and roses.

I'd been in charge of arranging small, rustic log pieces on the tables, completing them with candles, another wooden *Love* sign, and mason jars wrapped in burlap with flowers. Upon a large-wheeled wooden cart sat an assortment of cupcakes, arranged in pleasing tiers with plentiful flowers surrounding them. And by the door, an old-fashioned toaster alongside cloth-covered mason jars filled with specialty popcorn as wedding favors, a hand-painted sign that said *Thanks For Popping By*.

I couldn't deny how helping decorate had cemented my attachment to this family. We'd laughed at Amie's overly-critical eye and her shrieking when things came together perfectly. Bronson's puzzled face when he couldn't figure out why the *Love* sign had to be hung exactly so. Even the way Amie had tactfully suggested she had a dress "just my size" when she realized—a few minutes before guests arrived—that my idea of changing for the party involved pulling on a clean pair of jeans and a fresh t-shirt.

I don't think any of us would soon forget Lizzie's expression of astonishment from the inside of Mrs. Martin's car when they'd pulled up the drive of the bed and breakfast to see a slew of friends and family spilling out of the barn doors, yelling "Surprise!" Neither would we forget her tears of happiness at the sight of those she loved gathered to celebrate her upcoming new life.

The entire morning made me long for my own mother and sister with a newfound tenacity. Mom had called several times over the last couple of months, and while I'd gone over for dinner frequently, I hadn't followed through on the invitation for a walk. There was still an awkwardness that hung between me and my mother, and while I wished for its absence, I didn't know how to go about vanquishing it, either.

"Don't forget to fill out the marriage advice cards!" Josie's sing-song voice broke through the crowd from where she organized Lizzie's opened gifts with the tenacity of a Marine Corps commander.

Amie picked up the card, pencil flying to her mouth in concentration.

Maggie grabbed up her own pencil, seeming to put serious thought into the task. After a moment, Amie folded her card up, and raised an eyebrow in my direction. "No advice?"

I laughed nervously. "I'm not exactly experienced in marriage." Or romantic relationships, for that matter.

"Me neither, but I think Asher will love my advice for Lizzie." She opened the card to show me.

Wear lots of lingerie.

I burst out laughing, wondering how Amie and Lizzie were even related. Still, I couldn't bring myself to write anything down. I wasn't funny like Amie, and even if I were, I didn't know Lizzie all that well. Safer to abstain.

After Lizzie had finished opening gifts and we'd sampled the delicious cake made by Mrs. Martin—chocolate raspberry truffle—the guests began to dwindle. Bronson's aunt walked up to us, Isabel's grandmother by her side. Miss Esther made her way around the circle, hugging each person goodbye.

As my turn came and the older woman wrapped brown arms

around me, I simultaneously wondered if she knew who I was, and if Isabel's mother would burst through the large barn doors any minute to rescue her mother from my embrace.

"It was lovely to see you, Miss Esther," I said.

She placed a weathered hand upon my cheek, her clear gaze heavy upon me. "Always lovely to see you, Miss Morgan."

So, she did know who I was today. I wondered if that meant she remembered *everything*.

I averted my gaze, wishing for an escape, but Miss Esther wouldn't have it. "Child," she said.

Quite suddenly, I felt horribly alone with her. Maggie and Amie and Mrs. Martin had dispersed to bid farewell to the guests. Aunt Pris had moved to sample a leftover cupcake. With no escape, I forced my gaze to the warm liquid brown eyes of Isabel's grandmother.

"I want to apologize for my daughter's behavior, dear. We all know you feel terrible about Isabel, and sure, Ruth has a right to be heartbroken. But holding a grudge won't change the course of things, Lord knows. We all miss her, Miss Morgan. We all wish things had turned out differently."

It wasn't a pardon, exactly. But, in her moment of clarity, Miss Esther acknowledging the sadness and hopelessness of the situation we shared was . . . something. It offered a strange sort of camaraderie. In an odd way, it comforted.

I swallowed down the emotion climbing my throat. "Thank you, Miss Esther."

She squeezed my hand, then looked around for Aunt Pris, her mouth falling open at the dessert in Aunt Pris's hand.

"Priscilla! Those cakes will go right to your hips, and then what will your Ed say?"

Aunt Pris glared at her friend, while shoving the last bite of cupcake into her mouth with much show. "I have never conformed my ways for a man, and I don't intend to now. Besides, if Ed only wants me for my beauty, I think we may have other concerns to discuss."

I smiled, turning to see Bronson enter the barn, a strikingly handsome man in a wheelchair at his side. Bronson waved and walked over to me.

"Wow. Not sure if it's unprofessional to say or not, but you look great." He grinned at me, seeming to consciously keep his gaze on my face.

I looked down at the yellow and white flowered dress, feeling suddenly foolish, as if I had played dress-up in Amie's clothes. "Amie insisted."

"Of course, she did. That girl has opinions on every matter under the sun, whether anyone asks for them or not."

I shook my head. "I don't mind. It was nice of her, really."

His jaw eased. "We're on cleanup duty. Think it's safe to start packing things up?"

"Better ask Josie. I don't want to give any wrong orders."

"I see you've got her pegged pretty well already." He winked, and I grinned at him, a part of me drawn to Bronson all the more after spending the morning with his family. They were a part of him, and in some ways, I glimpsed a deeper slice of who he was by being with them. Maybe that was foolish. Maybe I was a fool for harboring feelings for this man who, true to his word, had been nothing but professional since the day we'd almost kissed in the barn. We'd spent hours in one another's presence, planning for the camp that would kick off next week, and yes, nothing but professionalism from Bronson Martin.

If only that didn't disappoint me so much.

"Oh, Morgan. This is Asher, Lizzie's husband-to-be," Bronson said.

Asher gave me an easy smile and held out his hand. "Great to meet you, Morgan. I've heard you're doing an amazing job helping this guy with the camp."

I shook Asher's hand. "I'm moral support more than anything."

Bronson seemed about to argue, but was interrupted by a blur of two boys, maybe seven or eight years old, racing into the barn, oblivious of chairs or lingering guests. "Uncle Bronson!"

Bronson scooped one of them up, flipping him over in a complete circle in his arms before throwing him over his shoulder. "How's it going, buddy?" My heart squeezed at the sight of him with his nephew, effortless with genuine adoration.

The other boy hopped without reserve onto Asher's lap. "Can I call you Uncle Asher yet, Uncle Asher?"

Asher ruffled the boy's head. "There's nothing I'd like better, little man."

Bronson guided the twin in his arms to the floor, introducing the boys as Maggie's sons, Davey and Isaac. The one Bronson had returned to the ground—Isaac—surveyed the barn and its remaining guests surreptitiously. "Um, how come everyone's dry?"

Bronson cocked his head. "What do you mean?"

"I thought it was a shower."

I tried to hide a giggle while Bronson didn't bother concealing his hearty laugh. "That's just what they call it, buddy. Nobody takes a shower."

The boy's face collapsed in relief. "Oh good, because I don't think Mommy would like taking a shower in front of everyone."

Bronson's gaze flew to mine, his ears turning pink. Asher looked positively stricken.

I tried to save them both by pointing to the large pile of unwrapped presents beside the chair Lizzie had occupied. Towels and toasters and dishes and silverware and bedsheets. All the material objects Lizzie would need to start a life with her husband. I smiled at the twins, despite the unexpected lurch in my chest. "We all gave your Aunt Lizzie presents. We *showered* her with gifts for her new life with your Uncle Asher."

Understanding dawned on the boys' faces.

Bronson clapped his hands together, suddenly serious. "Okay, men. Did you bring your muscles?"

Davey and Isaac nodded eagerly, flexing their small biceps.

"Good. Go find your Aunt Josie and ask her which presents should go to Uncle Asher's truck. Got it?"

"Got it!" The boys ran off.

"It was nice meeting you, Morgan. I think it's time I find my bride-to-be." Asher wheeled off, his strong arms pushing him in Lizzie's direction.

I didn't realize the wistful sigh that came from my mouth until it was too late.

"Don't tell me you're hung up on Asher, too, after just meeting him." A twinge of jealousy peppered Bronson's words.

I squeezed my lips together, raised my eyebrows, and shook my head. "No—no, that's not it at all. It's simply nice to see them happy." What would it be like to plan a life with a man I loved? To belong to him, and him to me?

"Okay, because he has a way of making the women in my family swoon. And when he takes out his guitar . . . forget it, I'm catching falling women all over the place."

I rolled my eyes. If I swooned over anyone, it wouldn't be Lizzie's husband-to-be.

My smile must have lingered too long because Bronson tilted his head ever so slightly to the side, his gaze moving over mine in a probing, intimate way.

I cleared my throat and brushed my hands on Amie's dress. "Guess I'll go get changed so I can help clean up."

"Okay. We have one week to get this place in camp-worthy shape. Although I hate to see you take off that dress. Not that I wouldn't like seeing . . . I mean—" His tanned, handsome face developed a cranberry hue as he stumbled for words.

He'd never been more adorable. Knowing he was attracted to me, knowing he liked me, maybe even cared for me, sent a whirling top of emotions spinning around my insides.

I placed a reassuring hand on his arm. "It's okay, Bronson. I know what you meant."

And it was sending my heart into a confused frenzy just thinking about it.

⁂

BRONSON WATCHED MORGAN WALK OUT OF THE BARN, THE dress she'd slide out of in a few minutes clinging modestly to her curves. He swallowed, ran a hand over his face. Maybe there were some cold drinks left over. He could sure use something cold. Real cold.

His promise to be nothing but professional around Morgan grew harder and harder with each day. Not only was the woman beyond gorgeous—whether in jeans and a t-shirt or that incredible dress—she matched his drive and work ethic inch for inch. Though the camp hadn't yet begun, it transformed beneath their teamwork.

Too bad she'd made it abundantly clear she wasn't interested in him in *that* way. Why not? She hadn't mentioned a boyfriend. And he couldn't be imagining the long looks she gave him when she thought he wasn't looking, the way she smiled at him with her entire being. She wasn't repulsed by him, so what was the problem?

"She fits right in around here, doesn't she?"

Bronson blinked at the sound of Lizzie's voice. A mischievous grin adorned her pretty face, glowing from the morning's event. He slung an arm around her shoulder and pulled her close. "Shouldn't you be busy organizing towels and teapots or something, little sis? Asher was looking for you."

"He found me, but then Josie gave him the task of making sure Davey and Isaac don't break any plates."

They looked at Asher, wincing as Davey swung a box around, landing it squarely on Asher's lap.

Bronson laughed. "Guess I better go help them." He paused. "He's a lucky guy, Lizzie."

She blushed. "Actually, can we take a quick walk? I've been meaning to talk to you. They won't miss us with all the commotion."

He shrugged. "Sure. Maybe it'll all be done by the time we get back."

"With Josie in charge? I wouldn't be surprised."

They set off toward the orchards. Warm air wound around them, a slight breeze winding through the apple trees, some of the fruit on the outside of the trees already sporting color. He wasn't one to get sentimental, but the sight pulled a fierce sense of pride from him, almost enough to make him tear up.

"Dad would be proud of you," Lizzie said.

One corner of his mouth inched up in a smile. "I hope so. I wish he could see this, you know?"

"I know. I wish he could have met Asher. Dad would probably have him starting an entire school devoted to hiking and kayaking."

Bronson couldn't argue with that.

Lizzie stopped walking when they reached the slant of the hill. Below them, the waters of Camden Harbor stood calm and picturesque, Curtis Island green and vibrant in the middle of it all.

"Bronson, I wish Dad were here for so many reasons. To see your camp, to experience Josie's first published novel, to guide Amie through her spiritual uncertainties, to hold Mom's hand for their after-dinner walks." Her gaze flitted to mine. "I wish he could walk me down the aisle. But . . . well, he can't, and when I think of the person I'd want by my side to give me away that day, I can't imagine anyone better than you."

A foreign lump of emotion climbed Bronson's throat. Man, he'd just claimed he wasn't sentimental, but this day might take the cake for tugging at the feelings he normally pushed down with little effort. "Lizzie . . . I don't know what to say."

"I was kind of hoping you'd say yes."

He scooped her up in a big bear hug, lifting her off the ground. "Yes. Of course. I won't pretend I'm worthy, but I'll try my darnedest to stand in place of Dad." He set her back down.

"Bronson, I'm not asking you to be Dad. I'm asking you to be you—that's all I'll need that day. And, that's more than enough."

He kissed her on the forehead. "I am so proud you're my sister."

"I love you, little brother."

He swung an arm around her neck, dwarfing her with his solid arms and six-foot frame. "Little, huh?"

She giggled, and they started back down the hill.

"Okay, next item on the list."

Bronson raised his eyebrows. "Look who's all ambitious today. What do you have in mind?"

"A double date with me and Asher when we go to see fireworks this weekend."

"Double?"

"I had Ashley in mind, but seeing the way you've been looking at Morgan, I'm thinking she might be the better choice." Lizzie cocked her head, a playful question in her smile.

His mind barely registered the fact that Lizzie wanted to set him up with her best friend. Instead, he imagined sitting on a blanket with Morgan beneath a hot July night, fireworks bursting above them.

"What's with my sisters trying to set me up lately?"

"We just want you to be happy, Bron."

"I am happy. With teaching, this camp. When the right woman comes along . . ."

He couldn't avoid Lizzie's probing gaze.

"What?"

"You really like her, don't you?"

He raked a hand through his hair. "Yeah, I like her. But she's not interested in me in that way."

Lizzie squinted at him. "Not that I'm an expert in love or anything, but the way she was looking at you wasn't exactly . . . platonic."

Bronson straightened. "Really?"

"Really."

"I asked her out and she turned me down. I promised her I'd be professional after that. And I don't think inviting her to see fireworks with me would be considered professional."

"Good thing I already invited her."

"What? When?"

"I caught her right before we left. She was headed up to her apartment."

He couldn't stop the grin from inching onto his face. He threw an arm around Lizzie's shoulders. "Did I ever tell you you're my favorite sister?"

She giggled and they walked back down the hill, sunlight spilling onto their shoulders like a blessing from above.

❧ 14 ❧

Bronson and I had considered ourselves prepared. We'd
covered all our bases about possible worst-case scenarios
for our campers. If the weather gave us nothing but
downpours, we'd include extra indoor games and some simple
cooking creations. If one of us fell sick, Lizzie assured us she'd
drop whatever she was doing to come help. If a student forgot his
or her lunch, we'd store cold cuts and cheese to make a quick
sandwich.

We were prepared.

Or, so we thought.

As Bronson dealt with an unexpected camper, I forced a smile
for the twelve students sitting at two long tables in the cool shade
of the Orchard House barn. After studying their applications, I
almost felt I knew them personally. Daisy, her brown hair pulled
back into a French braid, sat at attention at the end of one of the
long tables. The twelve-year-old clutched the folder in front of
her, as if she couldn't wait to see what was inside but wouldn't do
so until given permission.

Beside her, Tommy, also age twelve, tapped a finger on the
table. He craned his neck toward the new, unexpected arrival at

the barn door. Beside him, Daniel fidgeted in his seat. Ned, also thirteen, scrunched his face at Daniel as if to silently say, "Don't you know how to sit still?" A rough-and-tumble girl named Anna sat back in her chair, arms crossed over her chest.

"Why don't you all look over the contents of your packet before we get started, okay?" I didn't know if I overstepped my bounds, but tension hung thick in the air—not a great way to start our first week of camp.

I walked to where Bronson stood at the small table outside the barn doors with the kid who'd sauntered up the drive just as our dozen students had finished a brief tour of the barn.

During the tour, Bronson had hummed with excitement as he told them the short story of the orchards, how they'd belonged to his great aunt but had been neglected for decades, how, with the students' help, they'd not only have tons of fun this week and throughout the summer, but they'd help start the next chapter for the orchard—a commercial one.

That's when someone by the door had cleared his throat. We'd glanced up to see a boy who looked older than our average camp attendees—at least fifteen. Sleek blond hair hung over one eye. No doubt he'd be a heartbreaker in a few more years.

Too bad he seemed to know it all too well.

From his canvas slip-on sneakers to his button-down collared short-sleeve shirt, he could have stepped off the pages of a J. Crew catalogue. He smelled of money and privilege, and I couldn't help but notice how the girls in the class—Daisy, Mikayla, Jessica, and even Anna—couldn't take their eyes off the newcomer.

Bronson's brow had furrowed. "Hello. Can I help you?"

"I'm here for camp." His clipped words spoke of confidence and he leaned casually against the massive frame of the double barn doors.

Bronson strode to the table by the door, where he kept his list. "That's strange, I'm positive we only signed up twelve students for the week . . ."

We had. He knew it and I knew it. Unless there had been a mistake sending out the acceptance letters. We'd been careful, though.

After flipping through his paperwork, Bronson opened his laptop. "What's your name, son?"

"I'm not your son."

Bristly as a porcupine, too.

Bronson raised an eyebrow. "Are you going to tell me, or are you going to waste my time?"

Something in the young man seemed to deflate. "Cameron Orwell."

The name registered in the depths of the applications we had gone through, though I couldn't remember the particulars.

Bronson pulled up the Excel sheet we'd used to compile the applicants' names, as well as whether we accepted or rejected them, whether they were rewarded a scholarship, which week (or weeks) they would attend, and whether they had any food allergies. He was so stinking organized—I found it hard to believe he'd make even one oversight.

While Bronson scanned the file, the boy named Cameron stood back, hands in his pockets, appearing nonchalant.

I wasn't fooled. The telltale way he shifted his weight gave away his nervousness. I wondered what had brought him here. He reached up for the leather cord at his neck, a small opened mouth bass hanging from its cord. Maybe he liked to fish. While he didn't seem like much of an outdoor kid, maybe I read him wrong.

"It looks like we had to deny the application you turned in, Cameron. I'm sorry, but we didn't plan for more than twelve kids a week."

Cameron pressed his lips together. "I won't be trouble."

Bronson looked at me, and I could see how uncomfortable this situation was for him. Yet, if he bent for one kid, what about all the others? And this kid hadn't even paid the camp fee.

Still, he came. To turn him away felt like it went against everything the Orchard House camp stood for.

I shrugged and hoped Bronson would read my look as, "What would it hurt?"

Bronson rubbed the back of his neck. "You can stay for today, and today only. And I'd like to speak to whoever dropped you off when they pick you up at the end of the day, understood?"

"I walked here, and I plan to walk home."

Bronson blew out a long breath. "Okay, I'll give your folks a call. Go take a seat, Mr. Orwell."

Cameron nodded and grabbed a seat away from the long tables, in the back corner of our informal classroom. No ignoring the air of entitlement the kid wore like cologne. Nevertheless, something about him made me think his smooth, clean-cut exterior hid some big wounds.

After Bronson made a call on his cell phone outside, he came back in and nodded at Cameron before taking a chair facing the students. He outlined our week—planting disease-resistant trees on the east side of the orchard and putting red sticky balls in the trees to protect them from pests (in place of using toxic insecticides, he explained, and in order to keep the orchard organic). Along with the work, we'd planned a mid-week kayak trip, an apple oxidation experiment to understand why apples turned brown, an early morning fishing venture, and the afternoon electives of writing, art, or music (Lizzie had jumped on board at Amie's prompting).

He clapped his hands together. "Any questions before we head out?"

Daisy raised her hand. "The description on the application talked about helping you run the apple-picking business. How are we going to do that?" Her prim manner had Anna rolling her eyes, but I appreciated Daisy's enthusiasm and straightforward way.

"I intend to teach you all about good business practices this week, as well as getting you involved in purchasing a trailer for hayrides up to the orchard for customers to pick apples. We need to build a simple stand to put outside the barn—a shaded place to take payments for picking apples, hayrides, and for serving customers baked apple goods. Obviously, we won't be accomplishing all this in one week, but it looks like most of you are attending throughout the summer. We'll see where your interests and strengths lie and go from there."

Tommy raised a hand. "My grandfather taught me everything he knew about agricultural mechanics, so if you need work on a tractor, trailer, weedwhacker, you name it, I'm your guy."

"I appreciate that, Tommy. It'll definitely be handy having you around."

Mikayla raised a tentative hand. "I'm a great baker. I didn't realize we'd be handling the business. I could bake pies and cakes and make caramel apples."

"I'm good at handling a cash register," Daisy piped up.

"I could drive the tractor for the hayrides," Ned said. "I visited my grandparents in Florida and drove the golf cart around all over. A tractor wouldn't be any harder."

I forced my smile away. Bronson had been careful to only hint that a few students would stay on to run the apple-picking business, but clearly, it excited the kids.

I noted the almost sullen silence coming from Cameron's direction in the back corner.

Bronson scratched his jaw. "You guys are an entrepreneur's dream, but let's take one thing at a time. First and foremost, this is camp—a time for you to put in some good work, have some fun, make some friends, and maybe learn a few things. We won't be bringing in customers until the end of next month, so let's take one day at a time."

Most of the kids nodded, save for Daniel and Cameron, the withdrawn two in the otherwise effusive bunch.

"If anyone needs to use the restroom before we head out, go

ahead and do so. It might be a good idea to grab some water, too. It can get hot out there."

◈

SEVEN HOURS LATER, I PRACTICALLY WILTED AGAINST THE BARN door as the last of the parents drove their children down the driveway of the Orchard House Bed and Breakfast. In the distance, Cameron took a right out of the driveway, walking home as he said he would.

Now, Bronson staggered into the shade of the barn and sprawled out on his stomach with a groan, his cheek pressed to a wide-planked floorboard. "We made it."

I released a tired laugh, lowering myself into a chair beside him. "Day one, down. That was . . . exhausting. Exhausting but satisfying."

He rolled onto his back, the chest of his t-shirt peppered in fine dust and bits of hay from one of Lizzie's bridal shower displays. "I concur."

"You're great with them, Bronson."

"So are you. We make a pretty good team, don't we, Dalton?"

I smiled. It wasn't the first time he'd made the remark, and I didn't think I'd ever tire of hearing it. "Your sisters didn't hurt things, either." In fact, Amie, Josie, and Lizzie may have very well saved the day. While both Bronson and I were accustomed to handling students inside a controlled classroom setting, venturing outdoors in an orchard with lots of hiding places and obstacles proved something else altogether. The boys wanted to climb trees. Daisy and Anna had gotten caught up in a gymnastics competition.

They weren't bad kids—none of them. Still, it took every ounce of watchful energy to direct their focus and enthusiasm. By the afternoon, when it was time for their chosen electives, Bronson and I had willingly handed the group over to his sisters.

"You think we need to hire another counselor?" Bronson asked. "Maybe I could find a college student pursuing a teaching degree."

"Not a bad idea," I agreed. "If it's in the budget. Or maybe we simply need to adjust. Did you ever go to camp? The first day was always exhausting, no matter how much fun. Jenna and I always settled in after a couple of days."

Still on the floor, Bronson turned his head toward me. "I never did camp. Too many kids, not enough cash—story of the Martin family since the beginning of time. Not that it mattered. Our house was almost a sort of camp. Josie with her books and directing us to put on plays, which I hated, by the way. Amie with her mudpies, Lizzie with her music."

"And what about you?"

"What about me?"

"Besides grumbling over Josie's plays, what occupied your time?"

Bronson stretched his arms over his head before propping them behind his neck as a sort of pillow. An insatiable urge to climb down beside him on the cool floorboards, to snuggle myself into the hollow between his body and his arm, crawled over me. The same inclination had consumed me when I'd sat beside him on a blanket last week for the Fourth of July fireworks, the lights bursting above us in scattering circles of celebratory festivity. Now, as I had done on that night, I tamped down the attraction simmering deep. But when he didn't answer right away, I slid from my chair to sit cross-legged on the floor beside him.

After a moment, he spoke. "I guess I was trying not to get swallowed up by it all, you know? To figure out who I was in the sea of women and creativity that was my house."

"What about your dad?" I hadn't thought before I asked the question, and once it drifted into the air between us, I wished to snatch it back.

Bronson had asked me about the night Isabel died, and I

refused to share. Why should he share the personal parts of himself with me? Why should I expect him to?

"Dad loved us, no doubting that, but he didn't show it with his time too much. Always busy starting some well-meaning charitable venture or serving the poor. He took me along when I was older. By that time . . ." Bronson shrugged. "It doesn't matter now, does it? He was a good father. I didn't mean to imply—"

I shook my head. "Bronson, it's okay. I'm not judging. No parent is perfect."

"What about yours?"

I bit my bottom lip. "I guess I was a little spoiled. That was the defense, after all." I closed my eyes against my bitter words.

"Defense . . . for your trial?"

I stood, my limbs ten times wearier than when I first sat down. "We should talk about Cameron."

He rolled into a sitting position. "Morgan, is that what you meant? The defense for your trial was that you were spoiled?"

Spoiled little rich girl. Poor thing, didn't know right from wrong. One could only expect she'd drink and drive.

What a joke.

"I shouldn't have brought it up." My tone held a hard edge. Too hard, maybe. "Please. It's nothing personal, it's just—"

"Personal," he finished, the corners of his mouth tight. "Not professional. I get it, no worries."

His words stung. I wanted to let him in—couldn't he see how much I did? But there was only pain there, only hopelessness.

He rubbed the back of his neck. "So, Cameron. I can't say kids showing up unannounced at the camp was a problem I anticipated."

"Me neither. You don't think we sent him an acceptance letter in error, did we?"

Bronson shook his head. "I triple-checked what we sent out. Something feels off with the kid. I'm not buying that he actually thought we accepted him. I looked over his application this afternoon. It was half-hearted, purposefully obtuse. He applied for a scholarship. When I spoke to his mother this morning, she didn't seem to know anything about it, but agreed to let him stay. Looking back, it was probably a mistake for me to go along with that—better to get something in writing. I'll call again and explain things, tell them he can't show up tomorrow."

I'd looked over Cameron's application as well. While the thirteen-year-old hadn't so much as made it on to the "maybe" list, I saw something in the boy today that made me question our initial decision. Something about him reminded me of my own teenage years as I watched him agonize over which elective to attend, as if it were a life-and-death decision. Whatever it was, a niggling feeling that the boy needed this camp wormed its way through me.

"I looked over the application, too." I dragged in a deep breath. This was Bronson's camp, not mine. What right did I have to disagree with him on a major issue like this? Hadn't I already pushed my luck in advocating for Marcus?

"And? What'd you think?" Bronson rubbed the spot above his eyebrow with his thumb.

Well, since he asked . . .

"I think we should let him stay."

Bronson studied me, those deep chocolate pools wearing me thin as he waited for me to elaborate.

"His essay wasn't great, I'll give you that. But I don't think he was trying to write badly. He showed up. He wants to be here."

"I actually know his family. Friends with the mayor, his dad's some hot-shot lawyer. He gave our family trouble about my dad's mission some years back. They could send him to whatever camp he wants."

I raised an eyebrow. "So, you have a personal vendetta against Cameron's family?"

"No, that's not it. Well, maybe that's it a little. My point is, the kid didn't get accepted. He's used to getting his way, used to the world being served to him on a silver platter, so he shows up here, entitled, when his parents can afford any number of other camps for the summer."

"But he came to *our* camp."

Our camp. That was presumptuous. Yet, with all the sweat I'd poured into the Orchard House camp, I couldn't deny I thought of it this way.

"So, we should accept anyone who comes waltzing into the camp regardless of our plans?"

A simmering flame crackled in my chest. "Now, who's being obtuse? How often do you think something like this happens? I'm simply saying, maybe it happened for a reason. Aren't you the one who believes God has a plan and all that? Is it outside the realm of possibility that Cameron's meant to be here?"

"That's great and all, Morgan, but what about order and the attention we can give these kids? There are rules and guidelines—and protocol—for a reason."

I stood, the need to flee the barn and Bronson surging over me all at once. "You know, it's not just the underprivileged kids who need camps like this one. Sometimes it's the kids who look like they have the world handed to them that need something solid to grasp onto the most." I turned toward the barn door and the stairs to my apartment. A shower would feel good. "Obviously, it's your call. I'll see you tomorrow, Bronson."

⚜ 15 ⚜

Bronson paced the floor of his makeshift classroom, phone tight to his ear, the hollow ringing echoing in his eardrum. He hoped Morgan was happy. He hoped she was very, very happy.

"Hello?" A deep, baritone voice answered.

"Hi, my name is Bronson Martin. I'm the director over at the Orchard House summer camp. Is this Mr. Orwell?"

"Speaking."

"Hello, sir. I'm calling because your son came by our camp to—"

"Stepson."

Bronson paused. Hadn't expected that one. And for the guy to point it out, to start the conversation off by distancing himself from Cameron.

"Okay, sure. Your stepson came by our camp today. We never sent him an acceptance letter, but after reviewing his application and reconsidering, we're willing to let him stay on this week if that's agreeable to you."

He gave himself credit for sounding more enthusiastic about the plan than he actually was. Truthfully, he was doing this for

Morgan. For Morgan, and maybe a little bit for Cameron. He admitted that something with the kid didn't quite add up.

"That'll be fine." Mr. Orwell's clipped voice sounded as if he were ready to brush Bronson off the phone for a more important call. Probably a call that would make him money instead of lose him money.

"That's great, sir. We'll look forward to having him back tomorrow. We'll just need payment to complete the application."

"Payment? The boy told me you were handing out scholarships."

"That's true, but Cameron didn't submit any financial documents. I'm afraid all of the scholarships have already been awarded." Not that the Orwells would have met the economic criteria.

Then again, neither had Ned, and they'd made an exception for him.

And though technically there was one scholarship he had in reserve, he wasn't ready to hand that out just yet. Surely, a few hundred dollars was a drop in the bucket for someone like Mr. Orwell. Certainly, worth the educational, worthwhile experience the camp offered.

"Tell me again what this camp's about?" The line went muffled as Mr. Orwell spoke to someone. Bronson couldn't make out the exact words but he caught enough to gather someone had gotten Mr. Orwell's coffee order wrong. And from the sounds of the urgent, muffled tones, he was none too happy about it.

Bronson cleared his throat. Was the guy even listening?

"It's a camp teaching kids how to run an orchard, sir. It includes field trips—a kayak trip is planned this week—as well as science experiments, fishing, business planning, and a time for electives. Writing, art, and music. A little bit of everything."

A pause. Probably Mr. Orwell sipping his new coffee, mulling over whether the server had gotten it right—not pondering the value of the Orchard House camp for his son—ahem, stepson.

"Sir, are you there?"

"Yes, yes, yes. How much did you say this camp will put me in the hole?"

This guy was a real piece of work. Bronson was about ready to pay for Cameron himself just to expose him to something that wasn't Nathan Orwell.

He named the price.

"I'm sorry, that's not in our budget at this time. I'll let the boy know. Rest assured, he won't be showing up to bother you tomorrow."

"He's not a bother . . ." In fact, the thought of Cameron not showing up the next day caused a heavy weight to settle in Bronson's chest. He cleared his throat again. "What if we worked out an agreement?"

"You have my attention." The lawyer in Mr. Orwell must have perked up at the word *agreement*.

"Part of the camp initiative is to start an apple-picking venture out of the orchards the kids will be maintaining. My plan was to hire on some of the students." Though he'd never considered Cameron might be one of them. Until now, anyway. "What if Cameron paid off the camp by working for us throughout the summer. Maybe into September as well."

A moment's pause. "That'll be agreeable, I suppose. The boy could use a little help in molding his work ethic."

Bronson swallowed. This was a gamble. He could very well be saddling himself with a problem—not just a camp problem, but now, a business problem.

Here it was, here is where he started down the path of being just like his dad . . . .

He closed his eyes, sending up a prayer for wisdom.

"Sounds like a plan, then," Bronson pushed out. "I'll just need you or your wife to sign some forms tomorrow morning when you drop Cameron off."

"My wife will be there."

"Thank you, sir."

The line went dead.

Bronson lowered himself into the chair Morgan had sat in ten minutes earlier. If only his last challenge of the day was over. But he had a feeling his next task wouldn't prove any easier.

He glanced up at the ceiling, where Morgan probably settled down for the night. Took a shower, perhaps made herself a simple meal.

There was no denying he couldn't run this camp without her.

There was also no denying that—as seemed to be the norm with all the women in his life—she was expecting a lot more work from him than he ever intended.

BRONSON RANG THE DOORBELL OF THE DAVIS HOME, HIS HEART picking up a steady rhythm.

Was he making a colossal mistake? Should he have left well enough alone? He thought of Morgan, of her refusal to share the details behind the night Isabel died or the trial. Whenever he drew close to her, she pushed him away.

He was a fixer. And more than once, one of his sisters had accused him of sticking his nose where it didn't belong, of forcing something to happen—or, in the case of Lizzie and Asher's burgeoning relationship, to *not* happen—when the situation didn't need his intervention.

Was this another one of those times? Or could this open up possibilities? A way for Morgan to heal from her past, a way to show her how much he cared.

The Davis door opened and Isabel's mother stood on the threshold, opening the screen door. "Bronson, so nice to see you."

"Thank you for agreeing to meet with me, Mrs. Davis."

"Why don't we sit on the porch? It's such a lovely evening. Hold on a minute, and I'll get my husband."

She ducked into the depths of the house. "Mike! Pris's

grandson is here!" In the background, he heard what sounded like a soap opera. Miss Esther sure did love her "stories." Aunt Pris was forever harping on her friend about how trashy the soaps were, but Miss Esther couldn't be dissuaded.

A moment later, both Mr. and Mrs. Davis slipped out onto the porch. Mr. Davis, a tall man with a bald head and dark-framed glasses held his hand out to Bronson. "My, son, you've certainly grown since last I saw you."

He smiled. "Aunt Pris's seventy-fifth birthday party, I think. Isabel whipped us all in a game of basketball."

Both Mr. and Mrs. Davis's faces fell, and Bronson bit the inside of his cheek. Should he not have brought up their daughter? Did they not speak of Isabel? Was it too painful? And yet, how could that be healthy?

He sucked in a breath, reminded himself he wasn't here to fix anyone. He was here to offer the camp once more to Marcus, to ensure he'd done anything and everything he could for not only the boy, but for Mr. and Mrs. Davis, for Morgan.

"Can we get you anything to drink, Bronson?" Mrs. Davis asked, and he had the horrible feeling she was already trying to escape him.

"No, ma'am. I'm fine, thank you. I won't take much of your time, I promise."

She gestured to the wicker furniture on the porch and he took the chair, allowing Marcus's parents to sit on the couch.

He placed his elbows on his thighs, leaning over his splayed legs. "I asked to meet with you in hopes you might reconsider allowing Marcus to attend the Orchard House camp. I realize there's a lot of history between your family and Miss Dalton, but I'm hoping that needn't interfere with the possibility of Marcus enjoying himself at the orchard."

Silence overtook the porch, and for a moment, Bronson wished he hadn't come at all. Better to leave well enough alone.

He really did think he was Superman, didn't he? Barreling in to solve the world's problems.

Mrs. Davis stared at the chipped paint of the porch floorboards. "What you're asking is impossible," she whispered.

Mr. Davis leaned forward. "We appreciate your efforts in this matter, Bronson. You and Miss Dalton are very persistent in showing up to try to convince us, but . . . it's hard for my wife—"

Bronson didn't miss the glare Mrs. Davis sent her husband.

He shook his head. "Morgan came here?"

"Even though I asked her not to come back." Mrs. Davis uncrossed her legs, tapping her feet on the wooden planks.

Mr. Davis continued. "It's hard for *us* to place Marcus directly in the hands of the woman who took our daughter's life. I'm sure Morgan has changed. I'm sure she's entirely responsible now. It's just too big a hurdle to get past. We hope you understand. It's nothing personal with you or your camp."

Bronson rubbed the back of his neck, tense from the stress of the day, from the hours he'd spent awake the night before, anticipating the first day of the first session of the Orchard House summer camp. And then, Cameron showing up, corralling the kids, his talk with Morgan . . .

"All right." He set his jaw. "We only wanted to be certain before awarding the scholarship to someone else. I wanted to clarify we have several other counselors on staff, including myself. Ideally, there will always be one or more counselors with your son. And my sister, Amie, is willing to serve as an aid to Marcus the week he's at camp. I showed her his drawing, and she was in awe of his talent. You know Amie, don't you? She sells her art at some of the local shops downtown. Her leaf lamp things . . ."

He was rambling. Leaf lamp things? He'd have to pay better attention to what Amie called the nightlights and lamps she made out of natural or recycled materials.

Mr. Davis glanced at his wife. "Do you think we should reconsider, Ruth? It might be a good opportunity—"

A wounded look passed over Marcus's mother's face. Quietly, but with enough tension to hold a tightrope across Niagara Falls, she stood and slipped inside the house, leaving Bronson and Mr. Davis alone and untethered on the porch.

Bronson stood. "I'm sorry, Mr. Davis. Please extend my apologies to Mrs. Davis also. I didn't mean any harm. I thought—"

"She's had a hard time letting Isabel go." Mr. Davis's soft voice lingered in the air. "It's not healthy, but I also don't blame her. Isabel was her best friend, her only daughter. She blames herself; I think. They'd been arguing a lot in the time leading up to that night. She's not simply angry at Morgan, she's angry at herself." He shook his head. "I've said too much. Thank you, Bronson, for coming by. I'll talk to my wife. I don't think it will make any difference, but can I give you a call by the end of the week before you award that scholarship to another student?"

"Of course, sir." That he hadn't closed the door on his offer felt like victory. And whether or not they accepted it, Bronson could continue the camp knowing he'd done all in his power to pave the way for the Davises, and maybe Morgan, to find some healing.

"It's important to wear the lifejackets at all times." A tick started in Bronson's left eye as he looked over the thirteen kids he was about to take out on Camden Harbor. He ordered his nerves aside. They were perfectly safe, especially with two guides from Paramount Sports, himself, Morgan, and Asher.

"Aww, come on, Mr. Martin. I know how to swim. This thing gets in the way of my mad rowing abilities."

Though they'd only gone through two full days of camp, Bronson was getting to know the kids and some of their quirks. Like thirteen-year-old Ned, a bit on the small side, who always seemed to look for a laugh and sought to prove himself at every turn.

While Bronson had an inkling the kid only pulled his leg, he gave him a stern look. Ned had complained about the tedious job of painting the Tanglefoot sticky coating on the red balls hung on the trees to attract maggot flies away from the real fruit. "You mess around and you'll be banned from Friday's picnic and games, and I'll have plenty of extra sticky balls for you to work on."

Ned held up his hands, a look of pure horror on his face.

"Enough said. Lifejacket plastered to body." The boy grinned, zipping up the flotation device.

He was a good kid. A bit of a goofball. Bronson couldn't imagine him at military camp.

"Any other questions?"

Anna tugged at the ponytail protruding from her Red Sox cap. She glanced at the kayaks waiting on the shore, shifting her weight from one foot to the other. "I know how to swim, but . . . how deep is the water?"

"Maybe twenty, thirty feet?" He didn't believe in lying to the kids to soften their fears, even if it might be easier. "But you'll have your jacket, Anna. Even if you did fall in—which you shouldn't if you follow the instructions of our tour guides—your lifejacket would keep you afloat and someone would help you in a matter of seconds. But you don't have to go if you don't want to."

She bit her lip. Bronson glanced at Morgan, who sidled up to the girl and leaned down, whispering in her ear. Warmth flooded through him, and for the tenth time that week, he thanked God he'd made the decision to hire her.

He turned to Asher. "Did I miss anything?"

Asher gestured to a tall guide with blond hair. "Leroy will be in front. Follow him and stay out of the way of boats. We should see some beauties today—cruising yachts, historic schooners. He'll show you all the points of interest around the island." He turned to a petite woman with light brown hair and a sunhat. "Mariah and I will take up the rear. You're all perfectly safe as long as you respect the water and stay between us." He glanced at Anna and gave her a kind smile.

The girl blushed.

"Okay, let's do this." Mariah pushed out onto the water first.

Bronson and Leroy helped the kids into their boats one-by-one—a happy mess of hats above white sun-screened noses, kayak paddles, and lunch pails.

Morgan was still standing to the side, speaking softly with

Anna. He hoped she could convince the girl to give the kayak a try. If not, one of them would have to return her to Amie at Orchard House, possibly missing out on the trip.

Tommy stood back, studying Asher as he used his muscled arms to lower himself from his chair into the kayak. "You ever fall doing that?" he asked.

Bronson winced. While Asher was open to talking about his disability and preferred acknowledging his wheelchair over pretending it was just another set of legs, Bronson couldn't imagine he enjoyed a twelve-year-old studying him as he tucked the dead weight of his legs into the kayak.

"Lots of times at first," Asher answered. "Just like anything new—riding a bike, rock-climbing, juggling. You fail at first, but it's part of the process of learning."

Tommy raised his eyebrows, seemingly impressed as he jumped into the boat, pushing out into the water with a shove from Leroy.

"You sure you didn't miss your calling as a teacher?" Bronson asked Asher.

"Oh, I'm sure." His soon-to-be-brother-in-law chuckled. "Kids scare me out of my own skin."

Bronson raised an eyebrow. "Lizzie know that?" His sweet sister loved children.

"Don't worry, man. I'm not against kids themselves, just teaching a classroom full of them. Which, by the way, don't you think you should . . ." Asher gestured to the empty kayak beside him.

"Right." Bronson pushed the red boat's nose into the water. After he situated his small cooler, he pushed against the sandy bank with his paddle.

He watched as Anna climbed into the front of the only double kayak, Morgan at the rear. They pushed off. The girl sat stiff as a post, her paddle tight in her knuckles as she held it suspended in the air.

"All right, Anna!" Bronson whistled his encouragement.

Asher joined in and the girl dipped her head, tentatively placing her paddle in the water, looking down into the depths as if expecting a fish to jump up and grab her fingers.

Bronson grinned at Morgan, who no doubt had struck a deal with the frightened girl. He gave her a thumbs-up and she rewarded him with a smile that could have lit the harbor on a cloudy night. He might not be overly experienced when it came to women, but he wasn't oblivious, either. Morgan felt something for him. Why then, wouldn't she grant him a single date?

With everyone out on the water, the group followed Leroy toward Curtis Island. A schooner slid by, the movement creating slight ripples that rocked the kayaks. Bronson breathed it all in and grabbed a water bottle from his cooler. The sight of his students rowing toward the picturesque Curtis Island Lighthouse was exactly as he'd imagined this trip. The lighthouse stood on the hunk of rock and grass, a beacon to ships entering the harbor, its white-washed lighthouse keeper's house set beside it. Quintessential Maine. He couldn't imagine living anywhere else. Couldn't understand why Josie had gone to New York City, why Amie often spoke of going there, too. Noise and smog and traffic and buildings so tall they blocked the sun. Nothing like this place, where the mountains met the sea, where open sky and untampered forest spoke of a history and timelessness all its own.

"Check this out!"

Bronson blinked to attention, turning to the voice a couple hundred feet to the side of him. His blood surged as he saw Ned standing up in his kayak, performing a rather risqué dance move that involved gyrating hips, one hand behind his head, the other moving in a sprinkler type motion in a semi-circle in front of him.

"Ned, sit down!" Bronson yelled across the water at the same time Morgan and Mariah did.

Ned startled and held up his hands. "I was just having a little fun is all. I—" Just as he was lowering himself, a crest from the wake of a yacht met Ned's boat, knocking the boy backward. He slammed his head on Tommy's kayak on his way into the water.

Bronson didn't think—he lunged. The sharp, cold water met his clothed body and he swam with powerful strokes toward Ned. Halfway to him, Bronson realized it probably would have been smarter to row closer to the boy and try to assist him with his paddle. But what if knocking his head had made him unconscious? His lifejacket didn't matter much if he didn't have the wherewithal to pull his face from the water.

Commotion surrounded them. Boats clamored. Tommy's stricken face grew ashen as he held onto Ned's lifejacket, trying to pull him into his boat.

"Let go of him!" Leroy said to Tommy. Either the boy didn't hear or he didn't realize Leroy spoke to him.

"Tommy, he's okay. His face is out of the water. Let go or he'll pull you in too." Morgan's voice was surprisingly calm, bringing a semblance of peace to Bronson's pounding heart. When he reached the boys, Ned was blinking his eyes, a dazed look on his face. He shook his head, his arms flailing in the water.

"I'm okay, Mr. Martin. I'm okay. Sorry. Really, I am."

Bronson gripped the armhole of the boy's lifejacket, helping him toward his boat. A moment later, Leroy reached them. After a few awkward moments, they managed to help Ned into his kayak. Bronson swam back to his. Thankfully, Daisy had the sense to grab it before it floated away from them.

Once he was in the boat, Bronson assessed the situation. He needed to bring Ned back to shore, get him checked out, call his parents. "How's your head, Ned? You whacked it pretty hard."

"I blacked out for a minute, but I'm okay. I'm super sorry, Mr. Martin. I didn't think it was so easy to get knocked over."

"And I didn't think I had to outline the rule about not standing up in kayaks." The corners of Bronson's mouth tightened. "I told you no goofing around."

The boy looked appropriately chastened. "I know."

"Let's go."

"What? Really? You're going to make me go back?"

"We have to get you checked out and call your parents."

"I'm fine!" Ned threw up his hands. "Please, don't call my parents. They'll never let me come back."

For a moment, pity erupted in Bronson's stomach. How many times had he stood in his kayak as a boy, trying to show off for his family, show off for his dad? Or that time he'd jumped from a tree branch onto their backyard trampoline, bouncing off onto the grass and breaking an arm?

But the boy had blacked out. He couldn't take that lightly.

"Listen, Ned. I get it. But I made a promise to your parents to keep you safe and take care of you. I have an obligation to them to report this, and an obligation to you to get you checked out and make sure you didn't knock any more sense out of your head."

Ned didn't laugh at the joke.

Morgan and Asher paddled toward them.

"You heading back?" Asher asked.

Bronson nodded.

"You want me to come?"

He shook his head. "I think you and Morgan should stay and finish out the tour with the rest. I'll call Ned's parents and see if they want me to take him to the hospital."

Asher nodded. "Let us know how you make out."

Bronson turned to Morgan. "You think you got everything under control until I get back?"

"Absolutely. Call me, okay?"

He began rowing back toward shore, Ned beside him.

"I didn't hit my head that hard, Mr. Martin. You don't have to call my parents. They'll send me to military camp, I know they will."

Bronson pushed his paddle through the water, propelling his kayak forward. "I hope they don't, Ned. I hope you get to stay at Orchard House, but it would be dishonest of me to keep this from them. And what if you did some serious damage? I told you no goofing around and you did. Now, we'll deal with the consequences together."

"You said not to take off my lifejacket!" the boy whined. "I didn't do that."

Bronson sighed. Maybe he wasn't cut out for this camp thing. True, he wasn't a stranger to the mischief middle school kids could get into, but maybe he hadn't planned well enough. Maybe he wasn't firm enough in the ground rules he'd set for the kids.

Maybe he was just plain lousy at all of it.

❧ 17 ❧

I clenched my fists as I entered the doors of the hospital emergency room. The last time I was in this place, I'd learned of Isabel's death. I still remembered the haze and pain of it all. The harsh scent of disinfectant, the thick bandage around my head where the windshield had cracked through my tender skin, my parents wringing their hands by the side of my hospital bed.

Worse than all that was the sound of Isabel's parents praying aloud in the hallway. Then, when they found out the horrible news that they'd never see their daughter again this side of heaven, their haunting wails pierced the hospital corridors, echoing the silent, soul-sucking moans of my own heart.

I spotted Bronson in the waiting room and wilted in near relief at the sight of him. His hair lay plastered in unruly waves, his t-shirt crinkled where it had dried slowly beneath the air conditioning of the hospital. I should have asked Mrs. Martin or Amie or Lizzie for an extra pair of clothes for him after the parents had picked up their kids. But I hadn't realized he'd come straight to the hospital. Had Ned hit his head that badly?

I reached for Bronson, and he squeezed my hand.

"How is he?"

"He seemed fine, but they won't tell me anything. His parents are with him now."

"He'll be okay, Bronson." I slid into a seat beside him, not at all sure of my own words. Bad things happened at hospitals. People died. Lives were changed forever.

Bronson touched my cheek ever so gently. "He *will* be okay. Don't worry, Morgan. Kids bump their heads every day. My mom used to joke that I was actually a goat with how often I was knocking my head against things. His parents weren't even sure about bringing him to the hospital—said they could monitor him at home. But with it happening while at camp, I encouraged them to get him checked out."

"They won't blame you."

Bronson shrugged. "I hope not."

I recalled Bronson's determined strokes to Ned, how he'd confidently handled the situation with firm compassion. I loved that Bronson knew what he was about. He didn't doubt his actions, his faith, his place in the world. He'd never questioned whether they should simply go about their day, pretend the incident with Ned never happened.

I remembered Cameron and his mom walking up to the Orchard House barn the morning before. When I'd given him a questioning glance, Bronson only shrugged, the edge of his ears growing endearingly pink.

"We cut a deal."

Only later did I find out the deal Bronson had "cut" with Cameron. He risked so much—not only Cameron's admission fee to the camp, but a whole lot of headaches if he didn't prove to be a good worker for Bronson's apple-picking venture.

And yet, Bronson had gone out of his way for the sake of giving the kid a chance. He'd listened to me. So much so, that he put his neck on the line for a kid we hadn't an inkling would prove his mettle.

I even offered up a prayer that Cameron wouldn't disappoint.

When I'd watched Bronson row away with Ned, his wet t-shirt highlighting those powerful arms, a longing had ripped through me, strong and sure, making me momentarily forget all the reasons we couldn't be together.

Bronson squeezed my hand. "There they are."

We stood as Ned—who looked no worse for the wear—emerged from the swinging triage doors, a couple in their forties behind him. Ned's father was dressed in army fatigue pants, a forest green t-shirt stretching across his solid chest. Short in stature, completely intimidating in stance. Ned's mother wore a flowing maxi skirt and a white tank top that showed off her glowing tan and bleach blonde hair. She kept a hand on Ned's shoulder.

Ned's father held a hand out to Bronson, then me. "Victor Abbendroth. My wife, Katrina. Sorry we didn't introduce ourselves when we first arrived."

"I understand why you didn't, sir. How'd everything go in there?" Bronson asked.

"Just a small bruise. Nothing most boys don't endure." Ned's father glanced at his wife, then at the plentiful patients in the waiting room. "Why don't we step outside?"

Bronson nodded, and we followed the Abbendroths into the parking lot, where they stood by a concrete retaining wall. I dragged in fresh breaths of the open air.

Mr. Abbendroth placed a hand on Ned's shoulder. "Ned here told us what happened. I wish to apologize for the trouble my son has caused you all and your camp. I want you to know we're withdrawing him immediately. We hope it's not too late for you to award his scholarship to another student."

My jaw dropped. Ned had been awarded one of the whole summer scholarships. His enthusiasm for the camp was contagious. Yes, he could be mischievous and a little too fun-loving, but after only three days, I couldn't imagine our camp without him.

Bronson shook his head. "Sir, that's really not necess—"

"I should have listened to my gut and sent him to the camp in D.C. to begin with. It's not your fault, Mr. Martin. Some kids simply need a firmer hand."

My jaw quivered until I couldn't hold my words back any longer. "Bronson doesn't let the kids get away with anything. He's a great teacher, Mr. Abbendroth."

Bronson's fingers brushed my arm. "It's okay, Morgan. Mr. Abbendroth didn't mean for us to take offense."

"I most certainly did not. I think your camp is a great idea—it just might not be for every kid."

"Dad, I really like it there. Please, could I have another chance?" Ned looked up at his father's imposing posture. "I promise I'll be good."

"No, son. My mind's made up." He held his hand out to Bronson. "Thank you for bringing him to the hospital, Mr. Martin."

"Sir . . ." Bronson began. I could almost see his mind scrambling for a way to convince Mr. Abbendroth, for a way to keep Ned.

Mr. Abbendroth paused, but when Bronson didn't speak, the older man nodded. "Good night. Thanks, again."

"Sir, what if there were a way for Ned to make it up to the camp for his actions? A little discipline, I mean."

Mr. Abbendroth straightened. "How's that?"

"I need workers for the apple-picking business we're starting over at Orchard House. What would you think of Ned putting in an hour or two after camp and on Saturdays to help out?"

Mr. Abbendroth spread his feet apart, arms loosely clasped in front of him as if just told by an officer that he could stand "at ease." "And you'd consider that discipline?"

"It's hard physical labor, sir. I'd need help keeping the weeds back in the orchards, keeping the pests away, turning compost, watering the trees."

"Isn't that what the kids at the camp are doing?" Mrs. Abbendroth asked.

"Well, yes, ma'am, to an extent. But the goal of camp is fun, of course. Otherwise, why would any of them want to come back? I'm talking real work for Ned. Something to build muscle and strength of mind. Something to show him that life's more than a game."

I raised my eyebrows at Bronson's words. Harsh words, coming from him. But they seemed to sing the tune Mr. Abbendroth liked to dance to.

He glanced at his son. "What do you think about this, Ned? If we give you one more chance at Mr. Martin's camp, do you agree to work—to the best of your ability—for him at his orchard?"

Ned's eyes widened. "Yes. I'll do a great job. I promise I will, sir."

Mr. Abbendroth turned to Bronson. "And you'll let me know if he steps one *toe* out of line, Mr. Martin?"

"I will, sir."

"I mean it—one toe. I will not have my son running around, wreaking havoc in this town. One incident, and D.C. it is."

For a moment, my heart went out to the boy. The last thing Ned was doing was "wreaking havoc." Okay, maybe he wrought a little havoc today. But he wasn't a bad kid.

Still, although I might not agree with Mr. and Mrs. Abbendroth's parenting approach, it was apparent they loved their son. Who was I, of all people, to judge them?

"You have my word, sir." Bronson held out his hand. "Thank you. I could really use the help in the orchard."

"Don't try paying him anything, either, understood? This is strictly a disciplinary act."

"Of course, sir. I wouldn't dream of going against your wishes."

"Very well, then. We'll see you soon." Mr. Abbendroth placed his hand on the small of his wife's back and they started toward their car. Ned trailed behind, turning back once to give us a small, grateful smile.

We stood there, watching until they climbed into their Jeep Cherokee and drove away.

I gave Bronson a sidelong glance, raised a single eyebrow. "So, your solution to every problem student is to hire them for orchard work so you have to manage them for *additional* hours of the day?"

The corners of Bronson's mouth tugged into a grin as he shook his head, casually propping a playful elbow on my shoulder. "Morgan, Morgan, Morgan. There are no problem students. Only students with gifts they haven't quite harnessed yet."

"That's . . . profound."

He let his arm fall. "My dad used to say it. But he also said, 'The less routine, the more of life.' I could never get on board with that one."

"You do seem to like your schedules." I'd noted how he never allowed the kids extra time on an activity if it wasn't in the plan. While the camp endeavor had begun as a way to simply get the kids outside, enjoying good honest work, it very quickly evolved into a regimented camp. Not that I blamed Bronson. Thirteen kids needed routine.

"How about something not on the schedule, then?" he asked.

My skin prickled at his words.

"What'd you have in mind?" I may have asked the question, but I already knew I'd agree to whatever Bronson Martin had up his sleeve if it meant spending more time with him.

$\mathfrak{H}$ 18 $\mathfrak{K}$

"Maybe we should have taken the kids here instead." Bronson pushed his paddle through the clear waters of Megunticook Lake. The sun began its descent, shining on the water, though the July days would leave them with hours of more light.

In front of him, in the double kayak he'd borrowed from Asher, Morgan slid her own paddle into the water on the left side of the boat. "It's peaceful, that's for sure. So, what'd we need to talk about during this impromptu teacher's meeting?"

He cleared his throat. No better time to test the waters— since she was surrounded by them and couldn't run away. "This isn't a meeting, it's more of a date. I just told you it was a meeting so you'd agree to it."

She dipped her hand into the water and splashed him. "Bronson Martin, I thought you were a man of integrity."

"Integrity, yes. But also, desperation. I put on my professional hat when we talked about our plans for tomorrow with the kids. Oh, I forgot to mention, Mom said she'd give us a hand with the apple pies after she was done serving breakfast. There. That covers the meeting portion of our night. Now, onto the date."

Morgan shook her head, and although he couldn't see her face from where he paddled in the back of the kayak—only the slender outline of her back, her auburn hair pulled in a ponytail that came a couple inches past her shoulders—he could imagine the smile on her lips.

Man, he loved to make her smile. He loved to make her happy. He was, he realized, beginning to love everything about *her*.

He cleared his throat, attempting to dispel such notions from his head. Yet, what was so wrong about the thought? Whoever she'd been in high school wasn't who she was now. The woman two feet in front of him was compassionate, a deep-thinker, beautiful . . . and struggling. Was that what he was attracted to? That blasted desire to help? To make things better? To assuage the guilt she clung to surrounding that night eight years ago?

On the not-so-distant shore, a King Rail spread its feathers in the sun, embracing the carefree, unburdened summer evening. If only he could get Morgan to open up to him. Would she allow him to share her burdens?

"Since you conveniently trapped me out on the water before you informed me of the night's agenda, I suppose I have no choice but to capitulate." Morgan dug her paddle deep in the water.

"I suppose you don't."

"You know, I like you better when you're not quite so full of yourself."

"And I like it better when I can see your face when we're talking."

She twisted around in her seat and scrunched her nose at him. "If you wanted to talk to me face-to-face, you should have suggested a business dinner."

"Okay, will you have a business dinner with me Friday night?"

"No!" She faced forward, cutting her paddle into the water again. The sun slipped behind a thick forest of trees—the foothills of Mount Battie—as they rowed forward. "Do you enjoy rejection or something? Is that it?"

How could he tell her he'd never felt this way about a woman before? That he wanted to spend all his waking hours with her, that he loved how she worked tirelessly in the orchards with him, and now alongside the kids. That he'd walk to the ends of the earth if it meant she'd give him just a small chance . . .

A horsefly landed on the smooth, pale skin of Morgan's arm. He leaned forward, hand raised. "There's a horsefly on you. Wait a minute, hold still."

Wrong choice of words. She dropped her paddle in the water, wiggling around and flapping her arms wildly, screeching and squealing.

A laugh erupted from deep in his chest. "I said hold still, not dance around like a banshee. There, it's around me now, you happy?"

She twisted around. "It's on your head." She raised her hand, leaned toward him. "Come closer."

"Words I've been waiting to hear all night."

"Now, this might be a little harder than"—she brought her hand down on his head—"necessary."

"Ouch. Did you get it? Do I need to come closer again?"

"Missed it. Wait." It landed on his shoulder and she lunged, tilting the boat.

"Easy there, killer," Bronson grabbed her arms to steady her, but she jerked free, causing the boat to rock more.

She turned around, half standing in order to readjust as she faced forward. "My paddle!" A few feet away, her paddle floated in the water. She leaned out over the side, extending her fingers toward it, but the motion was just enough to prod the rocking boat sideways. With a splash, she fell into the lake, coming up spluttering a moment later. Her auburn hair plastered to her forehead and in front of one eye. She pushed it aside, her skin glistening with droplets of water.

She was still the prettiest sight he'd ever seen.

Bronson reached for her, trying to tamp down his laughter. "Wait until Ned hears about this."

"You will not speak a word of this to anyone," she ground out, attempting to haul herself back into the boat with Bronson's help.

Once she'd managed to secure her arms in the boat, he grabbed for her waist to heave her up. The kayak rocked precariously. "Pardon my hands . . ." he managed, a moment before the boat overturned, sinking him into the water beside her. The cold climbed beneath his ballcap and clung to his shirt and pants. One of his flip-flops slipped from his foot.

One hand on the kayak, Morgan threw her head back and laughed, splashing him. "That's what you get."

"Oh, that's what I get, huh?" He reached out to poke her side as she continued splashing.

She wiggled away. "Maybe one of us should get on one side and one of us on the other."

"Worth a try." Bronson swam around the kayak. "Ready? One, two, three." He struggled up, but when Morgan lost her grip, the kayak rocked back, splashing him in the water again. Two more tries, and they both laughed so hard they didn't have the strength to try again. Bronson ducked beneath the kayak and popped up beside her. "For the record, this is the best first date I've ever had."

She screwed her nose up in that adorable way of hers. "This is *not* a date."

"Well, we sure aren't having a teacher's meeting out here. What else would you call it?"

"A disaster. A . . . horribly funny disaster."

He slid his hand along the side of the kayak, a bit closer to her and studied her shining green eyes and wet lashes. Somehow, hidden behind the kayak, no one around as far as the eye could see, the moment felt incredibly intimate.

He licked his lips. "Morgan, I really like you. I know I told you I'd be nothing but professional—"

"Yet another reason for me to doubt your integrity."

"But if I don't at least tell you how I feel about you, I'll be wondering forever if we could have happened."

⚜

IF WE COULD HAVE HAPPENED.

I had never known that innocuous little word—we—to pack so much punch. In it, I saw possibilities. I saw Bronson's desire for me, the past few months of getting to know him, a glimpse of a future that could be ours.

But I couldn't go there. Better to stick to jokes and teasing. Better to escape this water, where the slight swishing and swirling movement of Bronson treading the lake brushed against my skin, driving me to distraction.

I'll be wondering forever if we could have happened.

I cleared my throat, searching for a suitable comment to guide this conversation to safer ground. "And I'll be wondering forever if some giant fish is going to grab my ankle and drag me to the bottom of this lake. Let's get out of here." I grabbed the rope at the front of the boat and began swimming toward the shore, tugging the kayak away from the seriousness of the moment, away from Bronson.

After retrieving the paddles and tossing them onto the kayak, Bronson swam up beside me, taking the rope. "Here, I got it. Why don't you push from behind?"

I didn't put up a fight. Better to have the separation of the kayak between us. Better not to face Bronson and the brave thing he'd done, serving his heart on a platter for me to spear with a steak knife.

By the time we'd reached the small shore, my limbs ached and I gasped for breaths. Bronson dragged the kayak onto the sand

and I flopped beside it, pulling my wet t-shirt away from my body.

While I didn't normally put extra effort into my looks, I wondered what Bronson thought of me. Then again, why did I concern myself? If I cared for his heart at all, which I did, then I *should* attempt to repel him.

He lay beside me, sucking in deep breaths, not appearing concerned about my appearance in the least.

"For the record, I'm *totally* telling Ned that you stood up in the kayak and flipped us over."

I slapped him on the arm, then snatched my hand back. I couldn't flirt like this. I couldn't say one thing with my words and another with my actions, no matter how my body betrayed me.

We grew quiet. The sound of a woodpecker echoed across the lake. In the distance, a group of kids laughed as they swam to the floating dock near the beach. They jumped off and splashed into the water. Beneath the vibration of it all, I closed my eyes, more relaxed than I'd been in a long time.

"Morgan."

My eyelids fluttered open as my body hummed to life, a siren wailing through me.

Bronson turned on his side, propping one hand against his head as he stared down at me with those chocolate eyes. "Any chance you could tell me what you find so terribly undatable about me? That way, the next time Amie tries to set me up with her yoga instructor, I can give her some reasons why the poor woman doesn't need to waste her time."

The corner of his mouth hitched up in a halfhearted smile, and a pinch of jealousy squeezed my insides at the thought of Bronson with Amie's yoga instructor. A fit, lean, confident woman, of course. Someone who *deserved* Bronson's attentions.

Well played, Bronson. He succeeded in making me jealous.

I inhaled and exhaled a long breath, conscious of my chest rising and falling, of the t-shirt that clung to my body. Again, I pulled it away from my wet skin in hopes it might dry faster. "You're not *undatable*, Bronson. Clearly. You're—" I stopped. Amazing, is what I wanted to say. Passionate. Caring. Incredibly hot.

"Just undatable for you?" he said, guessing at my words and getting them all wrong.

I huffed, suddenly frustrated with myself, with the entire predicament. I had let him get too close.

"No, Bronson. *I'm* undatable, okay? I don't date."

He blinked. "Why not?"

"Because . . ."

Could I make him understand?

"Because . . .?" He dipped his head, as if to urge me on, but I didn't miss the fear in his eyes. Suddenly, he laid back on the beach. "You're kidding me, right? You're married. Is that it?"

I couldn't manage to snatch back the small laugh that escaped my mouth. "No, I'm not married."

"Did you take a vow of celibacy, then?"

I threw an arm over my face. "No vows here, unless you count the one I made to myself after Isabel died."

There. I'd said it. Perhaps I should have censored myself better, but there was a sort of relief in coming clean.

We stared up at the sky as my words lingered, the light from the late afternoon sun illuminating a crisp blue against the vibrant green of the trees above.

"What sort of vow did you make after Isabel died?" His solemn voice broke the sacred silence.

I sat up. "Never mind. You wouldn't understand. No one understands."

It was *my* problem. My cross to bear. No one needed to judge me about it.

I crossed my legs to wiggle into a sitting position, but he grasped my arm with enough tenderness to convince me to stay.

"Morgan, tell me. You shouldn't be alone in this. Maybe I

won't understand, but I'll try like heck to do my best. Let me in. Please?"

Looking at him now, with his dripping hair, his own t-shirt plastered to his muscled chest and well-defined biceps, the penetration of his gaze a tangle of question and concern, I understood the depths of what I denied myself. For I had never longed for a man like this, never wanted one to enfold me in his arms as badly as I wanted Bronson to do so now.

I settled my clasped hands on my stomach, working up the right words—and the courage to speak. "Not a vow, exactly. More like a knowing. A sense that I can't be trusted with another person's heart."

"Morgan, that's crazy. Why—"

I shook my head. "Please, let me finish." This wasn't easy. Best to get it done in one fell swoop.

He nodded, clamping his mouth shut.

"After Isabel died, I thought I'd go to prison for fifteen years at least. Twenty, maybe. I deserved at least eighteen. One year for every one of Isabel's life. They gave me two lousy years, Bronson. Two years."

Could I say this aloud?

Bronson's hand inched for mine, and when his pinky finger wrapped around my own, I couldn't bring myself to release it.

A wobbly breath shivered up my airways. "When they released me, I told myself I would give my life in honor of Isabel. I'd pursue the career she wanted. I'd give any extra money I made to the scholarship fund her parents had set up." She swallowed. "I didn't let anyone get too close. Even my parents I've kept at a distance. I guess I'm afraid I'll hurt someone again."

My words simmered between us long after they'd faded out.

Although I shrank from the tension, I couldn't bear to sit up and suggest we return home. A bubble of emotion climbed my throat and I pretended to rub my face with my hands when in reality, I simply wanted to hide. "You think I'm crazy."

He pushed up to a sitting position, swinging his legs around so he faced me. Bits of sand clung to the sleeves of his wet t-shirt, still plastered to his muscled chest. "No, Morgan, no. Of course not."

"It's not like you to be speechless."

The joke caused a sad smile to inch up his handsome face. "I don't want to say the wrong thing. I don't want to hurt you."

"So, you think I'm touchy." I stood, brushing off the sand that clung to my body, not because it bothered me, but because I needed something to do. Anything, to hide the emotion welling within me.

Bronson stood and placed both his hands on the sides of my arm. "Don't run away. We should talk about this."

"Why? It won't change anything." I looked off to the woods behind us where thick, lush trees climbed up a gradual incline.

"I care about you, Morgan. Even if you can't date me, let me be your friend."

Friend.

The word caused uninhibited sobs to wrack my body. Isabel had been my first real friend. My only friend. I hadn't let anyone get close since she died. Of course, I had Jenna. But Jenna was busy with her husband and her new baby, her job at the bakery.

How long had it been since I'd had a real friend?

19

"What? What did I say?" Bronson shook his head. "Whatever it was, I didn't mean to make you cry. Please, don't cry." There was nothing that could undo him faster than a woman crying. Particularly *this* woman crying.

She swiped the back of her hand across her nose. "It's nothing you said. I appreciate you, is all."

Appreciate might not exactly be *love*, but he'd take what he could get.

"So, will you sit back down and talk to me?" He ran his fingers up and down the sides of her arms, wanting to do so much more, wanting to pull her against him and never let go. To heal the deepest parts of her.

She sniffed and shrugged but sat back in the sand. He did too, not close enough to scare her away but close enough to let her know he wasn't going anywhere.

To his relief, she spoke. "I deserved more time. My parents' lawyer—*my* lawyer—argued that I didn't know better, that I was just a poor spoiled rich girl. I can't believe the jury bought it."

He wanted to rush in with words of reason, convince her that the best way to honor her friend was to live a full and joyful life, serving others, loving a man if he came along, building a life with him. With *him*. But it was careless to shove aside her concerns. He wasn't in her shoes. Maybe if he could understand . . . "Tell me about that night, Morgan."

She swallowed, surprising him when she did indeed take him back to that night. To a party and the realization of the stress Isabel put on herself—that she worried she wouldn't live up to the expectations of her parents, her coaches, herself once at college. To Isabel begging Morgan to drive them home instead of calling her parents.

"I've wondered many times how things would have been different if I didn't take that first drink. If we'd called my parents. But I can't take it back. I deserve to live with the guilt forever."

Bronson pressed his lips together. It would be so easy to say the wrong thing. What wisdom did he possess in the face of such tragic circumstances? He lifted up a prayer for discernment in the face of Morgan's pain.

"Morgan." He spoke slowly, as if testing the waters of his words. "I'm not saying you don't bear responsibility for what happened that night. Drinking and driving—yeah, that's serious stuff. But how will beating yourself up over it for the rest of your life change anything or make it better for anyone, including you?"

She hung her hands over her knees and stared out at the water. "I don't know how else to deal with this horrible guilt inside me."

Bronson cleared his throat. "Isabel was drinking too, Morgan," he said softly. "She's as much at fault as you."

Her fingers stopped fidgeting. He could see this was a new thought for her.

She shook her head. "But I'm the one who got behind the wheel. We both knew better."

He licked his lips. With this much guilt after so many years, was she placing her past in God's hands at all? Wait. Maybe she didn't even know she could. But she'd told him she prayed, hadn't she? She'd told him she'd asked God to take her burden. She'd even mentioned something about angels. He'd spoken of his own faith, but although she never disagreed with his words, neither had she echoed them.

Could he have been assuming what he wanted to assume when it came to Morgan and her view on life?

A heaviness settled in his chest. He chose his words carefully. "I can't pretend to know how I'd feel in your position, and I don't know what you believe about God and eternity, but I do believe forgiveness is possible. It's possible for you, Morgan."

She shook her hand. "Forgiveness is fine for people like you and your sisters and even my family. But I'm a murderer, Bronson. A traitor to one of the people I loved most in the world."

"I believe God can forgive anything. Even murder."

She calmed for the first time since her confession. "I don't know," she whispered. "I used to believe in . . . something. A Being of love and light. Isabel told me about Jesus once, and I liked the sound of Him, but after we went to high school, we started talking more about boys and basketball, our dreams for the future." She threw up her hands. "What does any of this have to do with . . . with—"

"Your vow to punish yourself for the rest of your living days?"

"It's not punishment. It's fear. Fear that I'll hurt someone again. I can't risk that. One is enough."

He hiked in a deep breath, let it out slow. "Maybe our best lessons are learned not through our successes, but through our failures. When you come to the end of your life and you've lived completely and wholeheartedly in honor of Isabel, will that make up for her death?"

"Of course not."

"Then what's the point?"

She placed her hands on the sides of her head. "I don't know! All I know is that this feels right."

"What about letting people in? Accepting God's grace and forgiveness? Jesus had a special spot in his heart for the outcasts. He made the ultimate sacrifice so anyone can live in freedom—from those who think they have it all together, to those who know they don't."

"You're preaching at me." She stuck her bottom lip out.

"I don't know how else to help you except to point you to Someone who can."

Another sob bubbled up from within her. "Don't you think I wish I was free? Don't you think I want. . ." Her gaze entangled with his, and in the depths of those beautiful green eyes he saw how much she wanted to give in to him. Those green orbs dropped to his lips, and more than anything, he longed to inch closer.

But he refused to take advantage of her distraught state. Besides, was it wise to feel so strongly about a woman who was intent on keeping herself from God's forgiveness? With much effort, he forced some space between them. He didn't miss the way her eyes dimmed, desperate.

"Bronson," she choked out, as if pleading with him for something unspoken.

He rubbed his eyes, stared out into the water, the setting sun casting rays of light across the far end of the lake. "I don't understand why you'd choose the memory of someone you loved—someone who would want your happiness—over a real, living human being. Not just me, Morgan. But yourself. What you're doing—trying to walk around like the living dead—is not doing Isabel or her parents or you or anyone else in your life any good."

He reached out and squeezed her hand, the gesture somehow feeling inadequate. "Life is a gift, Morgan. I'll pray you see yours as such. Every morning, every night. Whenever I see you, know I'm begging God to heal the broken parts of your heart. Please, don't push away everyone who loves you."

She swiped her nose with the back of her hand, her bottom lip trembling.

As much as he wanted to take her in his arms, as much as he thought she might even let him, he abstained. Instead, he stood, holding out his hand. She needed time to think, surely.

"We should head back." He'd try like the dickens to act honorably, even in the depths of his disappointment. In the depths of her pain.

She slipped her hand in his and he pulled her up. Moments later, they paddled toward home in silence.

20

I settled a large blanket beneath the grassy shade of one of the largest trees in the orchard. Beside me, Bronson did the same as he spoke to the kids.

"You guys did a great job today. I can't believe I'm actually saying this, but in three more weeks we'll be open for business."

Their fifth week of the Orchard House summer camp had come and gone. From all accounts, the camp was a wild success. After they'd worked out the kinks that first week, things had gone smoothly. Orchard work, science experiments in the barn, fishing on Tuesday mornings, kayak trips on Wednesdays, baking apple pies on Thursday, and field games and a picnic on Friday.

While new kids came and went with each week, a core group stayed. A group I was becoming attached to. Along with Cameron and Ned, Bronson had recruited Anna, Daisy, Daniel, and Tommy to help out with the apple-picking business. We'd built a stand, bought a trailer, stocked the barn with hay, and accrued an assortment of recipes to be used when we officially opened for apple-picking season.

Everything was going swimmingly. If only Bronson would look at me with more than a professional, passing interest, my world would almost feel right again. But ever since that day on Lake Megunticook, he'd kept his distance. Sure, we worked alongside one another, planned the activities, toiled in the orchards beside the kids, and discussed incoming students, but there was no denying we'd lost something that day on the lake, and I couldn't pretend I wasn't to blame for it. I was sticking to my decision, and he said he'd respect it.

And respect it he was doing.

I sat on the corner of the blanket alongside Anna and slid a tuna sandwich from my brown paper bag.

If only I could stop Bronson from entering my dreams. If only I could stop imagining the what ifs of a future with a man I could love. A man like Bronson.

Our best lessons are learned not through our successes, but through our failures.

Whenever I see you, know I'm begging God to help you find healing.

I don't understand why you'd choose the memory of someone you loved —someone who would want your happiness—over a real, living human being.

Bronson's words from that day replayed over and over in my mind.

In a twisted attempt to make myself feel better, I'd pushed my parents and Jenna away over the last eight years. I'd hurt them, choosing to stew in my own bitterness.

I'd vowed to be the best person I could be, so how was hurting the people I loved accomplishing that?

The kids flopped onto the blanket and a slight breeze blew Daniel's napkin a few feet away. He scurried to get it. "Miss Amie will go mad if she thought I was littering."

Amie was very passionate about the environment. And yoga. And eating healthy. And "finding herself."

"Aw, you just like her is all," Tommy said.

It was no secret Daniel had a crush on Bronson's younger

sister. He didn't try to hide it much, and the boys constantly gave him flack for it.

Ned continued the teasing by fluttering his eyes. "Miss Amie, could you *please* show me how to make those shadows? I want my trees to look real. *Really* real."

Daniel tried to punch Ned in the gut but missed when the other boy rolled off the blanket.

"Hey, quit it, guys."

Bronson's stern words stopped the boys' antics. There'd been an argument or two over the last several weeks. With some of the kids being together so much—particularly the ones who worked extra hours in the orchard—it almost felt like a big family with plenty of sibling rivalry to go around.

"At least I don't fall out of my kayak dancing like an idiot," Daniel muttered. The kids hadn't easily forgotten Ned's mishap from the first week of camp.

"I said, that's enough," Bronson gave them a look, then took a bag of potato chips and popped it open. I knew from experience that he'd peel his bread apart, mayonnaise thick on the slice, and layer his chips on top of his ham until there were only a few left in the bag. Then he'd close the sandwich and crush it down with his palm.

I smiled, and he caught it, tilting his head to the side as if to say, "What's so funny?"

I shook my head, brushing him off.

Daisy placed her sandwich on top of her brown bag and looked out over the orchards, sighing. "It sure is pretty here. I'm going to miss it when camp is over."

"Lucky for you, we still have three weeks left," I said, though I felt the same. The arrival of August had ushered in slightly cooler nights. The feel that fall was around the corner filled me with both anticipation and sadness. I still hadn't found a teaching job. Then again, I hadn't been all that diligent about looking.

"What will you miss most about the camp, Daisy?" Bronson asked.

I couldn't tear my eyes away from him as he chewed his sandwich, waiting patiently for the girl's response.

"I'll miss our morning walks in the orchard. The sunlight is pretty at that time of day. And all of you," she said shyly.

"I know what Danny here will miss," Ned said, wiggling his eyebrows and fluttering his eyelashes again.

"Ned, that's enough. Another word out of you and I'll be calling that D.C. camp myself."

Bronson's words served to clamp Ned's mouth shut.

I braced my own mouth to stop a giggle. I loved these kids. I mean, legitimately loved them.

Bronson cleared his throat. "Isn't it interesting how we each have gifts, but those gifts can become our downfall if we're not careful?"

Some of the kids sensed a lecture and seemed to tune out, but some listened.

"I had a goldfish once. His name was Bubbles, and—"

"How'd you know he was a boy?" Tommy asked.

Bronson grinned. "I guess I didn't. But I was always outnumbered with girls growing up, so I figured God would at least give me a man goldfish."

"A man goldfish, huh?" Ned asked, looking as if he might crack another joke.

Bronson held his finger up and it seemed to be enough of a reminder about Bronson's earlier threat, which I doubted he'd ever carry through, no matter what Ned did.

"Anyway, I decided I'd be the best goldfish owner in the state of Maine. I fed him three times a day, changed his water daily, I even read him a book before bed."

A couple of the kids giggled. One of the boys rolled his eyes.

His gaze met mine, but I looked away. "Anyway, one day I woke up to find poor Bubbles belly up. I was mortified. Couldn't figure out why he'd died. Then my dad explained to me that fish can actually overeat, and that changing his water every day probably made the pH levels out of whack."

Ned shook his head sadly. "Poor Mr. Bubbles's manhood wasn't enough to save him."

The corner of Bronson's mouth twitched. "I want you to each think about your strengths. Think about what you're good at, but also think how that could be a weakness as well. Think about how best to harness and use your gifts."

Bronson had told me once that a true teacher defends his pupils against his own personal influence. It took me a while to wrap my head around that one, but I think, after watching Bronson the last few weeks, I was beginning to understand.

More than anything, he wanted the kids to learn about themselves. To be openly curious, to question the norms. That's why I was sometimes surprised he seemed to write Amie's ideas off as silly. Sibling rivalry? Either way, I hoped she didn't take it to heart. After being with the family for months now, I could see that at least one of Bronson's strengths was also one of his faults—he cared about his family so much, he wanted to protect them *too* much.

I looked at the kids scattered on the blankets beneath the shade. Were any of them seeing Bronson's point?

"Like me being funny, you mean," Ned said. "Sometimes I can go overboard."

"You ain't funny," Daniel said.

"Aren't." Anna corrected before beaming at Ned. "And yes, you're very funny, Ned. But sometimes you hurt people's feelings."

"Making people laugh is a gift." Bronson bit into an apple. "But so is discernment—knowing when and how to use that humor."

Ned stared solemnly at the picnic blanket. "With great power comes great responsibility."

The group tittered, and Bronson placed a hand on Ned's shoulder. "That's right. Okay, who's next?"

"Don't you think it's bragging to be saying what we think we're good at?" Anna asked.

"I think it's healthy to evaluate ourselves every once in a while." Bronson swigged his water. "You're all at a great age. You have your entire lives before you. Who you'll become as adults will be shaped over these next few years. But the most exciting part is that you have a say in who that is. You get to decide what kind of crop you want to grow, and me and Miss Morgan and all the other counselors here are willing to help you grow it. You tell us how we can help."

Daniel tapped the bottom of his own water bottle against his knee, sending liquid splashing inside of it, turbulent and bubbly, his look sullen. "Sometimes our circumstances decide who we'll be more than we do." His bitter tone stabbed my heart. At the same time, I couldn't help but agree with him. Who I was had been cemented the night of Liam Baker's party. One bad decision had made me the irresponsible girl.

I studied Daniel, remembering his application essay, his question about good apples coming from bad ones. A part of me ached to answer that question for him, however inept I was at it.

I swallowed down my hesitation. "Someone once told me that our best lessons are learned not through our successes, but through our failures. Maybe that includes how others have failed us, too." I thought of Mr. and Mrs. Davis failing to forgive me. Would it have made any difference?

The weight of Bronson's gaze lay heavy upon me.

"That's right," he said. "There will be times in our lives when people fail us. Sometimes people we love will let us down. And I wish I could tell you guys that everything will work out, but we can't know that."

He paused, looking around the group, letting his gaze rest on each student. "What I do know, is that each of you are incredibly bright individuals. And each of you have gifts planted in you from the beginning. Overcoming the hard stuff isn't fun, but for those of you who choose to accept the challenge, the reward can be great. It can build honesty, integrity, faith, good work ethic, a willingness to learn. No one can take that away from you."

We talked a few more minutes—a surprisingly deep conversation with the group of kids we'd gotten close to over the last several weeks. I could see the relationships we'd built. I could see the ultimate vision Bronson had for this camp—not just to provide fun or even a profitable business—but to plant seeds that would stay with the kids forever.

As we packed up our dirtied napkins and empty water bottles, Tommy slapped Daniel's arm with the back of his hand. "I heard Miss Amie will be helping full time pretty soon."

Daniel's face grew a fiery red. "Yeah?" He looked at Bronson. "That true, Mr. Martin?"

Bronson's gaze flew to mine. "Last week in August, yes. Miss Amie will be helping full time. But she'll be occupied with a student, so keep your goofing around to a minimum."

Prickles shot up my spine, sending the tiny hairs on the back of my neck upward. What was he saying? Was Marcus coming to camp after all?

That would be *amazing*. What had changed the Davises mind? Surely not my visit . . . I sniffed, watching the kids barrel down the hill. Would they notice a change in me when Marcus was around? I'd have to be careful not to get too close to him. Mrs. Davis would have a fit if I broke any unspoken—or spoken—boundaries.

We trailed back down the hill toward the barn, the sun warm on our backs, the kids walking out in front of us.

"I received a call from Mr. Davis last week. It seems they've agreed to let Marcus attend camp. I guess between the both of us knocking on their door and arguing our cases, they couldn't refuse."

He knew she'd gone there? "You went there?"

His face colored. "Well, yeah. I knew how important it was to you, and I think it will be great for Marcus. I admit, I didn't realize you beat me to it."

But I was certain he was the one who had managed to win them over.

"Bronson, I can't believe it."

"I hope this will bring about something good, Morgan."

I looked at the ground. "Me too," I whispered.

Was there any way this could be the first step in closing the gap between me and Isabel's family?

Bronson tucked the picnic blanket under his arm and hung back as the kids walked in front of us, a couple of the boys rolling sideways down the hill. "Maybe Amie helping us out wasn't a great idea."

I raised an eyebrow at the sudden change in subject. "Because she's pretty? That hardly seems a reason to disqualify her."

"You're pretty. But you're professional. Amie has this . . . flirty air to her."

Though I didn't think of Amie as flirty exactly—simply care-free—I could see what he meant. Floating through life with an insatiable thirst for her interests, attracting people to her passionate, fairy-like qualities.

"She's doing a big thing helping us out," I reminded him.

"You're right." He grinned at me, and my face heated.

You're pretty.

How was I ever going to get over Bronson Martin by being around him every day, by hearing his sweet words and observing that charming smile?

21

I pushed my hair behind one ear as I entered the hair salon I frequented as a teenager. Lizzie's wedding was the following week, and I hadn't gotten a haircut in two years. My split ends had split ends.

Though I had first tried to politely turn down Lizzie's invitation, she'd insisted.

"Please, Morgan. It would mean the world to me."

I had to admit, we'd grown close as the summer progressed. Working at the camp with Bronson's sisters had forged not only friendship, but something more. We weren't family, I knew that. Yet living so close to them, working at the camp, even ducking into the gift shop and chatting with them at the end of the night, had paved the way for an affection I had come to think of as sisterly.

I opened the door of the salon, the bell above the door jingling merrily. I wondered if Sherry, my old hairdresser, still worked here. Though they accepted walk-ins, the amount of bodies inside indicated I probably should have made an appointment.

The salon smelled of bleach and hairspray and shampoo. Four

hairdressers worked over the heads of their clients, but I didn't recognize any of them.

The hairdresser closest to me, an older woman with a hunched back and bleach blonde hair, glanced up at my arrival. I thought I recognized her as one of Miss Esther's Quilting Club members. Dot, I think her name was.

"It's a half-hour wait at least, darlin.'"

The woman she worked over, who had to be close to eighty, tugged on Dot's sleeve. Dot leaned in, her eyes growing wide.

My heart ricocheted around in my chest as I felt the gazes of everyone in the salon heavy upon me.

Dot straightened. "You're Morgan, isn't that right? Morgan Dalton?"

I swallowed and nodded.

"Maybe it's best you go on over to the salon across town. It's nothing personal, of course."

My mouth grew dry. "I don't understand."

But I did, didn't I? Perhaps these ladies thought they were being loyal to Miss Esther or Mrs. Davis by turning me away.

I shook my head. Forget it. I'd gone two years without a haircut, I'd go another two if it meant steering clear of these ladies.

I turned on my heel, when I felt a presence beside me.

My mother.

"You can have my spot, honey. Sharon, would that suit you?" Mom called boldly to the hairdresser in the back corner, daring anyone to deny her. With her ramrod straight back, no-nonsense pantsuit, and raised chin, I doubt anyone would.

"That's fine by me. I'd love to get my hands on that gorgeous hair. Where'd you get that color, honey? Certainly not from your Mama."

"Her father." Mom smiled and led me to sit by her in the small waiting area.

I blinked back tears, forcing my emotions away as I'd learned to do in juvie. "I don't want to take your spot, Mom. I can come back."

"Nonsense. This will give us time to catch up. Besides, Clara will take me if no one else walks in. We can get our hair done together. Just like old times."

"Thank you," I whispered.

I hope she realized I was thanking her for more than just giving me her spot in line.

⁂

AN HOUR LATER, FRESH FROM A CUT AND BLOW DRY, I WALKED out of the salon with my mother.

"How about some ice cream? My treat." The hopeful expression on Mom's face was enough to break my heart.

"Okay."

We walked the short distance to the Camden Cone. I ordered pistachio, Mom ordered her usual mint chip. We strolled down the boardwalk, crowded on this beautiful Saturday afternoon.

"How's the camp going?" Mom asked, and I was grateful she hadn't opened up our conversation by interrogating me about a teaching job. Though I continued to search the websites of the local schools, no openings for a special education teacher had popped up yet. Neither had I received a call from the superintendent's office about substituting. Considering it was still summer, neither should come as a surprise.

"It's good. Great. I'm really enjoying it."

"I'm so glad, honey." She opened her mouth, then closed it.

"How's work with you?"

She finished chewing a bite of her cone. "I'm thinking of slowing down, actually. Moving to a part-time schedule."

I straightened. "Wow. I thought you'd never slow down."

My mom had started her interior design firm before Jenna and I were born, and it had taken off with wild success. She'd juggled raising the two of us and handling the business like a pro. She wasn't even sixty yet.

"What made you decide that?"

"Jenna's going back to work soon, and I've offered to watch Amelia two days a week."

I blinked, a warmth spreading through my chest as I imagined my goal-oriented mother choosing her granddaughter over her career. "That's awesome, Mom."

A soft smile curved her lips. "I'm looking forward to it." She swallowed. "I've been thinking a lot, about not being around for you girls when you were younger."

"We didn't lack for anything, Mom."

"I know. But it goes by so fast." Her tone grew wistful and she seemed to blink back tears. "I blame myself for you staying away these past several years, Morgan."

"What? Mom, no. It had nothing to do with you. I had my own stuff to work out."

"I should have been more persistent about you coming home. You needed your family."

"I couldn't," I choked out.

"But why?"

I glanced down at the last of my cone. "I didn't want to hurt you more than I already had."

"Oh, honey."

We'd stopped walking, and she placed a hand on my arm. "We wanted nothing more than to walk with you through the fire."

Silence hung heavy between us. I licked my lips before finally speaking. "Did you really believe the defense my lawyer came up with? That I didn't know better, that I was too spoiled?" My words came out bitter, for they were at the heart of this wall between us.

Mom lowered herself to a nearby bench. "I struggled with that question for a long time. The honest answer is no—I don't think you made your decisions that night because you were spoiled."

"Then why did you go along with it?"

She could have asked me the same question.

"You're my baby, Morgan. *My child.* In the end, your father and I were willing to grasp whatever defense we could. I'd lie for you, Morgan. I'd *murder* for you. I only wanted to protect you." A single tear slid down her smooth cheek.

My throat grew tight. I thought of little Amelia, the fierce need to protect her that I'd felt when I first held her. I lowered myself to the bench. "I'm sorry, Mom. I'm sorry I put you in that position."

"Honey, no more apologies. We've gone round and round with that. It's time to move forward. To start living. Please, Morgan. Don't push me away any longer. I won't be able to stand it. Whatever you're walking through, let me be a part of it."

My bottom lip trembled. I'd separated myself from my family in an attempt to protect them, but had I gotten it all wrong? Had I been punishing all of us? Could the last eight years have been made more bearable if we'd wrestled our demons together, instead of separately?

"Okay," I said.

Mom glanced at me through her tears. "Okay?"

I nodded. "I won't push you away anymore. I don't want to push you away. I want you in my life, Mom."

She threw her arms around me, squeezing me tight, and I sank into her warmth, remembering how she'd stood by my side in the hair salon.

I vowed this would be a new beginning for us.

❧ 22 ❧

"I t's showtime." Maggie carried Grace, her one-year-old daughter over to me and Amie.

I shimmied the hem of my dress toward my knees.

"Stop it, you look great. You've got killer legs." Amie elbowed me. Her hair was pulled back in an elegant French knot, blonde curls falling from the sides amidst a waterfall of flowers. She wore an off-the-shoulder sea-blue bridesmaid's dress that came mid-calf and matched Maggie and Josie's. The Martin sisters looked as if they'd stepped off the cover of a bridal magazine.

I was about to whisper that the dress Amie had let me borrow simply wasn't my normal attire. But of course, it wasn't—jeans and a t-shirt wouldn't cut it for Lizzie's wedding.

I looked out at the sprawling lawn unrolling to the blue waters of Penobscot River. A dry summer had caused water restrictions and drought warnings to pepper the midland coast, but one wouldn't know it for the luscious green grass stretching out to a cottage-like gazebo perched at the edge of the water. There, a beaming Asher sat in front of its stairs, anxiously looking down the lamp post-lined path of cobblestones. On either side of the aisle, guests sat in white chairs, awaiting the bride's arrival. A slight breeze chased away the humidity of the day.

Maggie handed Grace to me. "Thanks for watching her, Morgan."

I cradled the small girl in my arms, thinking of my niece, and missing her already despite having just visited Jenna and Amelia at Mom and Dad's the day before. "My pleasure."

"If she's fussy, I'll come sit with her."

"I'm sure we'll be fine." I planned to stay in the back so I could bounce and entertain Grace while her parents stood up with Lizzie and Asher.

Maggie planted a kiss on her daughter's head before I walked as gracefully as I could in my wedge sandals with a toddler in my arms. I found a spot in the very back row and sat, offering Grace a hardcover book entitled *Rainbow Fish*.

Moments later, the music began. Asher's parents strolled down the aisle, distinguished and elegant, followed by Mrs. Martin, stunning in a lacy mauve dress that dipped in the back. I hoped to high heaven I looked that good when I was her age.

Maggie and Josh walked up the aisle next, followed by Amie and Tripp. I thought it sweet that Asher had grown so close with Lizzie's brothers-in-law.

Next came Asher's best man, his brother Ricky, escorting Lizzie's matron of honor, Josie. Her chestnut hair was pulled halfway up, stray tendrils blowing in the breeze. Though just as pretty as her sisters, Josie's was a natural, windblown beauty I found refreshing.

When the bridal procession music began, we rose to see Bronson and Lizzie standing some paces down the walkway. Grace squirmed, and I bounced her on my hip, praying she wouldn't fuss.

She quieted when I settled her pacifier in her tiny mouth. Emotion bubbled in my throat at the sight of shy Lizzie in a stunning white gown that cinched at her waist, clinging tastefully until it flared outward at her thighs. Beneath a lacy veil, her brown hair fell in graceful waves to her shoulders.

But my breath didn't catch until my gaze landed on the man beside the bride. Tall and handsome in a gray tuxedo and gelled hair, Bronson bit the inside of his cheek, something he did when either in deep concentration or preparing himself for an important task. It endeared him to me all the more.

As Bronson escorted Lizzie up the cobbled path, I forgot time and place. It was as if I'd entered a fairytale, as if I'd found myself in a place where happy endings were possible.

When they passed, Bronson winked at me. A flurry of fireflies erupted in my middle. I swallowed and turned my attention to Asher, seated in his chair, eyes shining for his bride.

This wedding was the beginning of something beautiful for Lizzie and Asher—something magical. I realized my loss anew. In choosing not to allow myself to be close to anyone, to be close to a man, I would never have a moment like this for myself.

Was that really what I wanted?

No, that was the wrong question. Was that what Isabel deserved?

I shook my head and turned my attention to the ceremony—to Bronson giving Lizzie away to Asher, where she grasped his hand in eager anticipation. Grace grew heavy with sleep in my arms. Tripp, and then Maggie, took turns reading scripture verses and poems to the attendees.

As the minister spoke, I settled back in my chair, the comfortable warmth of Grace on my chest and the soothing scent of salty sea air making it easy for me to tune into the words.

"Any love can be a beautiful reflection of God's love, but the love between a husband and wife—this vow can prove especially sacred. Today, Asher and Lizzie not only declare their present love to their friends and family, but they vow to promise a future love as well. An agape love. The kind of love God shows all of us. True, unconditional love."

I listened with rapt attention, having never heard marriage described in such a manner before. Having never heard *God* described in such a manner before.

If God truly held unconditional love for me, how did He think of my past mistakes?

And marriage. A reflection of God's love. I didn't understand it, but right now, I allowed myself to be captivated by this moment, by the tiny hope that it brought.

When it was time for Asher and Lizzie to say their vows, Ricky and Tripp each took a chair, sitting on either side of Asher. A moment later, they had strapped each of Asher's legs to one of their own.

The crowd watched with intense interest, and I craned my neck to see Asher place his arms around his groomsmen. Ricky counted to three, and they helped him stand, Josh behind, supporting Asher's waist.

Lizzie put a hand over her mouth, blinking back tears along with her guests as she looked up at her groom standing, for what I guessed, was the first time. I shimmied a tissue from my purse and pressed it to my eyes as Lizzie recited her vows, looking up into Asher's eyes. He in turn, promised to love her forever.

After Ricky and Tripp helped Asher back into his chair, the minister declared the happy couple man and wife. The guests clapped and cheered. Asher pulled Lizzie onto his lap and rolled her down the aisle, both of them grinning as if they'd just won the lottery.

And they had—a lottery of love.

I sniffed as the rest of the wedding party filed down the aisle. Maggie retrieved Grace, the twins scurrying around in a whirlwind at her legs. Beside me, Amie sighed at the sight of Lizzie and Asher setting up for pictures on the distant shore. "Do you think there's happiness like that for everyone?"

It wasn't a question meant to be answered, but it seemed a bit forlorn coming from the normally spunky Martin sister.

Josie elbowed Amie. "Let's get over to the tent. I saw them putting out the cheese and crackers. You too, Morgan."

Amie rolled her eyes. "You'd have thought marriage and motherhood would have tamed your stomach."

Tripp, carrying Amos, approached us and swung an arm around his wife. "This girl? Never. One of the best things I love about her is the way she can eat."

Josie pushed him away playfully. "Well, you don't have to make me out to sound like a cow, Mr. Colton."

He tapped her nose. "No one could ever mistake you for a cow."

Amie huffed. "Okay, okay, enough of the mushy stuff. Let's go."

We started for the grand tent across the lawn, connected to a beautiful terrace with stone walls bordering quaint lamp posts and hydrangeas.

I thought of the happiness of which Amie spoke. Did it have to be romantic happiness that ultimately fulfilled a person? Could it be love for humanity, love for one's students, love for family, even love for a friend long gone?

I'd come to Camden determined to make amends with my past. But while the Davis's hadn't forgiven me, I sensed a new beginning taking root in my spirit. I felt it working at the Orchard House camp. I felt it living alongside the Martins. I felt it in my niece's cuddles and in weeping with my mother.

I turned and caught Bronson walking toward me. My stomach flopped.

And I felt it now, as I realized I was falling head over heels in love with Bronson Martin.

Could growing closer to the people I cared for actually be a way of honoring my dearest friend? Could I make myself believe it so?

BRONSON BREATHED DEEP, GRATEFUL HIS BIG JOB FOR THE evening was behind him. He watched Lizzie and Asher make their way down to the beach for pictures. She was in good hands. He couldn't imagine giving his sister away to a better guy.

He searched the crowd for his family, his gaze falling on Morgan. His breath snagged in his throat. Of course Lizzie took the cake that day—she was the bride.

But Morgan . . . .

His mouth grew dry as he allowed his gaze to wander over the black dress she wore snug at her thighs and tightening at the waist and . . . other areas. Man, did she have any clue how she tortured him? With those beautiful green eyes? That smile that lit up like the Milky Way?

And her hair. Normally pulled back, it flowed down her back in goddess-like waves.

He sucked in a breath and started her way.

"Bronson! Good job, up there." Josie came out of nowhere, kissing him on the cheek. "I thought you were going to faint, but you surprised me, little brother."

Tripp placed a firm hand on his shoulder. "I had faith in you, man. Well done."

A tug came at his pants leg. He looked down to see Amos smiling a toothy grin. Bronson crouched to his nephew's level. "Hey there, little man. I'm looking forward to seeing some of your dance moves later, okay?"

Amos started wiggling his body before falling back on the ground. Bronson took the boy's hands and lifted him up, sending the kid into a fit of giggles.

Out of the corner of his eye, Bronson glimpsed Morgan with Amie and Mom. "I'll catch up with you guys later, okay?"

With satisfaction, he saw Morgan twist toward him again. He jogged up to her. "Looking for me?"

"Maybe," she surprised him by saying.

"You look . . . amazing."

Her smile highlighted a slight dimple in her right cheek. "You're looking pretty sharp yourself."

A tightness in his chest he hadn't realized was there loosened. After their time on the kayak that day, things had been tense, to say the least. They avoided one another outside of camp and only spoke of necessities when in session. This felt easy, though. Good. Right, even.

"You feeling okay about this week?"

"This week?"

"Yeah, you know, Marcus's session and all that?"

It was what she wanted, wasn't it? But although she'd seemed pleased after he'd told her the Davises had finally agreed, she'd grown more and more distant in the days following.

He swallowed. "It'll be a big week for us, of course, with Lizzie on her honeymoon and Josie on her book tour, but having Amie full-time will help. And I think we're getting the hang of it, don't you?"

She reached up and placed a cool finger against his lips. She smelled of lavender and seagrass. Intoxicating. Her touch—her nearness—sent waves of shock through him. How in tarnation did she expect him to keep his distance when she did things like that?

"Bronson?" Her tone was low and sultry, working a tremor through him. Thundering turtles, he needed to get a grip.

"Yes?" He spoke the word against her finger.

"Let's not talk about work for just one night, okay?"

He swallowed. "Okay."

He'd do whatever she asked. And right now, it seemed she was inviting him into something he wanted very much.

"Does that mean you'll dance with me tonight?" His words came out husky.

"I'd like that." She gave him a coy smile before turning to catch up with Amie.

Oh, man. This woman might be the death of him. Seemed she

couldn't make up her mind whether she wanted him close or not. Though he supposed he might say the same for himself. He'd vowed to keep his distance. Was it the atmosphere of the wedding, the heart-tugging vows Lizzie and Asher had said to one another? The beauty of the view?

Or was it something more? Had Morgan finally decided to live a life out from beneath her past and give him—give them—a chance at a future?

※ 23 ※

I didn't quite remember how we'd landed on this topic of conversation at a wedding reception, but leave it to the Martin family to see it through. Still, I winced when Bronson's brows rose in frustration as Amie prepared another long-winded diatribe, defending the faith gathering she'd been explaining to the table.

"I simply don't understand why you think a group like mine isn't warranted." Amie sipped her glass of champagne and then pointed the crystal at Bronson. "I plan to let anyone who wants to preach and share what's on their heart. Man, woman, child. And none of this concert worship stuff where you can only hear the people with microphones singing. It will be solemn and beautiful. A celebratory worship with dancing and poem reading and everyone would be welcome."

"Everyone's welcome at our church!" Bronson threw his hands in the air.

"We say they are—we even think they are—but if that were true, don't you think we'd have more diversity?"

"Have you looked around Camden, lately, Amie? It's not exactly the most diverse population."

She tapped her lips. "Maybe I'll start my group in the city, then. Maybe—"

Her words were cut short by Ricky, who stood beside Amie's chair, clearing his throat. The youngest Martin raised pretty blue eyes to Asher's brother, blushing slightly at his presence. I didn't know much about him, but from what I'd gathered he'd been in some trouble before moving to Maine with his brother. As Bronson told it, Asher had a big hand in helping Ricky get his life back on track.

"Would you like to dance, Amie?"

Amie glanced back at the table.

Josie held up her hands. "Please, Amie, go. We can continue this discussion another time."

The rest of the table nodded in agreement and Amie swatted at her family. "You'll all miss me when I'm gone," she pouted, though I couldn't tell if she joked or not. She stood, gave Ricky a winsome smile, and sashayed onto the dance floor.

Maggie leaned back in her chair. "That was exhausting."

"She's simply expressing herself," Mrs. Martin said, taking a last bite of stuffed fish.

Josie shook her head. "Mom, you'd be supportive of Amie if she expressed herself by doing a one-woman potato sack race naked across the lawn while singing *A Few of My Favorite Things*."

I giggled at the mental picture. Tripp pointedly moved Josie's glass of champagne away from her plate.

Josie didn't notice. "But does she have to express herself *all* the time? This is Lizzie's wedding, after all. And you!" Josie pointed to Bronson. "Egging her on like that."

Bronson sported a sheepish grin. "What else are brothers good for if not for a little egging?"

Tripp stood. "You're right, honey. It's a wedding. Enough talking, let's do some dancing." He held his hand out to her and she smiled, the hint of a blush forming on her pretty face.

A moment later, Maggie and Josh followed, Grace cuddled

between them. In the distance, Davey and Isaac and Amos ran in circles on the great lawn, performing a version of *Duck, Duck, Goose* I'd never seen before.

Can't Help Falling in Love began playing over the speakers, echoing out to the darkened river. Dusk descended over the party, the lamp post lights flickering on. A crescent moon hung above the water, creating a picture-perfect night.

Bronson turned to his mother. "What do you say, Mom? How about a dance?"

"Oh, I think I need to digest a bit first. I'm stuffed." She looked pointedly in my direction.

One side of Bronson's mouth hitched up in a half grin. "I do believe my mother's suggesting I ask you to dance, Miss Morgan. And I always listen to my mother. Would you do me the pleasure?"

Well, I couldn't simply sit here the entire night, could I? And I *had* promised Bronson a dance.

"Sure."

He led me onto the dance floor as Elvis crooned about love being inescapable. We tucked ourselves into a spot beside Aunt Pris and Mr. Colton, and Bronson turned to me, placing his hands on my waist. I positioned my own on his broad shoulders, the fabric of his dress shirt warm from the heat of his body.

"Hey, kids," Mr. Colton said. "Come to dance to some real music, eh?"

Bronson grinned. "No one can top the king."

"If that isn't the truth." Aunt Pris glanced up at her partner, her eyes twinkling.

Mr. Colton twirled Aunt Pris around.

"Showoffs," Bronson muttered good-naturedly.

"How's the camp going there, young man?" Aunt Pris asked.

"Sorry, Aunt Pris. I'm under strict orders not to talk about the camp tonight." He pointed at me, making a face as if he were threatened by my mere presence.

I rolled my eyes. "I don't think you can afford *not* to answer."

"Good point." He turned to the older couple. "It's going well. Very well, in fact. If you all want to stop in and observe sometime, feel free."

Aunt Pris shook her head. "No, no. This is the endeavor of young people. We only wish to support you."

"Actually," I cut in. "It might be interesting for the kids to hear what the orchard was like when you were growing up, Aunt Pris." My face heated. "I mean, Miss Martin."

She waved a hand through the air. "I'm Aunt Pris to everyone. You feel free to call me that, too, dear."

"You know, that's a great idea. What do you say, Aunt Pris? Will you come by some afternoon and tell us about the orchard in its heyday? This week would actually be great since we had to cut some of the electives out."

"That's right. Josie's book tour. She was talking my ear off about it yesterday." Aunt Pris readjusted her arms on Mr. Colton's shoulders. "Yes, I suppose I could stop by."

"Thanks. That will be great, especially with Lizzie on her honeymoon, too." Bronson absentmindedly stroked his thumb alongside my waist as he spoke, sending shivers up my spine.

Mr. Colton grasped Aunt Pris's hands when Elvis's song puttered out. "How about a drink, my dear? Before they start some crazy shuffle or Magdalena or some such nonsense."

"I think you mean, *Macarena*, Mr. Colton." I giggled.

"Isn't that what I said? You two kids have fun." They slid off the dance floor as the hauntingly romantic tune of *Unchained Melody* began.

"And I was really looking forward to showing you my *Macarena* moves." Bronson leaned closer to whisper in my ear. "This is a good one, too, though. Dance with me again?" He pulled me an inch closer when he spoke, and my arms wound around his neck of their own volition in answer to his question.

I looked after Bronson's aunt and the man who made her smile as if she were twenty years old again. "How cute."

"I know I am, but it's nice to be told sometimes." Bronson sighed, feigning seriousness.

I shook my head. "Not you, them." I jerked my head in the direction of Aunt Pris and Mr. Colton, holding hands as they wound their way back to their table.

"Oh, yeah. They're okay."

"I know you can be serious when you want to be, Bronson Martin."

He pulled me even closer, leaning down until his breath warmed my ear. "I like it when you use my full name."

My body flushed, my palms suddenly sweaty where they lay at Bronson's collar. "So, what's their story?"

"Second chance at love with the one that got away. They were sweethearts before the war, and Aunt Pris's parents tore them apart."

"How sad."

"But they're together now, which is their happy ending. Still, I'd rather not wait until my eighties to have my own happy ending —you?"

I sighed, unable to avoid the smile tugging at my lips. The wedding ceremony, the music, the food, the champagne, it all served to tempt me to think it was possible.

"I can't get what the reverend said out of my head."

"What's that?"

"About God loving us no matter what. Doesn't seem it could be that simple."

"It is, and it isn't. It's why He sent His Son, why He asks us to trust Him."

"I'm trying," I whispered.

What would it be like to fall into the hands of a God who loved me?

The guilt of Isabel's presence threatened to saw away at the edges of my happiness, but I pushed it aside, moving closer to Bronson. An insatiable urge to close the gap, to press myself against his strong chest and feel the security and strength of those arms around me, took over. I wound my arms tighter around him until our bodies touched. "You really think there are happy endings for everyone? For us?"

His cheek, with only the slightest stubble, pressed against my temple. "I sure hope you're not teasing me, Morgan Dalton. A guy can only take so much, and I think if I ever get to kiss you, I won't be able to settle for anything less than having you forever."

His words caused a pleasant rush of adrenaline and want to pulse through my body.

Forever.

What a word for someone like me. A word I thought impossible until now, but in this moment, I hungered for it. Hungered to chase after my own dreams for once, instead of Isabel's.

Ever so slowly, I pressed my temple against his cheek, moving my face upward until our lips met in a slow, soft kiss that left me gasping for breath with the intimacy of it.

No matter that we were surrounded by dancing couples under this moonlit tent. No matter that I thought I could never have this life, never have a man like Bronson. In this moment, anything seemed possible. I was flying, soaring with the possibility of it, drunk on Bronson's words, on his arms around me, his lips on mine.

The song ended, and a shift on the dance floor caused us to part. But Bronson kept his arms around me. "Can I have the next dance?" he asked, his voice gruff.

I swallowed and nodded as the upbeat music of the *Macarena* started.

Bronson grimaced. "The next *slow* dance."

I giggled, stepping out of the warmth of his arms. "Oh, you're all talk, I see. Don't have the moves for the *Macarena*?"

"Guilty as charged." He took my hand and brought me in for

another quick kiss. "But I'm holding you to your word for the next dance."

"I'll be looking forward to it, Mr. Martin."

He lingered, his thumb caressing the top of my hand until Amie scooted up to us and grabbed my arm. "Unless you're doing the *Macarena*, off the dance floor, Bronson. You know it, don't you, Morgan?"

"Not really, but—"

"Oh, we'll show you!" Josie joined us, along with Maggie and Lizzie dragging a reluctant Mrs. Martin.

"I don't know . . ."

Mrs. Martin stood next to me. "I'll stay if you will," she said to me.

I shrugged and nodded, laughing. Joy bubbled up within me, the remembrance of Bronson's kiss fresh in my mind, the feeling that I belonged here, with this family.

By the end of the song, Bronson's mother and I were beginning to get the hang of the moves, no matter how ridiculous we looked. But when we jumped sideways to begin another round of the repetitious dance moves, Mrs. Martin suddenly dropped to the floor beside me.

❀ 24 ❀

Bronson paced the floor of the hospital waiting room in front of Morgan, thinking all manner of bad thoughts about his younger sister. *He* should be the one in there with his mom. But as always, Amie had pushed herself forward, thinking she knew best.

How was she qualified to be their mother's health advocate? Just because she knew what vitamins their mother took and how many scoops of collagen powder she put in her morning smoothie did *not* qualify her to accompany Mom back in the ER. Amie would be flirting with young handsome doctors or talking to a nurse about the benefits of yoga instead of putting her attention where it needed to be—on their mother.

If Dad were here, he'd be the one back there with her. But he wasn't. So, it was only right it be Bronson.

He sat, head in his hands, and prayed that their Mom was okay back there. She'd always hated doctors, and the fact that this place held hard memories for her after Dad died wouldn't make it easier.

"We should get frequent flier miles to this place, huh?" Morgan joked.

He managed a smile. "Maybe."

She placed a hand on his arm. "It's only her ankle, Bronson. She'll be okay."

He let his hands fall as he allowed her soothing words to ground him. "I know. But are you sure she didn't pass out? She seemed kind of out of it on the way here, you know?"

"I think it was the pain."

His phone rang and he pulled it out of his pocket. "Maggie," he told Morgan.

After Mom had fallen, claiming she'd simply twisted her ankle from dancing in such "foolish" high heels, it was decided that Bronson and Amie would take her to the hospital since Maggie and Josie had to worry about getting kids to bed after the wedding reception. Of course, Mom had refused to get checked out until after Lizzie and Asher had said their final goodbyes to their guests.

"No way on God's green earth am I missing the rest of my daughter's wedding," She'd sat beside Aunt Pris with a bag of ice propped on a rapidly swelling ankle.

No one argued with her, and although her face tightened in pain, Bronson was glad for Lizzie's sake that Mom stuck it out for the last hour-and-a-half of the reception.

He hadn't danced with Morgan again. Just didn't seem right with his mother looking on, suffering. It occurred to him then that this must be how Morgan felt in a much bigger way whenever she tried to be happy—as if it simply wasn't fair or right. Isabel's suffering, and that of her family's, had ruined her opportunity for happiness, just as, on a small scale, Mom's suffering at the wedding had ruined Bronson's opportunity to soak himself in Morgan's arms again.

A poor comparison, maybe, but it was the first time he'd glimpsed Morgan's viewpoint. And yet, if that kiss on the dance floor was any inclination, perhaps Morgan was beginning to think differently—to release her past and think of a future. To consider opening herself up to a healing God.

"Haven't heard anything yet," Bronson told his oldest sister.

"Amie's not answering her phone." Worry tinged Maggie's voice.

"There's probably not great reception back there. I'll let you know as soon as we find out anything, okay?"

He hung up as Amie walked out of the double doors of the emergency room, somehow still looking completely elegant and not out of place at all in her bridesmaid's dress.

Bronson and Morgan stood. "Well?" Bronson asked.

"She broke her ankle." She frowned. "She'll need surgery and she'll be on crutches for six weeks, but that's all it is. She didn't pass out. No head injury. She's sharp as a tack, the doctor said."

Bronson huffed. "I want to see her."

"They're taking her to surgery. I have to go back and get my bag."

"Okay. I'll let everyone know."

After Amie disappeared behind the swinging doors, he lowered himself to the chair, called Maggie, and asked her to call the others.

He hung up and leaned back in his chair until his head hit the wall. Sudden realization swept over him. "Oh no."

"What is it?" Morgan turned in her seat, crossing her long, shapely legs.

He straightened, then popped to his feet and paced again. "We have guests this week. Mom said she could get along okay without Lizzie and Josie, but there's no way she's able to make and serve breakfast, never mind clean the rooms, go to the market, keep up with the guests' other needs . . ."

"Maggie and Amie will help, won't they?"

"Amie's full-time with the camp this week. I guess she'll have to pitch in however she can at nights—I will, too, but no denying it'll be tight."

"I can help."

Overwhelming gratitude washed through him. He grabbed for her hand and wove his fingers through hers. "Maggie and Amie will take the brunt of the work. Mom will direct them, after all. It's nice of you to offer, though."

⁂

DIRECT THEM, ALL RIGHT. ONLY *THEM* TURNED OUT TO BE *HIM*.

"Just flip the bacon over halfway through cooking." At the dining room table, Bronson's mother arranged fruit cups in fancy glass dishes, her broken ankle propped on a nearby chair.

He'd never known a more stressful Monday morning in his life.

Amie had been vomiting all night—some sort of serious stomach bug he did not want to explore for himself. Maggie's father-in-law had scared them all with another heart attack. Denise, Josh's mother, was an emotional wreck, and Maggie didn't want her to be alone as they again operated on her husband.

So, that left him, his invalid mother, and octogenarian aunt to serve a five-course gourmet breakfast, clean six guest rooms, and —oh yeah, run a summer camp short-staffed on the only week he required a one-on-one aid for one of his students. Not to mention open up an apple-picking venture at the end of the week. No problem.

"No, honey. You have to flip them. Not just push them around." Mom grabbed a crutch, starting to hobble over to the oven.

"Mom, sit down. I got this." What did it matter if bacon was flipped or pushed? If less-than-perfect bacon was the one travesty the guests suffered this week, he'd count it a week of miracles.

He turned from the oven while glancing at his watch. "What's next? Kids will start arriving in a half hour."

Mom bit her lip. "Can you get the eggs out and put them at

the bar? I'll manage a quick French Toast casserole. Perhaps you can slice the coffee cake?"

Bronson clapped his hands together. "Coffee cake. Got it."

"Fridge," she directed.

"Fridge," he muttered, searching for the coffee cake. He winced. "You asked me to take it out of the freezer last night, didn't you?"

His mother held "baking days" where she prepared half a dozen coffee cakes and freezable desserts. This way, she could simply take them out the night before she planned to serve them.

"Yes . . ."

"I might have forgotten." He and Morgan had been planning the week, trying to accommodate, with the addition of Marcus and Amie, the loss of Josie and Lizzie in the writing and music electives. "Sorry."

Mom blew her bangs off her forehead as she settled on the bar and began cracking eggs into a bowl. "It's okay. Just pull it out and leave it on the counter. It should thaw quick."

He did as she directed. This really wasn't bad. Piece of cake. Ha. He even managed to make a corny joke, if only for his own amusement. As long as he was out of here by eight-thirty to greet the students. "What's next?"

"Go out in the dining room and ask what they'd like to drink. Mr. and Mrs. Rimeira will likely be up—they're the early risers."

Bronson pushed through the swinging door of the butler's pantry, pasting on a smile for the middle-aged couple seated by the fireplace. "Good morning."

They returned his greeting, and after he spoke to them, he made a mental note to bring tea and cranberry juice back to their table.

On his way into the kitchen, a group of five women in their sixties came down the stairs, laughing. Oh, yes. Mom had told him about the somewhat rowdy group of ladies having a reunion of sorts. They'd been friends since high school and vacationed in Camden once every summer.

"Good morning, ladies."

"Well, aren't you better than a fresh pot of coffee?" A petite woman with sea glass jewelry sauntered over to Bronson and fluttered her eyelashes.

Oh, boy.

"I bet he tastes better than coffee too, Ruth!" A stout woman with a large bosom elbowed the sea glass woman. They all burst into a round of giggles.

He cleared his throat. "What can I get you ladies to drink this morning?"

The sea glass lady grasped his arm. "Are you on the menu, darlin'?"

The women howled.

"That's enough, y'all." A tall woman with bright gray hair pushed them aside. "I'll take some coffee, honey."

"Tea for me."

"Do you have any of that orange-cranberry juice?"

He nodded, figuring it would be easy enough to mix the juices together if his mom didn't have anything prepared.

"Apple juice, please. Oh, and a glass of water. Nothing cleanses the system like a glass of water before a meal in the morning."

The stout woman brushed up against Bronson. "Oh, I think I know what can cleanse a girl better than some water."

He ducked away from the group. "I'll be right back with your drinks!"

He burst through the pantry doors to find his mother slicing cake at the bar. At the oven, hands covered in potholders, Aunt Pris grasped a pan of extra crispy bacon.

"Please, do not send me back in there. Those ladies are cougars ready to sink their claws into my tender young flesh."

Mom's mouth turned downward. "I was afraid of that."

"Seriously, Mom, they were touching me and saying they wanted to put me on the menu—"

Aunt Pris raised her eyebrows, setting the pan of bacon on a cooling rack. "That's entirely unacceptable. Leave them to me. I'll set them straight." She headed toward the guest area.

Mom placed a restraining hand on Aunt Pris's arm. "I'm not certain 'setting our guests straight' will earn us any five-star reviews, Aunt Pris."

"So, you're going to let them maul your son? Really, Hannah, I would have thought better of you."

Mom pinched the bridge of her nose, screwing her eyes together just as Morgan walked through the door.

"Morning!" she called. "Bronson, it's eight-twenty. I thought Amie might be over by now."

Right. Mrs. Davis would want to see the full staff. Especially the promised one-one-one.

"Amie's sick." How were they going to accommodate Marcus now?

Morgan's face paled. "Sick?"

As if on cue, a bell rang from upstairs.

"What the blazes? Mom—you gave her a bell?"

"You know how she is when she's sick. I didn't want her passing out and none of us knowing about it."

"How's she going to ring as bell if she's passed out?"

"Can you just go up and see what she wants, Bronson? Before you head out? Please?" She turned to Morgan. "Honey, is there any way you can help serve breakfast this morning?"

"Absolutely," Morgan said, a bit too enthusiastically. No doubt she'd do anything to avoid meeting up with Mr. and Mrs. Davis alone.

"Bronson, what did they want to drink?"

Bronson closed his eyes, trying to remember. "One of the cougars wanted cranberry apple juice—"

"Cranberry and orange juice, you mean?"

"Cougars?" Morgan asked.

"Long story." Bronson started in the direction of the stairs. "A couple wanted tea, one coffee . . . and I completely forgot what the Rimeiras wanted after I was traumatized by that group that calls themselves ladies."

Mom sighed and hung her head as Bronson started up the stairs, arranging his t-shirt over his face as a sort of mask.

The last thing he needed this week was to catch whatever Amie had.

❧ 25 ❧

Bronson dragged in a gusty breath when he finally managed to escape the Victorian. This was a nightmare. A legitimate nightmare. How would they survive the week?

He'd just finished swinging open the wide double doors of the barn when cars drove up, students spilling out of them. He pasted on a smile, lifted up a prayer, and told himself he had this. It would be fine. More than fine.

"Hey, Mr. Martin." Tommy jumped out of his dad's truck. "You'll never guess what I did this weekend."

Bronson marked Tommy as "present" on his list. "What's that, buddy?"

"Bought a '64 Camaro."

Bronson raised an eyebrow. "No way. What's a twelve-year-old like you going to do with a car?"

"Well, it's really my dad's. It's beat up, but we're going to fix it, maybe race it when I get old enough."

"That's awesome. I'd love to see some pictures."

Tommy reached for his phone as Mrs. Davis pulled up, Marcus bouncing beside her in the passenger's seat.

"You know what, Tommy? Let me get through attendance first and then I'll look."

"Sure thing." He went inside the barn, taking his usual seat between Daniel and Ned.

Bronson asked God for an extra dose of wisdom and grace as Mrs. Davis approached, Marcus by her side, towering over her.

He smiled brightly. "Hey there, Marcus. We're glad you're here." Marcus clapped and made an unintelligible noise, pointing to the top of the orchard. "We'll get up there soon enough, buddy."

Bronson turned to Marcus's mother. "Mrs. Davis, pleasure to see you again. I'm happy you decided to give the camp a chance."

Mrs. Davis's gaze shot back and forth, from the barn where the kids gathered to the orchards up the hill. "Yes . . . well, Marcus is quite excited about it."

Bronson swallowed, searching for words. "I do need to inform you that we've had a glitch this morning."

Mrs. Davis straightened, her entire body on alert. "Oh?"

The one word seemed to condemn Bronson, accusing him of failing. And, in a sense, hadn't he? He should have planned for this possibility, planned for a substitute.

"You see, my sister Amie—the one who was supposed to serve as Marcus's aid—came down with a stomach bug last night. I'm hoping she'll be on her feet by tomorrow, but we're still happy to have Marcus today. Morgan has adequate training, and this is a great bunch of kids—they're all very helpful."

Mrs. Davis grasped Marcus's arm. He rocked back and forth, one leg forward, facing the barn. "I really wished you'd called me this morning."

"I—I know. And I apologize for that. Things have been crazy. My mother's laid up with a broken ankle and I was helping her serve breakfast. Please allow Marcus to stay. We'll be making a volcano today and candy apples later."

Mrs. Davis stepped back, her hand still on her son's arm. "I don't know. Perhaps we should touch base tomorrow."

Marcus seemed to notice that his mother pulled him away from the barn. He made an unpleasant sound, pulling away from her.

"Marcus, that's enough. We'll come back tomorrow."

Bronson stepped forward, softened his voice as if speaking to a wounded animal. "Why not let him stay, Mrs. Davis? I give you my word he'll be in good hands."

She vacillated. "*You'll* be with him the entire time?"

Bronson didn't miss her implication. Mrs. Davis didn't want Marcus alone with Morgan. For a moment, he bristled. What did the lady think—that Morgan was going to get drunk while serving as a teacher at the camp, and then try and drive Marcus home?

He breathed around his frustration. That wasn't fair. He couldn't begin to imagine all Mrs. Davis had gone through. Wasn't her agreeing to the camp a big step?

"Yes, I won't let him out of my sight. I promise." Bronson stared into her dark eyes, trying to communicate how seriously he took his job, how seriously he took the responsibility of caring for each one of his students.

"I could bring him back tomorrow . . . one more day isn't all that much," she hedged.

Bronson swallowed. He wouldn't continue arguing with her. "Whatever you decide, Mrs. Davis. We're happy to have Marcus today, but if you'd feel more comfortable bringing him tomorrow, I understand."

She ran her fingers along the strap of her purse, up and down, like playing a musical instrument, trying to seek answers. "I suppose it would break his heart if I dragged him away at this point. And we've been praying up a storm that this would be a good thing for him."

Bronson smiled. "He'd have tons of fun."

"I could stay . . . I wouldn't mind, really."

Bronson tread carefully with his next words. Mrs. Davis wasn't a woman quite ready for a CrossFit session. He didn't want to offend her. "You are absolutely welcome to. We'll be doing a ton of walking around the orchards though."

She looked down at her flip-flop clad feet. "On second thought, I'm not quite prepared, am I? You'll take good care of him, won't you? And call if things aren't going well?"

"You have my word."

"Okay, then. Bye, Marcus."

But the boy was already taking long, jaunty strides toward the barn as soon as his mother released him.

Bronson followed after, waving to the older woman, breathing a sigh of relief when she ducked into her car and started down the driveway.

Now, if only his mother would release his co-teacher from breakfast duty, he might be in good shape.

❧

I PLACED A PLATE OF CAREFULLY-ARRANGED TEA BAGS BEFORE the ladies Bronson referred to as "cougars."

"There you are. I'll be right out with your coffee cake and fruit cups."

"Did we scare him away, darlin'?" A woman with seashell earrings asked.

"Of course, you did!" A woman with silvery hair scolded. "You near scared me away." She turned to Morgan. "I must apologize on behalf of these poor excuses I manage to call friends. Please tell that young man they'll be on their best behavior from now on. We're guests in your home, and they've behaved inexcusably."

A couple of the women at the round table looked genuinely chastened. A woman with the largest bosom Morgan had ever seen spoke. "Yes, doll. Please tell that young man we're sorry."

"Of course. I'll be back out with your first course soon."

Morgan walked away from their tittering laughter, unable to contain her own smile. She ducked through the butler's pantry and grabbed up the plates of coffee cake Mrs. Martin had set on the bar.

"Are they behaving themselves now?" Aunt Pris asked.

"I think they're appropriately mortified," I said. "One of them was giving her friends what-for while I served drinks."

"Good enough, then. Grown women acting like that. It's a disgrace, is what it is." Aunt Pris opened the refrigerator door, pulling out a package of strawberries.

"Thank you, Morgan. You're a lifesaver." Mrs. Martin said.

A life*saver*. Wow. That was a first.

I smiled at her, slipping back into the guests' dining room, feeling I contributed to something important as I served the ladies their cake and confirmed the Rimeiras' main dish orders.

I could get used to being a part of this family.

❦

IF ANYONE NEEDED A BLASTED BELL, IT WAS HIM.

Bronson had half a mind to march back over to the bed and breakfast and steal that annoying thing from Amie in hopes it would settle the kids down. Or in hopes Morgan would come running to help him.

Where was she, anyway? Surely breakfast was over by now?

And what had gotten into his kids? They were particularly rowdy for a Monday, and Marcus seemed to feed off the frenzy in the room.

Maybe he'd forgo the science experiment he planned first thing this morning. These kids needed to get outside for some fresh air and exercise. Burn off some energy.

He placed two fingers in his mouth and blew a long, strident whistle into the classroom barn. The room quieted. There, better than a bell.

"We're just waiting on Miss Morgan. Once she comes back, we'll head out to the orchards. For now, why don't we take turns sharing about our weekends?"

Ned raised his hand wildly, a newspaper clutched in his fist. "Did you see the article about our orchard, Mr. Martin?"

Bronson smiled, remembering the pride he felt when he'd unfolded yesterday's Sunday paper to see a picture of him, Morgan, and the students on the front page.

Camden Summer Camp Opens Apple-Picking Season, it read.

But none of that could compare to the tiny phrase Ned had just used. *Our orchard.*

This is what he'd envisioned. Not only a Martin family endeavor, but one these kids could take pride in.

"It was an impressive article." Bronson looked each student in the eye, deliberately taking his time to acknowledge them one by one. "This orchard is yours as much as it's mine. You all have made an amazing contribution to it. And I'm grateful for your help."

Ned turned the page to the rest of the article. "Did you see this picture, Daniel? You're practically drooling over Miss Amie. Maybe you'd want to take it and hang—" Ned stopped short, his gaze cutting to Bronson as he realized what he was about to say. "Never mind."

Bronson's chest swelled. It wasn't much, but it was a small victory. Ned thinking about what he was saying was actually a huge victory and showed a lot of growth.

A moment later, Morgan entered the barn. A giant balloon of relief deflated in his chest.

"Sorry I'm late."

The kids scurried for her attention, Tommy shoving his phone in her face to show Morgan his car, Daisy wanting to tell her about the camping trip she'd taken over the weekend, Ned waving the newspaper, Anna claiming she liked Morgan's hat. And above it all, Marcus rocked back and forth in his chair, yelling "Ehmmmmm!"

This time, Morgan whistled. They grew silent—all except Marcus, his insistent "Ehmmmm!" echoing in the back of the room.

Even Bronson straightened in silence at the sound coming out of such a tiny person. It was hot, pure and simple. Of course, anything Morgan did these days sparked a simmering flame inside him.

Bronson smiled at her, nodding his thanks. "Daisy, why don't you go first?"

Morgan slid into the seat next to Marcus as Daisy spoke of swimming in the Saco River and hiking Arethusa Falls. What he wouldn't give for a weekend on the Saco right about now. He'd been so busy planning and running the camp and the apple-picking business, he hadn't planned his usual summer camping trip. Now, with August well underway, and his mom's injury, he doubted he'd have time for such a trip.

After each of the students who wanted to share had done so and the new campers had been introduced, Bronson clapped his hands together. "We have a big week ahead of us. The trees are ready for business, and our grand opening is this Friday. We'll be taking our usual kayak trip on Wednesday, but tomorrow I'd like to do a trial run where you guys will be the customers. Sound good?"

They nodded.

"Can I drive the tractor up to pick the apples?" Tommy asked.

"We'll have to get clearance from your parents, but I don't see why not."

Bronson glanced at Morgan, who whispered something to Marcus. He admired how she'd calmed the boy down with little effort.

On the way up to the orchard, Morgan stayed at Marcus's side. He didn't miss how some of the kids—particularly Daisy and

Anna—kept glancing at Morgan and Isabel's brother. He hoped they didn't begrudge Marcus the attention Morgan usually gave to them.

They walked through the rows of orchards, Bronson pointing out which variety of trees were ready for picking and which would benefit from another week or two. When Marcus ran away from the group without warning, Morgan chased after him, calmly guiding him back and speaking softly to him. Some of the boys laughed, but one sharp look silenced them.

"Where's Miss Amie?" Daniel asked. "I thought she was going to be here full-time this week."

"Amie's not feeling well today. Hopefully she'll be back on her feet tomorrow."

Daniel's face fell. Poor kid really did like Bronson's pain-in-the-butt little sister.

"We could make her a card," Daisy said. "She'd like that. Especially if we drew something for her."

"That's a great idea, Daisy. When we get back to the barn, we'll do that while we're waiting for our special guest speaker."

Cameron raised an eyebrow. Bronson had to admit, the boy was a good addition to the camp—hadn't given them an ounce of trouble since he showed up that first day, and he was a great worker to boot. He had a penchant for building and the farmstand by the barn was his special project, ready to host customers in just a few days.

"Who are you making us listen to?"

"Hey—what's the deal here? I never make you do anything. You always have a choice."

"But the other choice always involves coating those sickening red balls with Tanglefoot."

Bronson shrugged. "It's still a choice. Besides, I think you'll enjoy this guest. She knows a lot about orchards. Particularly *this* orchard."

"Who is it?" Daisy asked.

"You'll see after we finish our inspection." Each morning, they toured different parts of the orchard, inspecting the trees for bug infestation and general health. "Man, we could use a good rain." It had been weeks without any, and some of the trees looked more tired than they should this time of year.

"But we water with the system." Daniel pointed to the thin hoses Morgan had helped set up in the spring. "Isn't that good enough?"

"It's helpful, that's for sure. But nothing can quite compete with rain. It soaks deep, saturating the roots of the trees. I've been praying for it, but so far God's seeing fit to make me wait."

Daniel scoffed. "You really think God listens to prayers for rain? If He exists, He's probably got better things to worry about. Hungry kids in Africa, or something."

"I'm certain He cares about the hungry kids in Africa, and yeah, if we think of God in human terms, maybe He doesn't have enough time for everyone. But that's a great thing about God— He made this piece of land with the same attention he gave to the Grand Canyon or the Redwood Forest or Mount Everest."

"What are you, some preacher?" Ned squinted at Bronson.

Bronson laughed. "No, but you don't have to be a preacher to share what you know."

He watched his words settle over some and roll off others. He prayed that what seed he scattered on their growing hearts and minds would take root somehow, someway.

He glanced at Morgan, and she bestowed a bright smile on him. Maybe, with all the praying he'd been doing, seeds of faith would take root in her heart as well.

❦ 26 ❦

"Ehmmmm." Marcus looked at me with excitement in his eyes as he pointed to the blank sheet of paper on the desk in front of him.

Did he know who I was?

Of course, I may never know for certain, but the way he looked at me with those shining brown eyes, the way he hummed an "M" noise whenever he saw me, and even the way he'd seemed distraught when I'd left his home after first arriving in Camden, made me think that, beneath the odds of it all, Marcus remembered me.

And he didn't do so with hatred or regret, but with joy.

I opened the box of colored pencils on the desk and Marcus grabbed for them, kicking his large legs in excitement and nearly upending the table. I placed a hand on his arm and made a gentle shushing sound so as not to interrupt the beginning of Aunt Pris's story.

"I was born in the house over yonder, and if the good Lord lets me have my way, I'll die there." Aunt Pris cuddled her dog, Cragen, on her lap. As she spoke, she pet his wiry white coat, a near color match for her own hair. Together, they commanded the attention of the classroom.

"Now, I didn't work in the orchard—my mother didn't think it proper for a young girl to be out climbing trees. But that didn't stop me from playing a game of hide and seek with my best friend, Esther, who lived and worked on our land."

Daisy raised her hand, waving it wildly.

Aunt Pris seemed half taken-aback, half-flattered over the girl's enthusiasm. "Yes, young lady, what is it? You best speak before you pop your arm clean out of its socket."

The kids giggled and Aunt Pris's mouth twitched upward, as if pleased that she had made a joke the students deemed funny. I shared a smile across the room with Bronson, and when he winked at me, it seemed that, just for a moment, we were the only two people in the world.

Strange how he could elicit so many feelings within me—hope that we might be together, joy that he seemed to reciprocate my feelings, and despair. Despair that maybe this was all simply a foolish summer romance. Sure, I'd considered actually making a go of it at Lizzie's wedding, but I'd gotten swept away with the ambiance of the night, the flowers and scenery, Bronson in that tux, the way he'd looked at me as if he'd never wanted someone more.

I sighed, forcing myself back to the present. Beside me, Marcus happily traded his red colored pencil for a green one.

"Did Esther's mother not care that Esther worked in the orchards?" Daisy asked.

Aunt Pris shifted in her seat, clearly uncomfortable with the question.

From where he stood in the corner of the classroom, Bronson cleared his throat. "Esther's entire family worked the farm."

Cameron's eyes widened. "Were they slaves? Did you have slaves?" he asked Aunt Pris.

"Of course not," Aunt Pris scoffed. "Don't they teach you any history in those schools? Slavery was long over by the time I was a girl." Her eyelids fluttered. "Of course, I wish I could say this orchard never knew slavery, but that wouldn't be the case. And, I'd be lying if I said Esther's family had it easy, being one of the few colored families in Camden."

Aunt Pris shifted Cragen in her lap and the dog's tail wagged once in a perfunctory fashion. "Esther's great-great-grandparents were slaves on this very orchard. When they were freed, they decided to stay on, as did Esther's family, right up until we stopped running it some thirty years ago. I saw firsthand how badly my friend's family was treated—not only by my own parents, but by many in town. I hope you all, being the next generation, will continue the work of rectifying the social injustices of our world."

Some of the kids seemed to be puzzling out the meaning of Aunt Pris's words. Some had taken to doodling on their notepads. But a small handful—the handful that had been with us for the entire summer and seemed invested in this orchard—listened with rapt attention.

True, this was not the discussion Bronson and I had planned, but I couldn't think of a better fit to the organic learning Bronson wanted for the camp, and for each of these kids.

"It would be cool if Esther's family could be a part of our apple orchard opening, wouldn't it, Mr. Martin?" Anna asked.

Daniel huffed. "Why would they want to celebrate a place that used them as slaves all those years ago?"

Anna glared at Daniel. "They kept working here after that. Maybe they *liked* working here. Maybe they thought of the orchard as theirs just like we think of it as ours."

"Or maybe they didn't have any other choice or anywhere else to go. Ever think of that, Miss Smarty-pants?"

"Hey, hey, hey. That's enough now," Bronson said. "But you two bring up an interesting debate." He turned to Aunt Pris. "Do you know why Esther's family stayed, Aunt Pris?"

Aunt Pris nodded, her mouth in a thin line that made her mauve lipstick a mere pencil mark upon her face. "I'm afraid what the young man says has a lot of truth to it. Esther's ancestors knew the work of the orchard. They felt comfortable. Certainly, they could have left if they'd wanted, but it was a big risk—starting over. Sometimes, it's too scary. Sometimes, it takes generations to birth something new." She looked out the window to the orchards, her thoughts in another time, another place.

Aunt Pris shook her head and continued. "Those before us made mistakes. We've made mistakes. But we don't have to be chained by them. We must acknowledge them, yes—own up to them even, repent of them, but then we must step aside and make way for God to do a new thing."

Aunt Pris's words wound around me like a warm blanket on a cold January morning.

Step aside and make way for God to do a new thing.

Something in those words tugged at the tangled knot of beliefs that I'd cinched the moment my jail sentence fell short of my expectations.

Could it be possible I was in the way of the new thing God wanted to do in my life? I thought of Isabel trusting in the same God as Aunt Pris and Bronson, of trusting in Jesus. If that were so, then all Bronson spoke of regarding his faith would be something Isabel would have believed as well.

I sat back, pondering this notion. If Isabel believed this stuff, was I dishonoring her memory by brushing God aside? If Isabel believed God wanted to forgive everyone, would she have wanted Him to refuse to give that forgiveness to the one who killed her?

I blinked back tears. Marcus's humming grew in intensity, and I placed a hand on his arm, holding my fingers to my lips as Isabel used to do when he became too excitable.

Marcus never gave Isabel anything, yet she loved him unconditionally. Because that's what her God did, and that's who Isabel was. Would it be a stretch to think that Isabel might also be the kind of person to forgive her killer?

The thought of Isabel acknowledging my status as a murderer but still wanting me to be forgiven caused a lump to form at the base of my throat.

If I had guts enough to ask God to forgive me, would He?

As Aunt Pris went on to speak of the workers washing the apples in this very barn and preparing to sell them downtown or ship them all across the country, Marcus tapped my arm, hard.

"Ehmmmm," he said loudly, grinning at me and pointing to the picture he drew.

I dropped my gaze, taking in Marcus's creation, my heart in my throat.

There, on Marcus's paper was a beautiful drawing of bright colors. In the foreground, he'd sketched brown hands that looked eerily similar to his own. The hands drew a picture of two girls playing basketball, one with hair as red as a fiery sunset, the other with skin as brown as a Hershey's chocolate bar. In the background, were Bronson's beautiful orchards, vibrant and green with dots of red apples ready for picking.

I raised my hand to my mouth, swallowing down a sob. Then, I looked directly into Marcus's eyes.

He *did* remember who I was.

I flung my arms around him. He sat stiff and awkward, allowing me the embrace without returning the gesture. "Ehmmmm," he hummed under his breath.

Maybe these orchards held a little magic after all.

$$\text{\ss} \quad 27 \quad \text{\ss}$$

Bronson waved goodbye to Marcus as Mrs. Davis drove down the driveway of Orchard House. Morgan busied herself inside the barn, obviously avoiding Marcus's mother.

With all the kids safely with their parents, Bronson trudged with heavy feet into the shade of the barn, leaning on the rough wood of the wall. "If we made it through today, we can do anything."

Morgan smiled. "Cameron and Ned were disappointed you didn't want them to stay."

"I know. But I can't supervise right now. Actually, I better run in and see how Mom's holding up."

"I'll check in when I'm done cleaning here?"

"That'd be great. And for the record, hiring you was the best decision I have ever made."

Beneath the dim light coming through the window, her face reddened. "I enjoy it, Bronson. It's a good thing what you're doing—"

"What *we're* doing."

She bit her lip, averting her gaze. "What we're doing."

"I better see how the B&B's holding up." He ordered his feet away from the barn.

In reality, he wanted nothing more than to stay and help Morgan clean up the remnants of their science experiment. He wanted to talk to her, take her to dinner that night. Hopefully finish what they'd started on the dance floor of Lizzie's wedding.

But as always, duty called. He grabbed up everything the campers wanted Amie to have before walking across the drive and swinging open the back door of the Victorian. He avoided the urge to call for his mother—Aunt Pris could be taking her afternoon nap.

His mother wasn't in the kitchen or dining room. He trotted up the stairs to their personal bedrooms. "Mom?"

No answer.

He knocked lightly on Amie's door. A groan came from within and he inched it open. The shades were half drawn, the window wide open, probably an attempt to wash away some of the stale stench soaking the room.

"Ame? How you feeling, champ?"

She tugged the sheet off her face. "I feel as bad as you usually look."

"Sounds like you'll live. Either that, or your sense of humor will kill you." He placed the card the kids had made her, along with the wildflowers Daniel had picked, on her nightstand.

"What's that?"

"Something from the kids. They missed you today. I told them maybe you'd be in tomorrow." He held his breath, partly to avoid inhaling Amie's germs and partly in hopes Amie would answer enthusiastically about the possibility of joining them tomorrow.

"Unless God's feeling like giving me a miracle, I wouldn't count on it."

His hopes plummeted. Well, they'd pulled it off today. What was one more day?

"Feel better."

"Thanks, big brother."

Something in him softened at her words. Maybe he was too tough on her. She was still young, finding her way. Maybe, being the only Martin sibling younger than him—the only one without a father for part of her teenage years—he felt she needed more guidance, more protection.

After all, Amie wasn't exactly responsible like Maggie, or cautious like Lizzie, or even driven like Josie. She was . . . Amie, willing to be swept up by whatever passing fancy caught her attention.

But she'd grown up a lot in the last couple of years. Maybe he simply needed to give her a chance.

His mother wasn't in her bedroom. Though he could have used the locked door that led to the upstairs hallway in the guests' living quarters, they tended to avoid it when guests stayed with them.

He jogged back down the stairs, through the dining room and kitchen, and through the butler's pantry where a ringing phone greeted him at the front desk.

He answered it. "Orchard House Bed and Breakfast."

"Hi. I'm looking to surprise my wife for our ten-year anniversary next weekend. Do you have any rooms available?"

Bronson glanced down at the desk, not seeing a calendar or any clue as to how Maggie booked rooms. "I'm sorry, I don't usually handle the bookings. Can I have someone call you back tonight?"

He took the man's name and number and left it at the desk before starting up the stairs. He rounded the landing, where a stained-glass window looked out beyond the orchards then stopped short at the heap of laundry on the stairs. Beside the sheets, sat his mother, tears wet on her face.

"Mom! What happened? Did you fall? Why are you trying to handle the laundry?"

Her crutch lay haphazardly beside the railing, her booted foot splayed out at a pitiful angle.

She swiped at her nose with the back of her arm and shook her head. "I'm fine, honey. Sorry about this." She gathered the sheets that had fallen out of the basket.

He could count on one hand the times he'd seen his mother cry. It twisted something vicious inside him.

He grabbed the laundry basket from her. "No more climbing stairs. Camp's over. Just tell me what needs to be done and I'll do it, okay?"

Anything to stop those tears.

"I hate to ask you—"

"Stop it, Mom. We're a family business, and right now I'm the only family in commission. I'm here to help."

True, when they'd started this business, he'd made it clear he wouldn't be anyone's chambermaid, but these were extenuating circumstances.

She sniffed, gaining control of herself. "Okay. I need to bring up new sheets and towels from the laundry room and make the beds. Just toss these downstairs—I'll wash them later. I need to clean the rooms." Her bottom lip trembled. "It's already so late. I'm lucky all the guests are still out, but they'll likely return any minute."

"I'll get this done in a jiffy. Stay here, I'll be right back."

Bronson flew down the stairs with the laundry basket, tossing it onto the floor of the laundry room as he rummaged through the cabinet for extra sheets. He pulled out a couple sets and raced back up the stairs. Meanwhile, his mother had managed to enter the Alcott Room and was in the bathroom, straightening stray hair products on the vanity.

"Here we are." He lay the sheets on the bed. "Does it matter which ones?"

With her crutches, Mom shuffled out of the bathroom. "Bronson!"

He shrugged. "What? Are they the wrong—"

"You didn't wash your hands after playing in the orchard? Look at those sheets!"

Shoot. He'd been in such a rush, he'd completely forgone washing up. A smudged handprint marred the sides of the pure white sheets, effectively staining nearly all of them.

He swiped at the marks with the back of his hand, hoping to rub them out. "It's just a small spot. Maybe—"

"You're making it worse!"

"I'm only trying to help. Here." He went into the bathroom and began washing his hands. "We can probably put the spot on the bottom. No one will ever notice."

"I refuse to put dirty sheets on our guests' beds. I'll simply have to wash these along with the others."

"They're not dirty, just . . . a little imperfect. You don't have extras?"

"Bronson—stop. Bronson!"

"What?" He shook the water off his hands over the sink.

Mom breathed deep and slow, attempting to harness whatever was threatening to come loose inside her. He tried to tamp down his own anger. He was doing the best he could, trying to help her. And all she could do was scold him for *playing* in his orchards?

"You're spattering the sink. I just cleaned it."

He glanced down at the water on the handles, all the dirty droplets on the inside of the sink.

His turn to breathe deep. He swished water around to wash off the dirt, then looked for something to dry off the sink, but only saw clean towels. He wouldn't make that mistake again. He swiped off a generous portion of toilet paper from the roll and dabbed at the handles.

Mom sighed, rearranging the end of the toilet paper in a pointed triangle.

He glanced down and clamped his eyes shut. "Really? We have beds to make and you have time for origami toilet paper?"

She gritted her teeth. "Bronson, this is important to me. Presentation is everything. Can you please bring those sheets back downstairs and start a load while I finish cleaning up here?"

He nodded and grabbed the sheets, jogging back downstairs, this time ignoring the phone when it rang. He swung through the butler's pantry just as Morgan knocked at the back door. He waved her in.

"I'm here to help."

"Are your hands clean?"

She looked down at her fingers. "Yes—"

"Great. You're golden, then. Will you go upstairs and help my mom?"

"Of course."

She started past him, but he grabbed her arm, brought her to him, and gave her a sound kiss on the cheek.

She pulled back, eyebrows raised and mouth parted. "What was that for?"

Because I love you, he wanted to say. "Just because."

She smiled and squeezed his hand. "Okay, I'll take it."

She scurried off to find his mother and he strode to the laundry room, hoping his brain wasn't too buzzed to remember the correct setting on the machine to wash white sheets.

❧ 28 ❧

I wasn't hiding when Mrs. Davis dropped Marcus off at camp the next day. Mrs. Martin genuinely needed my help serving breakfast.

Last night, after we'd finished cleaning the rooms and putting sheets on the bed, I'd sat down with Bronson and his mother. Fortunately, the two guests who had arrived in the middle of the sheet mishap had been understanding. By the time they had settled on a simple supper of scrambled eggs and bacon for themselves, I was bone tired and didn't turn down Mrs. Martin's offer of dinner.

"Mom, I'm not sure how long we can do this."

After we'd said a prayer of grace in which Mrs. Martin had asked God to help us through the week, Bronson stared at his eggs instead of digging in—something extremely out of character for him.

"Hopefully Amie will feel better tomorrow. And Maggie said Josh's father's doing well. With both of them back, things will go much smoother."

Bronson exchanged a look with me. "Amie's supposed to help

us at the camp this week, remember? Marcus is attending. We had a heck of a time today with only the two of us."

Mrs. Martin rubbed a hand over her face, pushing aside her bangs. "That's right. Well, we'll have to muddle through. I'll start cleaning the rooms earlier than I did today and leave the breakfast dishes for later."

I tossed my ponytail over one shoulder. "If Amie's better tomorrow, I could help out around here. At least until the rooms are cleaned."

Bronson had looked as if he wanted to argue, but his mother spoke first. "No, honey, that's not fair to you or Bronson. That camp is important to those kids. They need you."

I smiled. "But your foot will never heal if you're constantly on it."

"Morgan's right, Mom. Even when Lizzie and Josie are back, it's too much for you to be standing on your feet doing all the cooking." He swallowed. "Maybe we should close for a couple weeks. Just enough time for you to heal up."

Mrs. Martin blanched. "Bronson, absolutely not. Some of my guests booked eighteen months ago. It's far too late for them to find anything else now. That's not fair to them, nor helpful for our reputation, and plain bad business."

"Things come up. People will understand."

"No one *died*, Bronson. I broke my ankle. We'll manage." She gave him a half smile. "Besides, I know my limits."

Bronson sighed and took his first bite of eggs. "Whatever you think. I'm not sure how much I can help though, you know? I'll do what I can, but the orchard's opening this week and—"

She placed a hand on his arm. "I know. I'll plan a better system tonight. If I have you carry up the clean sheets and towels after they're done in the dryer, I can manage the beds and the cleaning myself tomorrow. And Maggie will be here." She spoke the last sentence a bit too brightly, as if Maggie's presence would fix everything.

"Sure, Mom. We'll work it out," Bronson had said.

Only this morning, when I'd knocked on the door of the Victorian, things had been in no less of a disarray than they'd been the day before.

"Can you serve again today, honey?" Bronson's mother asked.

"Of course, Mrs. Martin."

"Please, call me Hannah. I'm feeling old enough as it is these days."

I grinned. "You're not old, and I'm super impressed how you handle this place."

"I'm much more impressive on two feet."

We laughed, but I sensed the strain behind her words.

Bronson came thudding down the stairs. "Amie's still sick."

"Good morning to you, too," I said.

Hannah waved a hand through the air as she scooped flour into a measuring cup. "Don't mind him. He was never much of a morning person."

"Maggie on her way?" Bronson asked, ignoring his mother.

Hannah's mouth turned downward, highlighting the fine lines around her lips. "She just called. I'm afraid Davey and Isaac caught whatever it is Amie has. Must have been something going around at the wedding. Hopefully the rest of us can stay clear of it."

Bronson's face fell. "She's not coming?"

"Afraid not."

He rubbed the back of his neck. "Great. Why can't anything be easy?"

I exchanged a glance with Hannah. She placed her measuring cup down. "Maybe we should pray."

Bronson flung up a hand, as if to say, "Go ahead, it's not as if we don't have a million other things to do," but then closed his eyes.

I followed suit. Though praying with other people wasn't something I'd ever done, being with Bronson and Hannah in this way didn't feel awkward. Bronson's mother's words were heartfelt, begging an unseen God to place His hands upon our day. She prayed for the guests and the students, and for the three of us—that we would know a peace that passed understanding.

I sank into the prayer, questioning the peace that did indeed settle upon me. Was it wishful thinking? My imagination? Or was the God of the universe actually choosing to bless us—bless *me*?

As Bronson's mother ended the prayer, I inhaled a deep breath, feeling I had received an undeserved gift, been given a sudden knowing. I wanted to cling to it for as long as humanly possible.

But after the prayer, Hannah asked me to bring drinks to the early risers waiting in the dining room. I tucked aside thoughts of undeserved gifts for a later time.

AN HOUR AND A HALF LATER, I CLIMBED INTO THE BACK OF THE hay-filled trailer with a group of excited students. I guided Marcus to sit beside me, well away from the end so he wouldn't spill out. He clapped in delight.

Daisy sneezed once, and then twice. "I think"—another sneeze—"I'm allergic to hay."

Ned gave her a lopsided grin. "Better get out and walk then."

She returned him with a dirty look. "And let you wipe your grubby hands all over my perfect apples?"

Ned laughed, and I rolled my eyes.

"I think there's plenty of perfect apples to go around," I said.

The tractor roared to life and Tommy whooped. The scent of diesel wafted in the air and with a lurch, Bronson pulled us forward. Marcus fell against me and I braced myself on the railing of the trailer.

I loved this. It felt like something good and wholesome, simple and historic.

The diesel cleared away and I breathed in the fresh air, the faint scent of salty sea coming off the harbor. The sun shone brightly, warm but not suffocatingly hot. A perfect late summer day.

The kids laughed and joked, talking of the kayak trip the next day, the candy apples they planned to buy when the orchard opened for business.

Marcus began fidgeting in his seat when we reached the top of the hill. Bronson pulled the tractor to a stop beside a field where he'd started several compost piles. The kids climbed out, but Marcus sat rigid in the trailer, rocking back and forth, hands clasped between clenched knees.

"Do you want to get out and pick apples, Marcus?" I asked.

He shook his head and rocked harder. I sat beside him as the kids gathered around Bronson.

"What's the matter?"

He rocked more, then held out his fist, signing that he had to use the bathroom.

I suppressed an inward groan. "You just went before we left. Are you sure?"

He waved his fist with increasing vigor.

"Okay. Okay, buddy. Do you think we can find a spot in the woods over there?"

Not really woods. More like a couple trees by the hay field.

He shook his head, rocking back and forth and continuing to sign wildly.

I caught Bronson's attention and he came up beside us. "Everything okay?"

"He has to use the bathroom. I guess I'll have to walk him back to the barn."

Bronson looked at the kids, then at Marcus, seeming to vacillate between the two. "I'll take him."

"Bronson, there's no need for you to—"

He avoided my gaze. Was it my imagination or did he look guilty about something?

"Mr. Martin, can I start picking?" Tommy called.

"Wait a minute, kids." Bronson turned back to me. "I'm sorry. I promised Mrs. Davis I wouldn't let him out of my sight."

It shouldn't have hurt so much to hear his words, but they hit me with the force of a punch to the gut. It didn't surprise me that Mrs. Davis would ask such a thing of Bronson, but while I'd always admired his integrity, it would have been nice if he'd clued me in on the arrangement.

"It's the bathroom, Bronson. We'll be back in ten minutes. I think I can at least handle that."

"I know you can, but a promise is a promise."

I pressed my lips together and nodded. "Okay." I gestured to Bronson. "Mr. Martin will take you to the bathroom, Marcus."

He signed again, starting with hurried steps back down the orchard.

"Be back in a jiffy."

After they left, I gathered the kids. "As soon as Mr. Martin comes back, he'll show us which trees we can pick from."

Tommy kicked at the grass. "Miss Amie going to be better tomorrow? I'm not sure you two can handle all of us and him." He gestured to Marcus's fast-retreating back.

"Oh, I'm certain we can. Besides, you're all practically pros by now. And we trust you to handle yourselves and help one another, and Marcus."

There. That sounded like a good thing to say. Something Bronson would say—and believe. These were good kids. They simply needed a little guidance and responsibility to prune their characters, to draw out the trustworthiness we felt certain was in each of them.

Cameron elbowed Ned, but Ned slapped at his friend's hand. "*Ask her.*" Cameron said in a strained whisper.

"Cameron, you have something on your mind?"

Cameron glared at Ned. "Nothing, Miss Morgan. Just something we were wondering about."

"Well, if I can answer your question, I'm willing to try."

"It's nothing," Daniel said quickly. Too quickly, maybe.

"Okay . . ."

Ned stepped forward. "We heard something is all and were wondering if it was true."

Something about his tone caused a wall of caution to erect inside of me. I swallowed down my fear. Wasn't I just thinking how important it was to build trust with these kids?

"I'll answer whatever question you have as best I can."

"Did you kill a girl when you were our age?"

There it was. The worst question I could imagine. I took a step back, as if I could escape. My foot hit the wheel of the trailer. I leaned against it, hay sticking out of the slatted sides and poking my back.

The kids likely got their answer by way of my reaction.

One thing they didn't have was the whole story. Not that it would change the facts.

I rubbed my throat, attempting to massage the right words closer to my tongue. None came.

Daisy stepped forward. "Don't listen to them, Miss Morgan. We don't believe such ugly stories anyway. Come on, let's go find four-leaf clovers."

"I did," I said, my voice sounding foreign even to my own ears. "I killed my best friend."

The group grew dead silent, quieter than I'd ever known them to be. Tommy's mouth fell open as well as Ned's. Cameron raised his eyebrows, probing me with that inquisitive, intelligent gaze of his.

Worse was Daisy. Her brow furrowed and she shook her head, a look of pure disgust on her face. "What?" she croaked.

I bit my lip hard, then straightened. "I drove home from a

party after I'd been drinking. We got in a car accident, me and my best friend. Marcus's older sister," I whispered.

I didn't have to tell them all of this. I deserved my privacy.

But I wanted to tell them. I wanted to give them this piece of myself. Offer a grain of wisdom, if possible. A story they might remember if they found themselves in a similar situation in the next few years.

"You . . . she died?" Disbelief etched Daisy's face. She seemed to take the news personally. Still, I hadn't expected that falling out of her favor would hurt quite so badly.

"I'm sorry, you guys," I whispered. "I wish it wasn't true. I'm ashamed that it is."

Daniel stepped forward, reaching out a hand and barely touching my sleeve. "It was a long time ago, Miss Morgan. You're not the same person."

Tears pricked my eyelids. I remembered the last sentence of his essay question. *I'm wondering if you can teach me if it's possible for good apples to come from bad ones?*

Looking at the faces of my students, I wondered along with Daniel, if good could possibly come out of the bad.

I opened my mouth. "You're right, Daniel. It was a long time ago. And I'm not the same person. But the guilt and regret doesn't fade away. I'll have to live with it for the rest of my life."

The group grew silent, none of them meeting my gaze.

I cleared my throat. "Every day, we make choices. We never know when we might make one that will change the rest of our lives."

"But how do we know we'll make the right one?" Daisy asked, her voice tiny.

A small smile curved my lips. "We don't always make the right choices. No one's perfect, but if we're quiet, we can hear a small voice inside us. That night, I knew it was a bad decision to take that first sip, but I did it anyway. I didn't listen to the tug inside my chest that told me I was making a mistake."

"A tug?" Ned asked. "You mean, like God?"

I looked down the hill, gazing out over the crisp beauty of the orchards, the apples red and ripe on the trees. "I think so." I dragged in a deep breath, hoping they'd not ask much more—I wouldn't know how to answer.

The kids shuffled in awkward silence.

Had I lost the respect I'd earned from them? Whether I had or not, we couldn't just stand there. This was camp. "Why don't we scope out the trees for pests? Mr. Martin should be back any minute."

They turned their attention from me to the trees, but I didn't miss how Daisy's shoulders slumped. I hated that I'd let her down. But perhaps it was better if she knew the truth.

"Boys, you take the east line of trees, we'll take the west."

The boys sauntered off past the trailer, pointing to one tree, then the other. I went with the girls to the other side of the orchard, trying to distract them by asking what they planned to do with the apples they picked.

None of the girls gave more than a word or two worth of answer before we descended into silence.

I sighed as the girls scattered to scan for signs of pests and I was left alone. It felt good to tell the kids the truth, but had it been good for *them*, or just a way for me to clear my own conscience?

29

Bronson paced outside the door of the barn, waiting for Marcus to finish in the bathroom.

He knocked on the door. "You okay, buddy?"

Marcus let out an unintelligible murmur, but it didn't seem like a sound of distress. A moment later, he began humming.

"Try to finish up, okay? We want to get back and pick apples with the other kids."

When the boy finally emerged a moment later, Bronson asked him if he'd washed his hands, and he nodded. They walked toward the door of the barn together.

"Do you like the camp so far, Marcus?"

He nodded.

"Once Miss Amie feels better, she'll paint with you. She's looking forward to that."

Marcus held out his hand as if brandishing a paintbrush—or a sword—and swiped it wildly through the air.

"I think you're looking forward to it too, huh?"

The boy grinned wide, and Bronson acknowledged a connection with him. He didn't know how Morgan did it, honestly. But for the first time, he understood the reward behind it.

They were starting back up to the orchard when a banging on the window of the bed and breakfast caught his attention. A moment later, Aunt Pris shuffled out of the house, wearing a flowered housedress. "Bronson, thank the Lord you're here. Hurry. Your mother's fallen."

Dread seized his insides. He ran toward the Victorian, then, remembering Marcus, called him inside.

"I told her she had a death wish trying to navigate those stairs like she is," Aunt Pris said.

Bronson pushed through the butler's pantry and rounded the corner to find his mom heaped against the last step.

"Mom." He bit back an admonishment. She should have listened to him and closed this place for a couple of days.

"I'm fine. Just a little woozy."

That's when he noticed the ugly welt on her temple. "You hit your head?" He turned to Aunt Pris. "Did you call an ambulance?"

"She wouldn't let me. Ed's on his way. He'll drive us."

"I'm fine. I just need a little ice is all."

Bronson slid his hands beneath his mother and lifted her up. She curled around herself. "Bronson, go back to the kids. I'll be fine."

The kids. Had Marcus actually come inside? He raced back into the kitchen and found the young man had sat at the dining room table, drawing something on his mother's grocery list. Good.

Bronson ran back to the stairs.

"I'm not leaving until Mr. Colton gets here. Morgan's with the kids."

"The beds still need to be made."

"Forget the stupid beds, Mom!"

He'd had it with this bed and breakfast. The guests always came first. Well, what about his mother's sanity? What about his? What about the camp and the kids and his dreams?

Mom's expression . . .

"I'm sorry," he said a moment later. "It's just, this is too much. You're more important than a few guest beds. You're going to the hospital and I'm taking over. And I'm making the executive decision to close us down for a few days."

"You have no authority to—"

"Who will run this place, Mom? We need to close. Just for a few days until we all get back on our feet."

A few minutes later, Mr. Colton's truck pulled into the driveway. He parked as close to the side door of the Victorian as possible.

Bronson helped his mother outside, and with Mr. Colton's assistance, shimmied her into the truck.

"I hate being such a bother. I'm perfectly fine, really," his mother said as Bronson arranged her crutches in the bed of the truck.

"Nonsense, Hannah. Head wounds are a serious matter." Mr. Colton opened the back door of his truck. "Coming, my love? If so, I'm afraid it's coach for you today."

Aunt Pris's lips thinned. "Of course, I'm coming. Someone has to watch out for this stubborn woman."

"Something you can't relate to in the slightest, I suppose." Mr. Colton's eyes twinkled.

"Aunt Pris, there's no need—"

"It's not up for debate," Aunt Pris said in her clipped tone.

Bronson smiled at his aunt's feistiness before putting on a more sober, authoritative expression to get through to his mother. "I'll be at the hospital as soon as camp is done. I'll take care of everything."

"Hopefully I'll be back home by then."

He placed his hand on his mother's arm. "Don't worry about this place. Just take care of yourself."

"Bronson, do not close the B&B. I forbid it."

His heart went out to her. "It'll be okay. I'll see you soon."

The truck pulled away and Bronson looked toward the top of

the orchards, noticing a wispy trail of smoke rising to the sky. Their neighbor must be getting a jump start on burning his fields. Hopefully the smoke wouldn't bother any of the campers.

He strode back to the kitchen, breathing easy at the sight of Marcus still drawing on Mom's grocery list. "You ready, buddy?"

Marcus shook his head, pointed at the drawing of what looked like two girls playing basketball.

"That's really good."

Bronson dug his phone out of his pocket and dialed Morgan's number to explain why they weren't back yet. It rang, the hollow sound vibrating in his ear until her voicemail picked up. She probably had the ringer off—something they'd both took to doing during the camp day. He ended the call and turned to Marcus.

"Why don't we finish your drawing later and go back up to be with the other kids now?"

Marcus shook his head, slamming a fist on the table.

Bronson looked out the window to the orchards. "Marcus, we don't have time—" The thin plume of smoke was much bigger now, and it definitely looked closer—as if it came from the orchards.

Heart knocking on his ribcage, he glanced at Marcus, still doodling. He couldn't just leave Marcus, but what was he going to do, drag the boy up to the orchard? And if there was a fire, Marcus wouldn't be any help.

Bronson ran to the foot of the stairs. "Amie! I need you to come down and watch Marcus."

She wouldn't be happy, but this was an emergency. "Something's going on in the orchards!"

A faint sound and a creak came from the top of the stairs. Good, she was dragging herself out of bed.

"Stay here, okay, buddy?" He rushed past Marcus, trying not to sound panicked. "I'll be right back."

He took off out the door, letting it slam behind him.

❀ 30 ❀

I turned from the tree I'd been inspecting, the scent in the air confusing me. "Do you girls smell . . . smoke?"

Daisy gasped, pointing toward the sky. I followed her finger to the thick column of smoke mounting the tops of the apple trees.

"The boys!" I yelled, taking off in the direction of the trailer. My legs burned as I pushed up the hill of the orchard, the acrid scent of smoke becoming more and more pungent the closer we drew to the spot where we'd all gone our separate ways.

We couldn't have been separated for more than five minutes, what could have happened?

Once we reached the clearing, I stood frozen at the sight of flames engulfing the trailer. The fire consumed the hay with a hungry vengeance. Small flames crackled in the field beside it. Some of the boys had taken off their shirts and were trying fruitlessly to swat at the inferno.

"Boys!" I yelled. "Get away from there. Now!"

All listened except for Daniel, who continued swatting at the flames with his shirt.

"Daniel!" He didn't stop.

I turned to Daisy. "You remember how to turn on the hoses for the drip system?"

She nodded.

"Go turn them on, okay?" I didn't know if it would do anything to stop the spread of fire, but wet trees were better than dry ones, that much I knew.

She took off down the hill, her brown ponytail flying behind her. I approached the flaming trailer, heat searing my skin. "Daniel, leave! Now!"

I went to the trailer hitch, but realizing I had no clue how to unhook it from the tractor, I backed away, grasping at Daniel as I went, to no avail.

On a burst of wind, the flames shifted, growing hotter.

"Daniel, leave it!" Bronson's voice boomed out.

I'd never been so happy to see Bronson. He dragged Daniel away, practically throwing him on the ground since the boy fought against him.

"Back down the hill. All of you. Stay together."

Bronson ran for the tractor hitch.

"Bronson, no!" Emotion clogged my throat. The tractor had been an expensive investment, one he wouldn't want to lose, but his life was not worth the risk. "Bronson!" I yelled, my voice hoarse.

I dug out my phone, dialing 9-1-1.

He reached for the hitch, but his hands came away fast.

After I reported the emergency to the dispatcher, painstakingly going through all her questions after she'd assured me that fire trucks were on their way, I stayed on the line as requested and started counting the children. Two, four, six, eight . . . Ten. Only ten. I'd sent Daisy to turn on the hoses . . . there she was trudging back up the hill. But . . .

Marcus.

Fear clamped around my heart.

"Where's Marcus?" I yelled to Bronson.

He staggered closer, having given up on the hitch. "I yelled at Amie to come down and be with him."

So much for Marcus not leaving Bronson's sight.

"And you made sure she was with him before you left?"

"No, I didn't. There was a fire up here!"

"I'll take the kids down and check on him."

Bronson nodded, defeat lining his handsome features. He backed away, the trailer crackling and hissing as the flames consumed it.

Phone still pressed to my ear, the sound of sirens in the distance droned to life. They spurred me onward to see Marcus safe for myself. "Come on, kids."

⚜

ONCE THE CAMPERS WERE SAFELY SEATED ON THE PAVEMENT beside the barn, a first responder pulled into the drive. I ran into the house.

"Marcus?" I called. My gaze fell to his drawing on the table of the breakfast nook, crayons scattered. I ran up the stairs. "Amie?"

A moan came from a bedroom door decorated with a macrame hanging. I knocked before pushing it open, my heart sinking at the sight of Bronson's sister in bed.

"You're not downstairs watching Marcus . . . ." I backed over the threshold.

She shook her head, still groggy. "Was I supposed to?" She cocked her head toward the window. "Are those sirens I've been hearing? I thought my alarm—"

"Bronson said . . . never mind. I have to find him." I raced down the stairs, looking into every room with an open door as I went. "Marcus! Marcus, where are you?"

I ran back outside to see Bronson returning from atop the hill, where a loud pop caused an eruption of fresh flames and smoke to tunnel up to the sky. The water truck started up the wide tractor path.

"I can't find Marcus! Amie wasn't with him."

Bronson looked at me for a second as if not believing my words. Then he sprang into action, sprinting toward the bed and breakfast and ducking in the back door. He emerged a moment later.

"He was drawing at the kitchen table. He didn't want to leave. He was right here," Bronson said.

"Where could he have gone?" I cried.

Bronson ran a hand over his dirtied face. I didn't miss the swell of a bubble on one hand from where he'd tried to unhitch the trailer. "He was transfixed on his drawing. I thought Amie was coming down."

"Okay, so he's not where you left him. We'll split up. I'll stay with the kids, and we'll look around outside. Do you want to search the house?"

Bronson nodded, his face grim, sweat and dirt creasing the small lines near his mouth.

"Marcus!" he called, heading back into the bed and breakfast.

I turned to the kids. "We are not separating or going far. Understood?" They nodded, not one of the boys meeting my gaze. What had happened up on that hill? "We need to find Marcus. He's probably close by. Help me look for him."

The kids called out as we searched the inside of the barn. I even tried the door of the bookshop, though I knew it to be locked. We made a circle around the barn, checking behind bushes and barrels. Daisy promised Marcus one of her candy apples if he came out to play with her. Tommy told him he'd won the game of hide and seek and could come out now. The rest called his name.

Five minutes later, Bronson exited the bed and breakfast, huffing and shaking his head at my questioning look, defeat written on his face. "We need to call the parents." He tapped a few buttons on his phone.

I turned around to search the barn once more, desperate, praying we'd find Marcus before Mrs. Davis showed up. If not, I'd only increase the divide that already existed between me and the Davises. There was no way Mrs. Davis would ever trust me again, and I couldn't say I blamed her.

❧

BY THE TIME PARENTS STARTED ROLLING UP THE DRIVEWAY, THE water truck was descending the hill. All that was left of the fire was the smoke still hanging in the air. Parents spilled out of their cars, running to their children.

They ran their hands over their children's heads and shoulders, inspecting them for injury before hugging them fiercely when finally assured they were all right.

Daisy's mother took in my disheveled appearance and squeezed my arm. "Don't worry, Miss Morgan. The important thing is that everyone's safe now."

"But Marcus—we can't find him!"

"Oh, well . . ." Mrs. Lincoln looked to the fire chief, who had just come down from the orchard to report that the fire had been contained.

"I'm afraid our emergency isn't over. We've got a missing camper." I shook my head as I told him. How could we have lost him? I gave him a quick description of Marcus and where he'd last been seen.

Mr. Abbendroth organized the parents who'd arrived and all the students to spread throughout the orchards to look for Marcus.

My heart sank as Mrs. Davis pulled up the driveway in her old Buick.

The fire chief spoke into his transmitter, something about getting a police search started.

Mrs. Davis ran up to Bronson who was coming out of the barn where he'd gone to double check the boys' bathroom. I watched as he gestured with his hands, first to the orchard and then to the bed and breakfast. I approached, cautiously.

"What do you mean, my boy is gone?" Mrs. Davis's cry was shrill, her hands grabbing the edge of her shirt and twisting it.

Bronson shouldn't have to face her wrath alone. I approached them. "Mrs. Davis, I'm so sorry. We've checked everywhere, but I want to assure you, he was nowhere near the fire. Can you think of some place Marcus might—"

But a sharp sting burned my cheek, cutting off my words. I stared, slack-jawed, at Mrs. Davis's hand, still partly raised.

"I knew I shouldn't have left him with you! I should have listened to my gut."

I stumbled back, in shock, my hand raised to my stinging cheek. Had that really just happened? I deserved a lot of things, but never in my wildest dreams had I imagined Isabel's mother striking me.

Bronson placed a hand on Marcus's mother's arm. "Please, Mrs. Davis. Morgan had nothing to do with it. I was the one who was with him, but right now we need your help finding him."

Mrs. Davis's hand trembled. She stared off into the orchard, seeming to be in another time, another place.

It didn't matter that I hadn't left Marcus. In her eyes, I would always be untrustworthy. I staggered away from the woman, tears clouding my vision. I needed to get as far away from her as possible. I turned, bumping into the fire truck, skinning my shin. The bright red made me think of flames and sirens.

Sirens.

Marcus hated sirens.

All at once, I remembered a time I'd been over Isabel's house, doing our homework at the kitchen table. Isabel's parents had been grocery shopping, and Marcus had been watching a cartoon in the living room.

A police siren had sounded, followed by another, and another. Speeding past Isabel's house, when another awful sound had grated my ears. A deep wail, followed by heavy footsteps.

Marcus.

"I'll be right back." Isabel had left the room, and when she hadn't returned five minutes later, I went to search her out.

"Isabel?" I called, walking down the hall toward the bathroom.

"In here," came a muffled voice.

I followed it to the Davis's laundry room, where I found a huge, lumpy pile of bed sheets, comforters, and towels. The pile moved.

"Isabel?"

A corner of the pile lifted, revealing Isabel with her arm wrapped around Marcus. He clutched his knobby knees tight to his chest, his face buried in Isabel's shoulder. "Izz . . ." he hummed, over and over.

"He won't come out until I get in with him and tell him everything's okay," she said.

He doesn't come out until I get in with him.

I blinked, bringing myself back to the present. I ran toward the bed and breakfast, calling behind me to Bronson, "I think I know where Marcus is!"

I ran, huffing into the Victorian, veering right toward the laundry room.

Maybe I was wrong. Marcus wasn't in elementary school any longer. No doubt he had different habits, different fears than he had a decade ago. Maybe sirens didn't scare him any longer. Surely Mrs. Davis would have thought of this hiding place if they did. Although, her anger at me might have clouded her judgment.

I rounded the corner to the laundry room. A sob worked its way up my throat at the lumpy pile on the floor. Hannah's guest bed sheets, winter comforters, and towels galore all atop a most obvious lump—a lump much bigger than the one in my memory.

"Marcus?" I lifted a corner of the pile and crawled in, pushing aside stray corners of towels to get to him. He sat just as I remembered he'd done with Isabel that day long ago. Knees pulled to his chest. Head buried tight.

When I placed an arm around him, he nuzzled into my shoulder. The milky scent of his soap mixed with the lavender scent of Hannah's laundry detergent. "It's okay to come out now. The sirens are all gone."

"Ehmmm . . ."

I blinked back tears.

"Izz . . ."

I sniffed. "I miss her too, buddy. I'm sorry. I'm so, so sorry."

BRONSON CHASED AFTER MORGAN, MRS. DAVIS TIGHT ON HIS heels. They entered the bed and breakfast, cool air washing over them.

"Morgan?"

"In here."

They walked down the hall to the laundry room. When Bronson saw the large pile on the floor, he could have kicked himself. He'd checked this room but hadn't thought to check beneath the pile of sheets since it hadn't looked all that different from when he'd thrown them here the day before.

He peeled back the pile to see a sobbing Morgan with her arms around Marcus.

"Izz . . ." Marcus was saying.

Mrs. Davis's hand flew to her mouth.

"She loved you so much, Marcus." Morgan sniffed between her tears, giving Marcus one last squeeze. "Look who's here?" She nudged him. When he saw his mother, he climbed up and hugged her.

Mrs. Davis closed her eyes, clutching her son tight. "Let's go home, baby."

"Mrs. Davis . . ." Morgan scrambled to stand.

The older woman stared, her face void of emotion.

"I am so sorry," Morgan whispered.

Mrs. Davis tugged Marcus toward the door.

"Ehmmmm!" he yelled, but Mrs. Davis's didn't stop.

Morgan said nothing, didn't even look at him as she skirted him to look out the window. He came up beside her, practically numb as he watched Mrs. Davis speak to the fire chief, no doubt reporting that they'd found her son. Once everyone walked out of sight, Morgan hung her head.

"Bronson, I'm so sorry."

His chest deflated as the tragedy of the day sank in. How could something like this have happened? What might have happened, all on his watch. At his camp! "How could a fire have even started? Weren't you watching? Where were you?"

"Where . . ." She bit her lip. "I split the group up to check for pests. I went with the girls and left the boys alone. . ."

He dug his hands into his hair. No parents would allow their kids to attend his camp after word got out that a fire started on his watch. No campers would sign up after a child had gone missing. His apple-picking business would have to wait another season, maybe more since he hadn't enough in savings for a replacement tractor. All he'd worked for had been crushed.

Maybe he was better off forgetting the entire thing. Better to simply pay Aunt Pris and Mr. Colton back what they'd given him and get out on his own. Away from this blasted bed and breakfast that had nearly sucked the life out of him. Away from needy guests and kids he'd poured himself into only to find that they didn't give a darn about him or the things he cared about.

He turned to Morgan, her eyes still wet—glistening and beautiful despite the redness of her face.

Away from this captivating woman who seemed to find new ways to break his heart every day.

He rubbed the back of his neck, sighed. It didn't matter what Morgan had done or not done—she was the employee, he was the boss. "I don't blame you, Morgan. It's my fault. I tried to take on too much. I didn't plan, didn't prepare, and it blew up in my face."

"The circumstances this week have been impossible."

He nodded, shoulders slumped. What a mess. Was God showing him he wasn't cut out to run a camp after all?

"Things will look better in the morning, right?" Her gaze pleaded with his, but he couldn't find it in his heart to agree.

"I'm going to head to the hospital to check on my mom."

"You should get your hands checked out, too."

He looked down at his palms, raw and blistered from the hot metal hitch of the tractor.

"Can I . . . could I come?" Her tinny voice echoed in the empty bed and breakfast.

He hitched in a ragged breath. That probably wasn't a good idea, he needed time to think, time to berate himself good and proper. "I think I'd like to be alone right now."

He didn't miss the tremble of her bottom lip, and though he hated himself for causing it, neither could he find the gumption to take his words back. If he didn't get away from her, he might say or do something he'd regret forever. Not because he was angry at her so much as he was angry at himself. Angry at the world. Angry at his family. Angry at God.

"Okay. I'll call Paramount and make sure we're still good for the kayaks tomorrow."

He shook his head. "Don't bother. I'm cancelling the camp for the rest of the summer. I'll call parents tonight and let them know. I'll make sure they're reimbursed, and you'll be paid for everything I owe you."

A tear crept out of the corner of her eye and down her cheek. "Bronson, you don't owe me anything."

He sniffed, swiped an arm below his nose, and grabbed his keys from the hook by the door before walking toward his truck without looking back.

$$\text{❦}\quad 3\,2\quad\text{❦}$$

I didn't bother to stop the flow of my tears as I packed my suitcase in the apartment above the bookshop. What did it matter? No one was here to see. Not the kids or their parents, not Hannah or Aunt Pris or Amie or Lizzie or any other members of the Martin family I'd come to love over the past several months.

And most certainly, not Bronson.

A fresh wave of tears spilled from my eyes and onto the copy of *Little Men* I packed at the top of my suitcase. I'd purchased it from Josie's bookshop, certain I could see Bronson's vision for the camp in how Jo March and her Professor Bhaer related to their "kids." I'd been foolish to think that a story as satisfying as theirs could unfold in our lives. In *my* life.

I had proven long ago that happy endings were not in the stars for me. I'd been a fool to think otherwise, to believe my future could be different.

After I packed what little possessions I owned in my suitcase, I looked around the stark apartment. I would miss it. I'd loved these few rooms that I'd come to think of as mine—rooms above the bookshop with the orchard view.

But it was time to leave. Bronson had made it clear, and really, it was better this way. I wouldn't have the opportunity to hurt anyone else. I wouldn't have to see Bronson every day and be reminded of what almost was.

For the millionth time that afternoon, I scolded myself for leaving the boys alone. Perhaps what happened was my punishment for entertaining a future where I broke free from my guilt.

I dug out my cell phone and dialed Jenna's number.

"Hey! Didn't expect to hear from you this time of day. Don't you have a camp to run with that gorgeous guy you insist you're not interested in?"

Her words, words that would normally make me laugh, caused a sob to clamp over my throat.

"Morgan? What's the matter?" Her question came out more like a statement, a demand that I tell her what had caused me grief.

"I'm okay. Everyone's okay." I turned my mouth away from the phone in an attempt to muffle the sob that broke loose. A sob that testified to the truth.

I was not okay. Everything was not okay. Bronson, Hannah, and even Aunt Pris were at the hospital. Amie was still sick in bed. The camp was ruined. The apple-picking business was closed for the foreseeable future. The bed and breakfast had no one to run it.

My thoughts slowed at that last thought. I was the only one here. And while I didn't have a clue about making breakfast or booking rooms, I could make the beds, clean, and do the dishes.

But would my help even be welcome at this point? Did it matter? Guests shouldn't be made to fend for themselves.

"Hold on, I'll be over in a jiffy."

"No, Jenna. I'm actually wondering if I could stay with you a few days . . ."

I didn't have a plan. Jenna and Amelia were the two big reasons I'd come back to Camden. Could I leave behind my family, the niece I already loved so much, the mother I'd just reconciled with?

"Of course, honey. You know you're always welcome. Come on over and I'll fix us some tea and zucchini bread. With cream cheese, just the way you like it. We'll talk this all out. It'll be okay."

The thought of sitting on Jenna's shady patio with a slice of zucchini bread and Amelia in her high chair beside us, calmed my nerves already.

"Thank you. I won't be a burden, I promise. I'll help out and babysit and—"

"Morgan, are you kidding? I'm starving for adult conversation over here. Really, you'd be doing me a favor."

I laughed through my now-drying tears. "Okay. Thank you. I'll be over later, I have a few things to take care of."

I hung up the phone and dragged in a deep breath. Bronson might not want me around any longer, but Hannah would appreciate clean guest rooms and a clean kitchen, even if Bronson closed the bed and breakfast while she recovered. I loved this family and would perform this one last act of service in a pitiful attempt to show my gratitude.

33

To say I was surprised Daniel asked me to meet him in the courtyard amphitheater behind the library a week after the fire was an understatement.

In my mind, I was done with the camp, done with the kids. They were all better off with me being out of the picture.

I hoped he'd gotten the okay from his grandmother to meet me. I still didn't know how the camp parents felt after last week's events, and Bronson hadn't updated me.

I assumed he'd reimbursed the parents who'd paid for camp, but again, I didn't know. I'd been written out of Bronson's life as easily as I'd been written in, it seemed.

While I'd been enjoying my stay with Jenna, her already small house began to feel cramped. I needed to make a decision—find another place in Camden and continue searching for any job I could find or search through the school district job postings for anything still open in the state of Maine.

Out of the corner of my eye, a figure approached, walking a bike in my direction. I stood.

"Hello, Daniel." I forced a smile, and it seemed to mirror his own.

"Thanks for meeting me, Miss Morgan." He let his bike fall to the ground and shoved his hands in his pockets, scuffing the toe of his boot in the grass.

"Does your grandmother know you came to see me?"

He nodded. "She's okay with it. Especially since . . ." He cleared his throat and looked out in the direction of Curtis Island. With fondness, I remembered our kayak trips around the island, Ned's antics the first time we'd gone out.

"Since?" I asked.

"It was me."

My stomach grew nauseous, afraid for the words that might follow.

Daniel scrunched his face up, as if it pained him to speak. "I brought some cigarettes I wanted to share with Cameron, only I lost my lighter. While the others looked at the trees like you told us to, I took Cameron back to help me find it. It must have fallen out of my pocket on the drive up."

Sour bile filled the back of my throat, but I kept silent, waiting for more.

"I lit up right there in the trailer, but Cameron tried to stop me. I dropped the cigarette when he grabbed my lighter and then I punched him. We didn't realize the hay caught on fire until it was too late."

The news didn't surprise me exactly. But I hadn't expected it to be one of the kids who'd been with us all summer—who we'd poured our hearts and souls into day after day.

And right after I'd told them my own cautionary tale, no less.

Now, it made sense why Daniel had fought the flames with such vehemence. Not simply because he cared about the orchards, but because he had started the fire in the first place.

I rubbed the bridge of my nose.

"I'm sorry, Miss Morgan. I'm so sorry. I want to fix it though. I plan to work any job I can get until I pay Mr. Martin back for the tractor and trailer. I'll work at Orchard House for the rest of my life. I promise I will. Please say you'll convince Mr. Martin to let me work for him when I get out."

The desperation in his eyes haunted me for its familiarity. I understood him in that moment, understood the want and need to make amends. For that's what had driven me in so many of my own decisions since Isabel died. I'd attempted to chain myself to her for all of time, just as Daniel wanted to chain himself to the Orchard House.

He straightened, mouth firm. "I'm going to the police right now to turn myself in, but I wanted to let you and Mr. Martin know I was sorry first."

My heart went out to the boy. I swallowed, unable to resist asking. "Did you speak to Mr. Martin?"

Daniel shook his head. "Miss Amie said he's on a camping trip."

The news soothed a raw part inside me. Maybe Bronson hadn't tried to contact me because he was away. Somewhere without cell service.

I sat back on one of the steps of the amphitheater and gestured for Daniel to sit beside me. He did so, hesitantly.

"Daniel, second chances are only as good as our intentions."

I could see Daniel's heart, the good he coveted for himself. And yet I saw his struggle as well. The Martins would claim we needed help from Someone bigger than ourselves to win such a battle as this. I was beginning to think they were right.

Daniel stared at me, a blank expression on his face.

"I mean, I don't want you getting locked up." I smiled. "I can tell you're sorry, and I'm sure Mr. Martin will, too. But if you haven't learned anything from your mistakes, they will have been for nothing. What have you learned?"

The boy swallowed, staring at the ground as he hung his hands over his outspread knees. "That I need to think before I do stupid stuff. That my actions have consequences. Both the bad stuff I do, and maybe the good stuff too."

I dragged in a great breath, considering my own journey learning this very lesson. But I liked Daniel's spin on it—not only did the bad actions have the propensity to spiral and grow, but perhaps the good did as well.

"I think that's a good lesson, Daniel." I smiled, remembering Bronson's words to me. "Someone once told me our bravest and best lessons are not learned through success, but through our failures."

He nodded solemnly, but we sat in silence for a moment before he became incredibly fidgety. "But I have to do something to make it right, you know? It's like this feeling inside me that won't get quiet until I do something. Even go to jail."

Oh boy, did I know.

"Remember I told you about what happened when I was in high school? About my best friend?"

He nodded.

"I've felt the same way since she died. That loud noise you're talking about. Wanting to do something to right past wrongs, to make up for them."

"What'd you do?"

I sighed leaned back on my hands. "Tried to make myself miserable, I guess. Tried not to enjoy life too much."

His face scrunched. "Did it work?"

I let out a sad, sarcastic laugh. "Not yet."

"You think it ever will? Like when you're old?"

"I used to think so. Now, I'm not so sure."

A moment of silence overtook us before I finally spoke. Slowly, at first. Tentatively. "Maybe if we both work to do something good instead of punishing ourselves, that might work?"

He smiled. "Maybe."

Sudden hope latched onto my chest. I tapped my chin. "I wonder . . ."

"What?"

"I wonder if it's possible for us to help Mr. Martin still open his apple-picking business."

Daniel straightened. "I've been talking to Tommy. He has his grandfather's old tractor in his barn. Him and his dad got it up and running. He wanted to let Mr. Martin use it until he could buy another one."

A lump of emotion lodged in my throat. "Really?"

He nodded.

I licked my lips, my mind racing. "Do you think we could build another trailer?"

"All we'd need is some pallet wood, and I think Ned's dad has plenty. I think the frame and wheels are still good." The boys' eyes lit, igniting excitement of my own. "We could do it, Miss Morgan."

I didn't question his surety. Instead, I spent the rest of the afternoon making phone calls and plans. The next day, I drove up the driveway of the bed and breakfast, smiling at the sight of Tommy's father backing an old tractor off a trailer, Ned's father directing him. Beside them stood Daniel, Daisy, Anna, and Cameron.

I got out of my car, gushing my thanks to Tommy's father. He lifted his ball cap slightly before placing it back on his head. "It was just sitting in the garage, gathering dust. It was my dad's, but I don't have much use for it." He looked at his son. "This orchard business means a lot to Tommy, and to the rest of the kids too, I think. I hope you all will accept it as a gift."

I blinked back tears. "That's beyond generous, sir."

Ned pointed to the back of his father's pickup, full of wood. "And my dad's going to help us build the trailer!"

I clapped my hands together, my excitement growing. We *could* do this. "Okay! It seems we have a business opening to prepare for."

Hannah had told me on the phone that Bronson would be

home in two days. If we could get the trailer built, stock the stand, and maybe call the local newspaper, we might be ready for business by the weekend.

❧ 34 ☙

Bronson pulled himself up an iron rung that served as a ladder to help climbers navigate the Precipice Trail in Acadia National Park. His still-tender palms were slicked with sweat, and he wiped his right hand on his shorts before taking the next step. Once on firm ground, he swiped his wet temples with the back of his hand. He leaned over his knees, taking in the panoramic view of Frenchman Bay, the Porcupine Islands covered in thin clouds in the distance.

He closed his eyes and breathed deep, inhaling the scent of pine and dirt and salt and sea. The vastness of Acadia never ceased to amaze him. While growing up, his family had taken frequent camping trips here to visit Charlotte, a friend of the family's who owned The Beacon Bed and Breakfast—the very bed and breakfast that had sparked Mom's own dream for an inn.

But over the years, Bronson hadn't visited Acadia often enough. He'd been too intent on school, too intent on his future. Now, he was here to clear his head. Rethink things. Rethink his whole life.

He navigated a few boulders before reaching another set of iron rungs. The trail lay surprisingly clear this morning, leaving him with plenty of room for thoughts. As always, they strayed back to Camden.

Despite his intention to temporarily shut down the bed and breakfast last week, things had managed to right themselves before they'd had to cancel anyone's reservations. He'd come home from the hospital with Mom and Aunt Pris Tuesday afternoon to see beds made, rooms cleaned, and dishes done. Shortly after, Amie had stumbled out of her deathbed and Maggie had popped in to help, saying Josh was tending the boys.

By the end of the week, Asher and Lizzie had returned from their honeymoon, sporting new tans and sparkling eyes, and Josie was gushing about her book tour . . . and news of a baby to be born in the spring.

Despite everyone showing up and rallying around Mom, Morgan had disappeared. Up and gone. He'd memorized the note she'd left on the kitchen bar.

Thank you for everything. I'm going to be staying at my sister's awhile. Please feel free to rent the apartment to another tenant.

So businesslike and distant. When he'd first read it, he'd immediately hopped into his truck and headed south to the town Morgan had mentioned Jenna lived in. He'd intended to find her and bring her back. Tell her there was no reason to leave, apologize for how he'd acted the day of the fire, reiterate that he didn't blame her for any of it. Grovel.

Whatever it took to get her back in his life. What would he do without her and the camp?

He'd driven down Route 1 for fifteen minutes before he realized the desperation that drove him.

More than desperation. Almost the feeling that, without Morgan, without the camp, his life was meaningless.

He'd pulled into a shopping plaza, turned his radio off, and left his truck idling.

The camp and Morgan had become his everything. With their loss, despair had nearly overwhelmed him. He'd run after her without thought, believing Morgan alone could help him figure out what to do next, when in reality, that job belonged to God. He'd panicked at the thought of losing her despite the fact she'd told him more than once that she wasn't interested in a relationship.

He'd run after her instead of turning to God.

That's when he'd decided to seek out some quiet time to sort things out. To sort *himself* out. Just him and God in the midst of nature.

He'd booked a vacant camping spot on Mount Desert Island, dug around in the basement for the old family camping tent, packed a hiking bag and some simple food, and was gone before anyone could ask him to fetch towels or shingle a roof or stuff baby shower invitations or fold toilet paper rolls to a point.

Out in the wild of nature, soaking in the vastness of its beauty, the rugged terrain and infinite ocean, he got quiet and examined his heart. He'd lain beneath the Milky Way on Sand Beach, had lobster and beer down in Bar Harbor, read his Bible late into the night, and whispered more words of prayer than he had all year.

He'd confessed his shortcomings to God, and that peace of knowing the Creator of the universe cared and forgave washed over him little by little while he climbed the Otter Cliffs, observed the seals and puffins, took amazing pictures of Bass Harbor Lighthouse at sunset.

Basking in that peace, Bronson had tried to let Morgan go, yet thoughts of her just wouldn't go away. At one point, he'd scrolled to her name on his phone, had almost pressed the big green call circle.

In a particularly crazy moment, he imagined driving to her sister's and stealing her away so they could finish this adventure together.

But the trip would take on a different feel if she were there, for Morgan didn't see God in the universe or the Milky Way. She wouldn't pray with him or pore over the words in scripture with him.

As much as it pained him, they weren't on the same page. Morgan had been right, after all—they weren't meant for each other.

He reached the top of the ledge and began a short traverse upward on relatively stable ground. His thoughts turned back to his orchard camp, and he swallowed down the taste of sour bile in the back of his throat.

He'd believed they'd been doing something great—not only with the camp and the kids, but with the resurrection of Aunt Pris's childhood orchard business. Instead, he started something he wasn't quite sure he had a right to finish.

Was this how his father felt each time he failed at one of his own startup ventures? The soup kitchen, grief counseling, an annual charity ball for the historical committee that faded off after they'd skipped one too many years. Besides their family, the mission was the only lasting thing his father had built, and that was because he'd given the running of it over to someone more capable.

Maybe managing a successful business simply wasn't in God's plan for Bronson. Maybe he needed to stick to teaching at the public school and managing the grounds of Orchard House. His dreams had been too big to begin with, too unrealistic and without enough forethought. He hadn't even been able to afford it, had to bum money off his great aunt and her boyfriend. Just more people to whom he owed money.

He approached a steep ledge, scoping out the hundred foot-plus vertical drop to the right, straight down to a cropping of rocks and dirt. Gripping the iron bars with his left hand, he moved along the precipice, surprised at how hard his heart beat against his chest. This was nothing. After climbing Otter Cliffs? After shingling Josie and Tripp's roof without anything to hold onto but his own toolbelt? Nothing.

Halfway across, irrational anxiety overtook him. He tried to shake it off, but like a dog intent on grabbing a meaty bone, it wouldn't release him.

The ground swayed before him, and he considered backing up the way he'd come, but the distance to finish loomed less than the length to backtrack.

Even now, as his sweaty palms gripped the strongholds, he knew the anxiety wasn't simply about the hike.

It was about his failure. He was the fixer, the one always rushing to mend the problems. Whether it be a flat tire, saving a kid from military camp, taking in strays . . . or trying to save the woman he loved from the guilt of her own past.

He'd been so certain he could make a difference in the lives of those he'd invested in. But last week had proven him wrong. Maybe succeeding at dreams wasn't for people like him and his dad. Maybe success was for Josie and Lizzie and his Mom. Maybe even Amie. Maybe the Martin men were simply a cursed bunch. Maybe, like his dad, he'd die young from a failed heart, a heart that strove after the impossible.

Another bout of dizziness, this time accompanied by nausea, overwhelmed him. He slid his arm into one of the iron rungs and clutched tight with the press of his elbow, forcing his face against the warm rock of the cliff wall. He breathed deep, praying for deliverance. Praying that he not pass out and fall to his death.

He stayed that way, forcing breaths in through his nose and out through his mouth. Though he felt like a wimp, clutching the side of the rock, he refused to release his grip. He breathed deep around the nausea, praying for its release.

Without warning, a memory came to him. A time out in the woods with his father when he was small. Smaller than Davey and Isaac, even. Bronson had been frightened of snakes creeping out onto the path, as they sometimes did. His dad had scooped him up in his arms and swung him onto his shoulders.

"I'll carry you for a little bit, son."

Bronson had clutched his father's wavy, slightly graying hair. "I don't want to ever get down, Dad."

"Bronson, have you ever been bitten by a snake?"

"No."

"Do you know of anyone who has ever gotten bit by a snake?"

"I guess not. At least, not outside of books."

"Do you know there are no poisonous snakes in Maine? None at all."

"I didn't know that."

"We fear what we don't know. We fear what hasn't yet proven itself as truth. It's a waste of time, that fear. It robs us of enjoying what's right in front of us." He gestured to the thick forest, vibrant and green around them. "Best give that fear over to God and be done with it. And don't forget, I am with you."

Bronson had taken the advice to heart. When his father lowered him to the ground, he'd picked out tentative, cautious steps. And he hadn't been bitten by a snake. In fact, he didn't even see a snake for the rest of the hike. But even if he had, it wouldn't have been unbearable, because his father was with him.

Now, Bronson bit down hard on his bottom lip. Why'd Dad have to go and leave him? Leave all of them? Bronson was beginning his adult life after he'd not only lost his father but had taken on a boatload of responsibility when it came to his mother and sisters. Not that anyone had asked it of him. Or expected it. He'd done that all on his own.

I am with you.

His father's words echoed inside of him, welling up from someplace deep. Over and over again, the words repeated until they became the voice of another. Not his earthly father, but his heavenly one.

Gradually, the nausea released its hold, and after a few minutes, he opened his eyes to find the rock no longer swayed. He relaxed the muscles in his arms, glancing at the ledge in front of him. One step at a time, he inched his way to the other side.

Once on firm ground, he collapsed beside a rock beneath a tree and took a long swig of his water. He'd never tasted anything so wonderful.

He gulped it, rinsing his mouth and swallowing it down. What had happened on that cliff? He'd never been struck by such an overwhelming emotion. Never felt so incredibly grateful to simply be alive.

He rose, cautious at first, and continued the trek up the rest of the cliff, his movements certain, his arms pulling him up the iron rungs, his legs traversing the rock with surety, clarity overtaking his brain where cloudiness had consumed him on the ledge.

With each breath, he knew an overwhelming gratitude for life. For the grace God showed him every day as he worked and laughed and loved. For the opportunity to do it all alongside a kick-butt family. Camp or no camp. Business or no business.

He thought of Morgan, and then he thought of his father.

His dad's life hadn't been wasted. He'd lived it to the fullest, and although he might not have succeeded at much, he did succeed at the most important thing of all.

Love.

Though it wasn't wise to push Morgan romantically, that didn't mean Bronson couldn't love her. His father used to say that love was willing the good of another.

He could do that for Morgan, will her good without worrying what he might get out of it.

Love was what counted, and that's what Bronson would attempt to live out, starting this very day.

"Is that even?" I called to Daisy as she backed up a few paces from the stand.

"A little higher. Higher, higher. There!"

I stuck a nail in the corner hole of the banner and gently hammered it into the wood of our stand before climbing down and surveying our work. *Orchard House Apple Picking*, it read.

On the counters behind the stand were candy apples, mini homemade pies, apple doughnuts, apple jelly, apple sauce, and apple cider along with recipe cards for each Amie had printed out to include in the bags of apples. Some of the treats had been preserved from our batches over the summer. The rest Hannah had helped me and Daisy with from her seat at the kitchen bar.

"It looks great!" I clapped my hands together. "And you put the tickets in the register?"

Daisy nodded. "We have tons, so I hope they sell."

"They should with that amazing article printed this morning." The reporter I'd spoken to had listened to the story about the fire and the delay of the apple-picking business. She'd written a lovely piece about beauty coming from ashes. My mother had called me up in tears, saying she was telling all her friends about the business. No doubt the article would touch other hearts as it had mine.

"Mr. Martin will be surprised, won't he?"

I looked to the boys stacking hay on the new trailer, Anna polishing the hood of the tractor, and Aunt Pris and Mr. Colton sitting in the shade of the back patio.

Bronson *would* be happy when he came home the next day, wouldn't he?

"Look! It's Marcus."

I turned at Daisy's words, dread clenching my stomach. I swallowed, offering the most tentative of smiles as Mrs. Davis and Marcus climbed out of the car. Marcus ran to the trailer, clapping his hands in excitement. Cameron helped him climb into the tractor, cautioning him not to fall off the sides.

Mrs. Davis approached me.

My bottom lip trembled. "Hello," I squeaked out. "Bronson's away—he should be back tomorrow afternoon."

Mrs. Davis gave me a tight smile. "If it's okay, I'd like to talk to you, Morgan."

Something about the way she said my name caused hope to sprout in my chest. She hadn't called me by name since before Isabel's death. It was as if I'd been undeserving of a name after that, undeserving of a kind look, a moment of her time.

And hadn't I been?

"Okay." I turned to Daisy. "Why don't you check on that pan of apple crisp in Miss Hannah's oven?"

Daisy ran off, and Mrs. Davis shifted from one foot to the other.

She opened her mouth, then closed it before trying again. "I've been angry for a long time."

"I can understand why, Mrs. Davis. You have every right—"

She held up her hand. "Now, just let me say my piece."

I clamped my lips shut, nodded.

"I've been angry—not just at you, but at God, at myself, and even at Isabel. I shouldn't have slapped you the other day—that was inexcusable, and I'm so sorry for it."

I wanted to say something, to reach out to her, but I could see how each word cost her something, how each syllable was a hard-fought battle.

"Isabel was unhappy. I knew it, and I ignored it. I didn't do anything about it. When you testified in court to her drinking, too, to her having that small bottle of alcohol hidden away, I hated you for it. Not just because you were the one driving that night, but because it made me face what I knew deep down." A small sob broke through, but the sunglasses perched on her nose hid her eyes.

"She tried to talk to me, and I insisted her father and I knew best. Following through on that basketball scholarship seemed like the obvious path for her. I thought she'd get over her upset and move on once September came. But I was wrong, Morgan. She needed help. Help I didn't give her. Instead, we stuck to our plans. Our rules. Our curfews."

I closed my eyes. "She was my best friend, and I didn't realize until that night how off things were. I'm sure you did what you could."

"I didn't. Just like you didn't. We both made mistakes. Mistakes that cost my baby girl her life. But the other day . . . when you found Marcus, he said Isabel's name. It was the first time I'd heard him say it all these years. Eight long, hard years. We didn't talk about her enough after she passed. Mom always said it wasn't healthy. But I didn't realize it until the other day. We need to talk about her. *I* need to talk about her."

A tear crept out of the corner of my eye. "She was a beautiful person, inside and out. Mrs. Davis, I'm so sorry. I wish a hundred times a day that I hadn't gotten behind the wheel of that car. I wish I had called you or my parents."

Isabel's mother sniffed. "I know. And I'm tired of being angry at you for it. I don't think it's honoring to Isabel, and I don't think it's doing either of us any good."

It wasn't forgiveness exactly, but it was something. Acknowledgment. A little grace.

It was enough.

I searched for words but couldn't find any.

"I can see how you tote around my daughter's death, Morgan. You've lost your passion for life, your spunk. I understand because I have too. But let's agree to find it again, for Isabel's sake." She breathed in a long inhale, let it out slow. "After I hit you the other day, I realized how hard my heart has been when it came to you. I can't live an angry life anymore. It's eating me alive. Eating up my marriage, my relationship with my son, even. I'm done. And I want you to live the life Isabel would have wanted you to live, too. Will you do that?"

She didn't know it, but here and now, Mrs. Davis offered me freedom. This past summer, I'd sensed guilt wasn't my path forward. Would I be able to release it now, with Mrs. Davis's permission?

I swiped at my tears. "I'd like that very much, Mrs. Davis."

She looked around at the apple stand, the kids near the tractor and trailer, Marcus laughing at a small hay fight between Ned and Anna, and then at the orchards beyond.

"I'd say this place is a good start," she said.

I remembered then the history Isabel's family had with the orchard. Perhaps this truly was a place of redemption.

"If Bronson's agreeable to it, we're hoping to go ahead with the opening of the orchards for apple picking this weekend. I hope you and Marcus will come."

Mrs. Davis smiled. "Mom would love to see this place running again. I'm sure we'll stop in."

I placed a hand on her arm, remembering a blur of memories from my childhood. Mrs. Davis making us jambalaya or Mickey Mouse pancakes on the griddle. Helping us out of our muddy clothes after a fun day out in the rain, bringing us to the library and patiently waiting for us while we agonized over which books to check out. "Thank you."

She sighed, and nodded, squeezing my hand. Without thinking, I threw my arms around the woman. I counted the fact that she didn't draw back a victory.

❦

I watched Mrs. Davis as she left my side to attend Marcus. While I couldn't deny the relief that came with her words, a niggling part of me wondered what going forward might look like. For so long, I'd sought the Davis family's forgiveness. Now that I had it, would I finally be able to forgive myself?

It still didn't feel right, and yet, I wanted to shed the guilt —desperately.

With the help of her crutches, Hannah turned from the apple stand and started in my direction. I met her halfway.

"Hey, honey. How are you holding up?" She smiled, its warmth like that of homemade apple pie.

I gestured to her crutches, ignoring her question. She didn't need my burdens piled on top of hers. "You're really getting the hang of those, aren't you?"

She laughed. "I guess so."

"Thanks for all your help with the baked goods."

"The place looks amazing. Bronson will be so pleased." She reached out to me, peering up into my eyes. "Are you all right?"

We stood in silence for a moment before I shrugged and looked away. "Mrs. Davis just forgave me. Well, pretty much anyway."

"Oh, Morgan. I'm so glad."

"Me too." I scuffed the driveway with my sneakered foot. "Only I guess I thought that would take away the pain, you know?

But maybe it's just going to hurt forever. Maybe I'll never be able to forgive myself."

Hannah shifted on her crutches. "Maybe that feeling inside you is your heart longing for more than just forgiveness from Mrs. Davis, or even yourself."

"More?"

"From God, Morgan. He can set you free." She spoke so gently, I felt nothing but love and kindness in her words.

"But how?"

"By falling into His arms. By giving Christ all of your past, present, and future. Even the most painful parts."

My mind flashed to the night of Isabel's death.

"Bronson said something similar once. I guess, I just don't know if I believe that it's possible."

"How about we head in and I make us some tea?"

I nodded, sensing a draw toward whatever Hannah might share with me. I followed her into Orchard House, a bit nervous, a bit excited. If God could forgive me, I'd do whatever it took. I wanted what she had. What Bronson had. What Lizzie had. I wanted to believe forgiveness. I wanted to believe I was loved no matter what, as the reverend at Lizzie's wedding had said.

Was it possible to find true freedom?

❦ 36 ❦

Bronson turned into the Orchard House drive, taking in the sight of the apple trees, ready for picking. He felt like George Bailey in *It's a Wonderful Life*. Things that had seemed burdensome before he left had taken on new life.

Hello, Camden!

Merry Christmas, library!

Merry Christmas, apple trees!

Merry Christmas, you wonderful bed and breakfast!

Merry Christmas, you burned-down trailer and tractor!

Only it wasn't Christmas—it was late summer, apple-picking season.

A twist of longing for what almost was threatened to stomp down his joy. And yet, he realized, it wasn't simply the apple-picking venture and camp, it was carrying it out with those he'd come to care about. With the kids. With Morgan.

People. Relationships. His family. God. When it came down to it, through the thick mess he'd managed to make, that's what mattered above all else.

He pressed the gas harder up the slight incline of the driveway.

He glimpsed Amie first, wearing a ballcap and standing in front of an easel, Marcus—was it really Marcus?—at her side.

Then the apple stand, complete with the banner they'd ordered. But why had Amie set it up when the business was shot, at least for this year?

And then, although his brain couldn't make sense of it, he saw the kids surrounding a new trailer and slightly rusted tractor. Stacking hay, laughing . . . He blinked. But no, it was real. And there was Daisy bringing a baking pan from the bed and breakfast over to the apple stand.

What the blazes was going on?

Amie caught sight of him and seemed to call to the rest of the group, waving her paintbrush in the air. The kids scurried in circles, some of them jumping up and down around the trailer. Adults stood in the background. Mrs. Davis? Mr. Abbendroth? Tommy's dad? He caught a glimpse of red hair and his heart leapt.

Morgan.

Dazed, he pushed open the door of his truck and practically stumbled toward them.

"Surprise!" the group yelled.

"What . . . what is all this?"

"It's the opening of Orchard House Apple Picking!" shouted Daisy.

Bronson gestured to the tractor and trailer. "How . . .?"

"We built the trailer." Ned puffed out his chest. "My dad helped."

"And the tractor's from Tommy." Anna gestured to the red beast. "Isn't she a beauty? Just needs a coat of paint, but she's running great."

Bronson stared at Anna. "A beauty . . ." He shook his head. "I can't accept this. Thank you, Tommy, but it's too much."

Tommy's father stepped forward. "With all due respect, Mr. Martin, these kids have worked hard all summer to see this place up and running. This tractor's been getting no use in my barn.

The way I figure it, we help each other out and let these kids help you get things going. All of this was their idea. Well, theirs and Miss Dalton's. I just got on board."

Bronson looked around the group, immense affection mounting inside of him. They'd done all this without him.

His throat grew tight. All this time, he'd wondered if he'd made a difference in any of their lives—well, here . . . here was his answer. An answer he didn't quite expect. For not only had this camp made a lasting impression on these kids, the kids had imprinted their hearts on his very soul as well.

Daniel stepped forward. "It was me, Mr. Martin. I had a cigarette in the trailer. I'm sorry. Super sorry. I'll work for you every season for the rest of my life to make up for it."

Bronson laid a hand on Daniel's shoulder. "It sounds as if you've learned your lesson."

"I have, sir. And I feel terrible. I'm prepared to work until I save enough money for a new tractor."

Bronson glanced at Tommy's father. "Seems we won't be needing a new tractor quite yet, Daniel."

"I need to do something though. I'll go crazy if you don't let me."

"If you promise to never smoke again, that'll be enough for me," Bronson said.

Daniel's face scrunched. "That's it?"

"And then I want you to accept that you're forgiven. By me, by God, and I think, judging from your peers here, your classmates as well."

The group nodded.

"Okay . . ." Daniel said, not sounding certain. He glanced at Morgan, who nodded encouragement. He smiled. "Okay. Now, can we test out the tractor?"

Bronson turned to Tommy's father. "Would you mind taking them up to the orchard, sir? There's some business I need to take care of here first."

"Be glad to."

"Ned, why don't you grab some apple bags. Let your parents take as much as they want."

The kids and parents climbed into the trailer. Even Amie wriggled on, Daniel turning crimson when she sat beside him.

"Hope this can hold." Daisy clutched the side and Ned's father stood on the step at the end, blocking the exit so no one would tumble out.

"Ready?" Tommy's father started the tractor, and when it chugged away, hauling the load with little effort, everyone cheered.

Bronson turned to find only Morgan left, standing beside him.

"You . . ." he said.

She smiled, a gorgeous smile that caused his insides to turn to mush. With much effort, he restrained himself from enfolding her in his arms.

"I missed you," she said.

He stopped himself from placing his hands on the side of her face, from reaching out and touching her. "Morgan, I'm sorry for getting angry at you the day of the fire. When I was camping, as beautiful as it was, I couldn't help wishing you were there with me. I'm not mad at you—I want to make sure you know that."

She cocked her head.

"But you were right to keep your distance. I realized some things up north. I realized I wasn't loving you—not in the best way I know how, anyway."

She blinked, those green jewels shining up at him. "Bronson, there's something you should know."

He braced himself. Whatever it was, he could take it. Whatever it was, he'd try like the dickens to see her how God saw her.

Precious. Loved.

"I spoke to your mom yesterday."

His mom?

"We had a really amazing conversation and she helped me pray for forgiveness, Bronson. From the One I really needed forgiveness from. Not Mrs. Davis, not even myself . . ."

She stopped to take a breath, but her words kept replaying in his head. Such wonderful words.

"I don't know if I won't ever again feel like I don't deserve good things, but I know God released me. I know punishing myself won't change anything. I feel . . . light. Free."

Her words were the most magnificent music his ears had ever heard.

He uttered a silent prayer of gratitude, marveling at how God had worked in both of them these last few days. He'd used the ashes of Bronson's dreams to bring about something far more important than he'd ever dreamed for this camp.

Maybe even more than he'd hoped for only minutes ago.

"I love you, Morgan."

"And I love you, Bronson."

The words unlocked a key inside of him, sprouting wings in the center of his chest. Just when he'd resigned himself to giving her up, God blessed him with more than he'd asked for.

She came to him, then, and he inhaled the scent of apples and her lavender shampoo as he held her tight. There'd been a reason she'd felt so right in his arms.

"Well, aren't you going to kiss me already?" she asked.

The corner of his mouth twitched. "Oh, you want to be kissed?"

She tiptoed up until her lips met his in a kiss that whispered of dreams yet to come true and hopes on the horizon.

And it was theirs for the picking.

Read on for a glimpse of Amie's story, coming January, 2023!

WHERE FAITH BELONGS

Chapter One

Despite what my family says, I am, in fact, an understanding person.

Yes, I have opinions. But I like to think that simply means I have good taste.

That's it, that's what I am. A person with good taste.

A person who tries to understand why my older sister insists on wearing open-toed shoes without first polishing her toenails. A person who tries to understand how anyone could watch *The Notebook* without bawling their eyes out. How my brother can sleep at night knowing he didn't floss that day. How *anyone* could dismiss yoga without even trying it.

All these things and more, I try to understand.

But I will never—ever—understand what I've just seen on this crisp, sunny first day of May. I grappled with it. I abhorred it.

I am *appalled* by it.

I blinked, staring out the window of my old Jeep Wrangler. Surely, this would not take place in Camden, in broad daylight, in the Hannaford parking lot.

But no, I wasn't mistaken—the evidence lay on the ground in all of its coffee-stained, Styrofoam glory.

The driver of the black Ford truck parked haphazardly between two yellow lines had committed an inexcusable offense, punishable by at least a five-hundred dollar fine.

Littering.

And this wasn't any kind of littering. This was so much more than casual, throw-your-paper-napkin-out-your-window-in-the-dead-of-night littering. This was blatant, daylight *Styrofoam* littering.

I pushed open my car door, nearly forgetting my keys in the ignition. No doubt, he thought no one noticed his blatant disregard of nature and civilization. Little did he know, Amie Martin was on the prowl. Amie Martin—short in stature, perhaps having a bit of a bad hair day, but powerful in all things that involved the betterment of humanity.

I threw my shoulders back, the beaded earrings I'd made the night before jangling lightly in my ears. I pushed up the sleeves of my green army jacket and strode across the parking lot to the black truck.

"Excuse me!" I called as I approached.

Nothing.

I continued toward him.

Don't pretend you can't hear me with your window fully down.

By the time I reached the driver's side of the truck, I fumed. Men. Men, and their callousness toward people and relationships and innocent animals and the environment.

"I said, excuse me!"

A head of dirty blond hair turned toward me.

My steps faltered and my mouth grew dry, the fury in my chest changing to shock and, to my horror, a tiny bit of longing.

August Colton grinned at me with twinkling hazel eyes. "Amie."

My name hung in the air between us as his gaze tangled with

mine. I waited for something more. A "You look good," or "It's been too long," or "I've missed seeing you."

All the things I wanted to say to him.

I shook my head, scolding myself for faltering in my mission. Surfer-boy good looks tended to do that to me.

He shoved a box of chicken wings out the window. "Want one?"

I gritted my teeth. "I'm fasting."

His eyebrows rose. "Oh, is that part of your new . . . spiritual explorations?"

I blew out a breath, fanning the hair from my face. "No, it's not part of my *spiritual* explorations." I didn't mean for the words to come out so snappy. It wasn't August's fault my new idea to create a group for those seeking spiritual truth had flopped. Sure, I could have given it more effort. Could have been less *flighty* about it, as Bronson said. But a little support from August wouldn't have killed him.

Who knows, maybe it could have made all the difference.

"Whoa, sorry. So, is everything okay? Are you having a medical procedure done or something?"

A medical procedure? Oh. My face heated as I remembered Mom having to fast and drink some horrible-tasting fluid before having a colonoscopy last year. "I'm fine. Great, really." Great. "Fasting periodically is actually a great way to increase autophagy in your cells."

Autophagy . . . that was the word, right? Or was it autophony? I was forever mixing up words.

"Autophagy?"

"It's your body's way of cleaning out damaged cells to regenerate healthy ones. It's fascinating. You should google it."

"I will."

No, he wouldn't. Since when did he care about anything I thought important?

"You want to sit in my truck?"

It was a pretty truck. Several steps up from the beat-up Chevy he'd driven around in high school.

But no. I hadn't stalked over to play nice.

"You littered."

"What?"

I pointed at the Styrofoam cup, clear as day, on the patch of grass by the curb of his truck. "I saw you. You threw it right out the window without any regard for the birds who might chew it up and choke on it or the people who have to pick it up for you—"

"Amie—"

"You always were selfish though, weren't you August? Never giving a care about what's humane and right. Sauntering through life, worried about your hair and your stupid surfboard and—"

"Amie." My name came out in a near growl, his jaw firm and eyes smoldering as he said it. Without warning, I remembered those smoldering eyes fixed upon me in an entirely different way. I remembered the feel of his hands brushing along my sides, the scent of him all musky and sweet, the taste of his lips on my own.

I blinked, forcing the unbidden—and unwanted—thoughts away. "What?"

"I didn't litter."

I jabbed both hands at the coffee cup on the ground. "Oh, really? What would you call this, then?"

"My worst fear."

I cocked my head to the side, my head spinning. August's worst fear. Shouldn't I know what that is?

"An *empty* coffee cup?" I guessed.

"Come on, Ame, we dated for six months and you don't remember my worst fear?"

I swallowed. Maybe August hadn't been the only one less than invested in our relationship.

I shook my head. "I got nothing."

"Spiders."

My insides twitched. I wasn't much a fan of the eight-legged creatures, myself. I crouched down, cautiously, peering into the cup. Inside, perched at the very bottom, was a hairy black-and-yellow spider with a body the size of a quarter.

I shot up. "Ew!"

"If he didn't crawl out by the time I finished my lunch, I was going to dump him out. Figured it would be the most"—he cleared his throat—"humane thing to do."

My chest deflated. "You weren't littering?"

What did it say about me that I almost wished he had been littering simply so I didn't look so foolish?

"Nope. After I escorted our hairy friend onto bigger and better things than the inside of an old coffee cup, I was going to pick up my trash and be on my way."

I blew out a gust of air, fanning my long blonde bangs out of my face. "Guess I owe you an apology, huh?"

"No worries. I know saying you're sorry has never been your strong suit."

Something tiny but sharp pinched my insides. I racked my brain for what I might owe August an apology for. If anything, he owed *me* an apology for that horrible day we broke things off. He'd accused me of being lofty and selfish, inward-focused and spoiled. He couldn't see I only wanted the best for my family, the best for him, the best for my community, the best for the world, even. At the time, I accused him of being selfish, too, of refusing to see how his actions affected others.

But apparently, he still believed me to be in the wrong. Well, I'd show him I could give an apology.

"August, for what it's worth—I *am* sorry. I shouldn't have stormed over here like the litter brigade."

He raised an eyebrow. "Litter brigade, huh? Is that a thing, because I'd nominate you as president."

I rolled my eyes. "Thanks." Another silent moment passed

between us. "I guess I should get to my shopping. Mom sent me with a list a mile-long."

"How's things going at the good ol' B&B, anyway? Tripp said you all barely got a rest this past winter and things are in full swing again."

I don't know why—or maybe I do—but my gaze can't hold his at the mention of August's older brother. My sister's husband. True, I spent most of my teenage years mooning over the oldest Colton. But that ship had sailed the moment he'd chosen Josie. I was happy for them. *Of course*, I was happy for them. I was not the spoiled, can't-handle-not-getting-my-way youngest Martin child I'd been in elementary school. I loved Tripp like a brother, and that was that.

"We're busy. How about you? Congratulations on graduating, by the way. You going to be some big-shot architect, now?"

"No danger of that working for Grandpops and big brother."

Oh. "You're working for Colton Contractors? I didn't realize that." For some reason, the news niggled at me. I suppose, deep down, I'd wanted bigger things for August. A big city where he would build skyscrapers and bridges, make his mark on the world. Not boring little Camden, where each day looked almost identical to the next. Where one relegated themselves to the good ol' family business.

I swallowed. There was nothing wrong with small towns if that's what one wanted. If that's what *August* wanted. But I didn't have to hunker down and accept the same fate. My life could be different.

I could break free.

"Yeah, I'm happy about it. Grandpops isn't getting any younger and the company needs a good architect."

He'd grown up in the last year. He exuded a confidence and stability he hadn't possessed when we were dating. Something about that drew me at the same time my brain screamed for me to turn and run, fast. Talk about spiders. August was one web I refused to fall back into.

"That's good, August. Real good. I'm happy for you."

"What about you? How's your art selling?"

"It's selling."

Not a lie. My enviro-friendly lampshades sold in the Camden shops faster than I could make them. The problem was, I couldn't make them all that fast. My profit often ended up being less than an hourly minimum-wage. While I'd experimented with a price increase, sales had suffered drastically. Until I could figure out how to make my lamps faster, my profit margin would suffer.

"I actually got accepted to Parsons School of Design." I pushed my hair over my shoulder.

If I could save up enough money for living expenses, that is. While I'd qualified for financial aid, Mom had offered to help how she could, but I had refused. Mom wasn't getting any younger. Not that she was *old*, but she'd started the bed and breakfast only a few years ago. She needed to save for her own future, for the unexpected. I was a fully functioning woman who could provide for herself.

And once I found the perfect summer job, I'd do just that.

"Where's that?" Was I imagining the flash of disappointment in August's eyes?

"New York City. I'll be moving there in the fall."

Nope. Hadn't imagined it. Perhaps I was vain to relish the fact that August obviously still had feelings for me. Perhaps it was selfish and spoiled—all the things he'd accused me of the day we'd broken up—but in that moment, I didn't care. I relished the twinge of satisfaction that I meant something to August Colton after all.

We bid goodbye shortly after, and once I entered the foyer of the grocery store, I peered around to glimpse a last look. My heart swelled at the sight of him crouched low to the ground, gently dumping our eight-legged friend out of his coffee cup with care.

Then, he picked up the Styrofoam and climbed back into his truck. I might have imagined the last look he gave as he surveyed the Hannaford foyer, but I don't think I did.

August had always held a flame for me.

Too bad, in the end, he simply wasn't the man I thought he was.

August Colton pulled out of the Hannaford parking lot with a whole lot more on his mind than chicken nuggets and fries.

After nearly a year of living life Amie Martin-free, he couldn't deny how the encounter they shared shook him up.

Shook him up good.

He'd never been able to resist her—the classic American beauty—that long blonde hair and those blue eyes the color of a clear sky, her feistiness, her honesty, the way she challenged and provoked him. He even missed the way they'd argued. More so, how they'd made up.

He unrolled his window, allowing the cool air to rush over his face. No denying he'd come home with hopes they could start things up again. But was it wise to pursue a girl who'd dumped him once, who was probably still secretly hung up on his big brother, even if she would never admit it?

Amie Martin didn't admit weaknesses.

Neither did she like to admit when she was wrong, either.

His phone rang out on his Bluetooth, and he answered. "Hey, big brother."

"August, where are you? Grandpop is having one of his conniptions, and now that you're on board, I expect you to be here when the ball drops."

August rolled his eyes. "Chill, man. I went to grab some lunch. Isn't that allowed?"

"Not when the secretary's having her first grandchild and my wife is going to birth my own child any minute now."

He groaned. That's right, Eileen had called out that morning, saying her daughter was in labor. Since August had been out visiting customers this morning, he forgot the office was short-handed.

"I'm on my way."

Tripp allowed a burst of air to escape through the phone lines. "Good. I have a couple estimates I need to get to this afternoon, and between you and me, Grandpop either needs a nap, or some Priscilla Martin time. Maybe you can help me convince him to give it a rest when you get here."

August chuckled. "Sure thing." He didn't understand why Grandpop and Priscilla Martin, his high school sweetheart who just happened to be Amie's great-aunt, didn't up and get married already. They could take naps together. Much more fun than going solo if you asked August's opinion. "I'll be there in five. Maybe you can take a nap, too." No denying his brother had been on edge lately, what with the upcoming arrival of his baby.

"No time for naps. Thanks, August."

August.

Not "little brother" or "surfer boy" or "colossal screw-up"—all names Tripp had called him at one time or another. His ship had finally come in.

Sure, he may have had some rough teenage years. He may have had a little too much fun—maybe *way* too much fun—his first year of college, but he'd managed to straighten himself out. Thirteen months ago, he'd even thought he was on the road to settling down. With one woman. With Amie Martin.

But it had all gone wrong. His confession had thrown her over the edge. She'd whipped out her holier-than-thou card and flashed it in his face when what he needed most was understanding, not condemnation.

He pressed the gas pedal harder, gaining speed up Route 1. Yes, best to forget eyes the color of a clear sky, legs as long as California, and curves more enticing than thundering waves on a beach. He needed to focus on his new job, on serving the family business, and on proving himself to Grandpop and Tripp.

That was a full-time job in itself. No sense adding a firebrand like Amie Martin to the mix.

❧

I scanned the list of job search results on my laptop and sighed, taking a potato chip and munching it thoughtfully from where I sat at the dining room table of our living quarters in the Orchard House Bed and Breakfast. I had planned to break my fast with a protein shake and some trail mix, but the thought of job hunting called for something a little more comforting than nuts and raisins.

Truck driver, no.

Pharmacy Technician . . . that could work if I was certified, but no doubt such a certification would take at least a couple of months. A couple of months I didn't have.

A local burger joint position. Ugh. If I had to witness the behind-the-scenes of fast food I might keel over and die from disgust.

Cashier at a home improvement store. A possibility. If I got really desperate, that is. I suppose I could keep it in mind.

Marine technician, no.

Speech pathologist, no.

Pizza delivery driver . . . they made good tips, didn't they? As long as I didn't have to deliver to one of my peers from high school. I imagined myself donning a ballcap and shapeless polo t-shirt as I walked a Hawaiian pizza up to Jenny Simcock's house. I cringed as I imagined Jenny's conniving smile. Jenny, the girl all the high school guys had called "easy." The girl who couldn't name one element on the Periodic Table and who thought Macbeth wrote Romeo and Juliet.

The girl who had apparently pulled herself together and was now a practicing CPA in downtown Camden, handling other people's money while growing her own.

Oh, good grief. It wouldn't do any good wallowing in jealousy. I may have floundered through the last few years with a handful of college classes, a couple of boyfriends, and fits and starts with selling my art, but I had to help Mom with the bed and breakfast she'd started. And now, I was *really* going to do something with my life. Sure, it took me a few years to figure out what that was, but I'd done it. I was going to art school. And not just any art school. *Parsons*. In New York City.

I could be proud of that.

If I could just scrape up enough cash to afford a few months in the big city . . . .

Maybe my friend Lacy would hire me at the yoga studio. I tapped my fingers on the table. No, Lacy handled everything at the studio swimmingly on her own. She'd even complained her bottom line veered dangerously close to red after a bumpy start the year before.

I didn't want to burden my friend.

A loud knock on the back door made me jump and I knocked a few potato chips off my plate. I peered out the window, my heart skipping a beat at the sight of Tripp.

I swallowed, ordering it into submission. Enough was enough. Tripp was simply a silly schoolgirl crush I couldn't quite shake. Josie would positively die if she knew I still battled such ungodly feelings for her husband. It was wrong. Immoral. And certainly not Christian. Each of my angelic Martin family members would be mortified.

I was mortified.

It wasn't as if I dwelled on him, or even dreamed of him. It was just my body's reaction to seeing him. Like now, when I opened the door and took in his easy smile and steady stance. After Dad died, he'd stepped in to help us in so many ways. He'd let me cry on his shoulder more than once.

Was that what was wrong with me? Was I mixed up in some weird crush due to the loss of Dad? I'd have to Google that later. *Dad-loss crush.* Or *Romantic feelings and vulnerability*, or more appropriately, *How do I stop crushing on my sister's husband?*

"Hey, Tripp." I attempted a breezy air. "Josie's not here."

His face fell, reminding me how much Tripp was completely and unabashedly in love with my sister.

When they started dating, Josie had told me she would stop seeing him if I didn't want her to. She said sisters were more important.

Of course, I'd rejected her offer. And August thought I was selfish . . . selfish would have been denying my sister happiness. Denying Tripp happiness. I had not done that!

"She's not answering her cell. Why wouldn't she answer her cell when she's nine months pregnant?"

"Why don't I get you a drink of water? Come on in."

He obeyed, looking at his phone for what I guessed to be the tenth time in the last five minutes. I pressed a clean glass to the water dispenser in the refrigerator and held it out to him.

"Thanks." He took a long swig.

"Tripp, Josie's fine. If she went into labor, you'd be the first one she'd call. Why don't you track her?"

His eyes lit up and he slapped his head. "Amie, you're a genius."

I shrugged. "That's what I keep trying to tell everyone around here."

He shook his head, tapping on the "Find My Phone" app. "Why didn't I think of that before?"

But before he finished, his phone jingled out an upbeat tone and he swiped to answer. "Josie?"

I returned to my computer and the mess of job offerings on my screen to give him some privacy.

"You've been at the house all this time?" A long pause. "Yes, yes, I understand, but it'd be nice if you'd answer your phone, honey . . . okay, see you later. Love you, too. Bye." He hung up the phone and shoved it in the pocket of his jeans. "Your sister is going to be the death of me."

"Let me guess. She was deep into the writing of her latest book and didn't even hear the phone ring."

"You got it." He shook his head, but the gesture held more fondness than frustration. His gaze landed on my computer. "What's that? You're looking for a job?"

"Just something for the summer to help me get to the city."

"You think you could handle secretarial work?"

I perked up. "Yes . . ."

"Eileen asked for some time off to help her daughter get settled with the new baby. I've been running around like a chicken with its head cut off trying to keep up with scheduling and phones. You interested in filling in?"

I popped up out of my chair. "Yes!" I flung my arms around his neck, then, realizing the awkwardness this incurred, at least on my end, snatched my arms back. "Thank you, Tripp. I won't let you down, I promise."

It meant so much to me that he trusted me. A real job. Not cleaning at a bed and breakfast or serving fries at McDonald's or even putting my art on consignment at one of the shops down the street. This was a legit job. I scrunched up my shoulders and squealed. "I'm so excited!"

"Okay, why don't you stop by the office tomorrow morning, say eight o'clock?"

"Perfect."

He placed his glass in the sink. "I better run. I have to meet up with August and Grandpop."

"Thanks again, Tripp."

I closed the door behind him, excitement bubbling up within my chest as I watched him climb into his truck. Only after he'd pulled out of the drive did I realize that in accepting this job, I'd be seeing on a daily basis, the two men who caused me the most romantic grief I'd ever known. My girlhood crush, Tripp. And his brother, August, the one man who'd crushed my heart with a secret I simply couldn't learn to live with.

ALSO BY HEIDI CHIAVAROLI

The Orchard House

The Tea Chest

The Hidden Side

Freedom's Ring

The Edge of Mercy

Hope Beyond the Waves

The Orchard House Bed and Breakfast Series

Where Grace Appears

Where Hope Begins

Where Love Grows

Where Memories Await

Where Dreams Reside

Where Faith Belongs (January, 2023)

ACKNOWLEDGMENTS

Thank you to editor Melissa Jagears for her indispensable help on this one. Melissa, again and again I am amazed by your insight and writing skill. Thank you for pouring into me.

A huge thanks to critique partner Sandra Ardoin for her writing wisdom and listening ear. Thank you to Erin Laramore for her great eye in proofreading this book! Any remaining mistakes are mine alone.

To my husband, Daniel, for making me laugh. When Bronson was giving me trouble, you suggested I kill him off and retitle the book *Accident at the Orchard*. I hope readers are glad I didn't take your advice, sweetie!

And to my sons, James and Noah, who always cheer me on. Lastly, to the Author of life. You write the best stories. Thank you for allowing me the privilege to join in for a scene or two.

ABOUT THE AUTHOR

Heidi Chiavaroli (pronounced shev-uh-roli...sort of like *Chevrolet* and *ravioli* mushed together!) wrote her first story in third grade, titled *I'd Cross the Desert for Milk*. Years later, she revisited writing, using her two small boys' nap times to pursue what she thought at the time was a foolish dream.

Heidi's debut novel, *Freedom's Ring*, was a Carol Award winner and a Christy Award finalist, a *Romantic Times* Top Pick and a *Booklist* Top Ten Romance Debut. Her latest Carol Award-winning dual timeline novel, *The Orchard House*, is inspired by the lesser-known events in Louisa May Alcott's life and compelled her to create The Orchard House Bed and Breakfast series. Heidi makes her home in Massachusetts with her husband and two sons. Visit her online at heidichiavaroli.com

9 781957 663906